Different

Jungles

Damian Ward

Copyright © 2024
by Damian Ward

Table of Contents

Acknowledgment

About The Author

<u>Dedication</u>

For David and Margaret. 'What will survive of us is love.'

PART 1

RESPECT

CHAPTER 1

Monkey Business

The jeep hit a deep rut in the road and shuddered violently and the thing in the cage in the back-seat squealed.

The driver slowed down and looked back to see if the animal was okay. It was standing on its hind legs, its front paws gripping the bars of the cage, looking straight back at him with those creepy pink eyes. The driver turned his head back to the road, taking the next few ruts much more gently. Ahead, he could see the edge of the rainforest and he drove as near to it as he could take the jeep.

He didn't like the animal, the *rata blanca*. He didn't like rats in general – dirty vermin - but this fat white rat was like a thing from a laboratory, not natural. But it was worth a lot of money, apparently. The message on his phone the previous night was clear: five thousand dollars, in cash, to collect a caged animal from the airstrip at Los Arroyos, the abandoned one that the *narcos* used to use, then deliver it to the edge of the forest and set it free; then wait for another message to collect it again from the same place.

The driver did exactly as he was told. He woke early, drove to the airstrip before dawn while it was still cool, and waited. In the quiet, with the sun coming up, he heard the plane from a long way off and watched it land. Without even turning the engine off, the pilot got out, holding a cage and handed it to him, along with an envelope of money.

He made sure to count it: fifty one-hundred dollar bills.

Over the roar of the propellers, the pilot told him:

"Check your phone for another message. You get another five thousand if you bring it back."

Then he climbed back in the cockpit and took off.

Ten thousand dollars! It was money from heaven. Some company called 'Differentjungles'. So, while he didn't like the white rat at all, he was taking very good care of it.

He pulled over and turned the engine off. It was hot already, even though it was still morning. He took a handkerchief from his pocket and wiped the sweat from his neck, face and forehead. He popped the door, stepped out of the jeep, reached into the back, grabbed the handle and lifted out the cage. He opened the door and put his hand inside, palm up, half-expecting to get bitten. The rat climbed into his hand. He brought it out, put the creature gently on the ground and left the cage there too.

"*Suerte,*" he told the rat. 'Good luck'.

He watched the rat walk into the forest until its white rump and pink tail disappeared into the green.

Pobrecito. he thought, *You'll be dead within the hour. Then I only get five thousand, not ten.* The money he did have, though, would go straight to Maria, his wife. Maybe she would buy pretty dresses for their daughters. Whatever, tonight at least, he would be happy to see them all so happy. He climbed back into the jeep, started the engine, turned around and headed for home.

Sai didn't wait for the human to leave but started straight into the forest. With the opening of the cage, a GPS tracker was activated and now he had to get in, find what - or rather, who - he was looking for, and get out again in one piece. That had been two hours ago. Sai felt very differently about the rainforest now that he was actually in it. Now that he was actually here, he wished he was back in the cage, safe.

"Stupid! Stupid! Stupid! I'm going to die here in this horrible hellhole! Oh, damn it! Damn it! What was I thinking?"

Waddling through the rainforest undergrowth, seeking a path, Sai was talking aloud to himself, as he often did when he was alone, or puzzled, or panicked. His words came out as a sorry whimper, and although he knew it was dangerous to make any sound that might attract the attention of something hostile and hungry, he couldn't help himself. He had never been as miserable and as afraid in his whole life and now he regretted absolutely his stubbornness, his whole ludicrous plan. Now that he was here, in the rainforest itself, for real, it was so unpleasant, so threatening, so very far from his previous, deluded idea of what it would be like; he almost wished the humans *would* just cut it down, pulp all the wood and turn it into books.

It's your own fault, Sai, he told himself: *You're overweight and unfit because you've spent your whole life reading and eating too much and now you're in one of the most dangerous places on earth and you're scared.*

He sighed and stopped to look around him, wiped the sweat from his face with a filthy paw and looked up, hoping to see the sky, wishing with everything he had that he could feel a cool breeze in this dank, hot, dark, stinking, claustrophobic forest. Specks of sunlight peeped through the canopy of leaves, sparkles in the dark, like light rippling on black water. The trees around him, giants towering above, all but blotted out the sun, spreading their leaves wide to absorb every joule of the life-giving energy of sunlight, and the floor of the forest was in their shadow. Four billion trees, over fifteen thousand different species were here, and even they were all trying to kill each other: everywhere he looked, lethally-intentioned vegetation was trying to outdo its competitors to survive by rising higher to the sunlight or by throttling a neighbor's roots. The ground beneath his paws was a wet, sucking, foul-smelling mulch; every few feet, the floor was spattered with

3

dung and bird-droppings. The stench was that of decay and death, and of life, too, springing up unstoppably, feeding on the rich humus; everything striving, climbing, living, dying, then returning to the soil to feed more life. And while death might be all around him, so was life, in superabundance. Sai could hear screeches, howls, birdsong, insect buzz, calls and cries, screeches, shrieks and roars. He hoped that amid all this noise, his passage through the jungle would go unnoticed.

"Oh, well, nothing for it," he said aloud.

He moved on until he came to a fallen tree-truck blocking his way. Gasping and struggling, he gained hold with his front claws and, grunting with the effort of lifting himself up, scrambled up the rough bark until he was standing on top of it, thinking about how to get down the other side. Then something large landed on the trunk next to him, a dull thump vibrating through the wood.

One moment, it wasn't there; the next, it was. Sai had no time to see what it was before it reached for him, grabbed him in a strong paw and raised him to its mouth. Sai screamed in terror. The thing simply reached out its other paw and pinched Sai's jaws shut. His scream was snuffed out, reduced to a thin, weak wheeze from his nostrils. Whatever had caught him now lifted Sai so that he could look at him, and Sai could see what had him in its paw: some kind of monkey.

Then it put one finger to its lips and whispered:

"Ssshh!

Then, holding Sai firmly, it leaped up onto a nearby branch, jumped to another, and another, and another, and then reached out to yet another and swung up even higher into the trees.

As the ground fell away, Sai closed his eyes, terrified of the fall, thinking:

4

So this is how I die: I'm going to be eaten by a monkey.

The monkey landed on a broad branch and put Sai down. Sai squeezed his claws into the bark as hard as he could. The ground was now far, far below: a fall would kill him.

"What are you doing?" Sai gasped.

"What am I doin? I'm savin' your ass, pal! Have a little gratitude," the monkey said. "What the hell are ya doin'? Trynna get y'self killed?"

DOMINO

The monkey peered at Sai. Its face was black; its paws were black; its eyes were black, but its fur was dark brown. It seemed neither friendly nor unfriendly. It looked at him until Sai began to get nervous… surely it was a vegetarian: monkeys were, weren't they?

Then it spoke.

"What are ya?" it asked. "Wassya name? Where ya from? Whaddya doin' here?"

Sai took a deep breath.

"My name is Sai. I'm a rat. I'm from… somewhere else… and I've..."

"Sai? That's your name? An' you're a rat?"

"Yes."

"Nah. You ain't like no rat I ever saw. Y'got white fur: rats here ain't white, pal. An' rats don't have pink eyes; you do. You ain't no rat."

"I am a rat, I assure you."

"Yeah? Really? Cuz the rats here ain't dumb an' you are. Rats I know are smart: They stay out of sight. You got white fur. You wanna walk around here in white fur? Did ya ever hear o' camouflage, buddy? Me, I can move through the trees an' ain't many guys could get me as long as I pay attention. I'm the color of a shadow an' if I'm still ya don't see me, an' at night ya don't see me either. I got camouflage: you don't. An' in case ya didn't know, there's a lotta hungry things aroun' here an' you're some guy's idea of plump 'n' tasty. If I hadn't seen ya first... you'd've been offed. Cuz from where I was watchin', up inna tree, I could see two snakes 'n' an ocelot comin' for ya. Did you see 'em?"

"No."

"No, ya wouldn't have: cuz they got camouflage. An' they know how to hunt. One of the snakes was poison: he's called Sizzle. The other coulda swallowed you in one bite: he's called Emilio. An' that ocelot? She's called Obie, and she's kinda mean: she woulda played with ya before killin' ya."

Sai thought about that: death by poison or death by claws and teeth and then being eaten.

"Thank you," he said. "I suppose I owe you my life."

"No 'suppose' about it, pal. This is the jungle: there's a million ways to get offed, snuffed an' dead, an' a million guys 'n' ladies who'd do it to ya. Folk gotta eat, right?"

"What's your name?"

"Domino."

6

"Well, thank you again, Domino."

"Y' welcome, Sai. So. Why are you here?"

"I need to talk to the most important animal here. I can help."

"Help what? Help how?"

"I can help stop the humans from cutting down the forest."

The monkey laughed sourly.

"Ha!"

Then he went quiet.

Sai waited.

"We been worryin' about that too," said Domino. "How the hell we stop 'em."

"I have an idea."

"An' you need to talk to the top guy about this?"

"Yes."

"Do you know who the top guy is?"

"No."

"His name's Carlo. He's the boss. Then there's Mauro. He's a hummingbird. He's the boss's eyes 'n' ears. Then there's Emilio, the big guy I just maybe saved ya from. He's an anaconda, maybe the biggest snake in the whole place. He's Carlo's *consigliere*. An' his muscle, too. Ya don't wanna tussle with Emilio."

"Emilio. A *consigliere* is an advisor, isn't it?"

"Yeah."

"Do you know him? Carlo, I mean," asked Sai

"Sure, I know him: I live in the same neighborhood, don't I?"

"What is he? Another monkey?"

Domino laughed.

"Carlo? Nah, Carlo ain't no monkey. Carlo's a sloth."

Sai gaped, stunned: a sloth ran the rainforest! A sloth! Sloths barely moved, sloths were gentle tree-dwellers, sloths didn't – couldn't - kill anything. Sloths could barely move. How had a sloth become the most powerful creature here?

"Carlo runs the forest. For now, at least. Since a long time back. 'Cept that might all be about ta change."

"Change? Why?"

"Cos of the sit-down happenin' today. The heads of the Five Families are havin' a meet about what you say you're here for: wadda we gonna do about the humans tearing the place down."

"And what happens at 'a sit-down'?"

"Guys, talk and try to agree on stuff. They're all bosses, so they got, y'know, families an' influence; they can make things happen."

"Ah, good", said Sai. "Who do the other animals want to be in charge?"

"Carlo. He don't ask for tribute. Carlo has *respect*."

Respect, thought Sai. And the way Domino said the word as if it were the most important word in the world… *Respect… more or less exactly what I don't have in my family.*

Domino was still talking.

"Except it won't just be about the humans burning the place down. Lotta bad blood between the families an' that'll be there too. An' it'll come out first. When guys whack other guys, then the other guy's family is gonna wanna whack 'em back. That's how it is here."

Domino rose from his crouch.

"So listen, Sai... I gotta go, got things I gotta do an' I can't take you. You gotta stay here. I'll be back in a while an' I'll try ta bring ya something ta eat. You should be safe up here. I don't think a snake would get up this high but don't count on it. But... there's something else ya should know. There's birds round here will snatch ya an' eat ya if they see ya. One in particular: she's called Griselda an she's got chicks ta feed so she's always huntin'. Everyone's scared of her. She's an eagle, the biggest y' ever saw, an' she can see from miles away an' you'd never see or hear her comin': you'd jus' be dead. Maybe she's stayin' at home today cos of the sit-down, but don't count on it. She's kinda too tough to take orders from anybody. So stay very still. Don't fall off. Don't make no noise. An' don't get seen."

"Where are you going?" asked Sai.

Domino shrugged, then grinned.

"I'm gonna go see what the hell's going on. Hey, it's the sit-down: big day. Ciao."

And with that, he leaped to a branch on a neighboring tree, then did it again, and again, and again, until Sai couldn't see him anymore.

EMILIO

"And remember, Emilio: there isss no sssuch thing as a dumb animal. There are only quiet onesss."

Emilio didn't know why his father's words should come back to him, now of all times, but as the great snake considered the awful possibilities of what lay ahead that day, he took some comfort from them.

Making his way through the undergrowth, Emilio moved quickly, propelled by easy, liquid, flexing oscillations down the length of his body. The grate of soil and the sigh of stems against his supple frame, the rustling leaves, scratching rocks, cracking twigs and squelching mulch of the jungle floor were deafeningly loud. On any other day, he would have made no more noise than a light breeze and moved with utter stealth: the stealth of a hunter, not the timidity of the vulnerable, for he was one of the least vulnerable animals he knew of. Fully thirty feet long and powerfully-muscled, he was also camouflaged, tree-climbing and amphibious, long-lived and intelligent, hypersensitive and rightly feared.

Still, the coolness at the base of his long belly gave the lie to the outward appearance of calm and self-confidence. It told a different story: Emilio was afraid. Not for his personal safety — that was as sure as sunrise — but for the safety of everyone else. *Am I strong enough for this?* he asked himself again.

The undergrowth started to thin out, and Carlo's tree came into view. Emilio stopped and rose up on his belly, and anyone who saw him might have thought that a fabulous tree-trunk with emerald bark had sprung from a seedling to a deeply-rooted adult in little longer than it took to blink. Then, he began to sway from side to side. But Emilio was on the lookout. His black eyes scanned ahead, his skin felt the caress of the warmth and the moisture in the air, while with his tongue, he sensed the vibrations of the forest itself — the background noise of vegetation growing, the thrumming of life going on all around — with the music of the river reaching him between the notes of the forest. His tongue flickered, tasting, filtering, processing the air for information. No sign of any of the others yet. *Good.* Before they arrived, Emilio wanted to talk to the Don. He needed to tell him of his fear of failing him, of giving bad advice. *Give me a sssip of your ssstrength, Don Carlo,* he thought. The Don would expect him to be early on such a day, and Emilio was hurrying, though the Don had warned him to be wary of hurry.

"Why hurry?" he had chided Emilio one day as they talked at the top of his tree. "Must we live like *men?*"

Emilio smiled now to remember Carlo's permanent grin until the thought crossed his mind that the smile would probably be the only genuine one that day, a thought that immediately killed off his own smile.

But was Carlo right? Slothi, the shining example of inertia and yet the most powerful animal in the rainforest, never hurried. And apparently never worried. *Or doesn't worry enough,* mused Emilio. Because Carlo was not invulnerable. Just like any other animal, *capo* or no, Carlo answered to his bowels once daily. And when he did, he had to come down from his tree to the ground, where he was completely defenseless.

But it was not for this reason that Carlo was coming down to the ground today. He was coming down today for much more important matters, matters that made him extra, extra-vulnerable. Emilio hastened on to the meeting-place, his mind fixed on one thought. *Don Carlo should be very careful on the ground today: very watchful, very worried. I am.*

SAI

Sai peered over the edge of the branch and experienced a sickening rush of vertigo and head-spin. He shut his eyes and pulled his head back and did not open his eyes until the dizziness passed. He breathed deeply to regain his calm and relished the air: it was sweeter and cooler than it was on the forest floor. Above him, the roof of foliage still covered a lot of the sky, but he could see more blue than he could from the ground, and it raised his spirits.

He took stock of his situation: he was several hundred feet off the ground, and while he felt safe, he could not get down without Domino's help. As for his reason for being here – to talk to whoever was in charge, to share his plan for saving the forest, there was nothing to do but wait for the outcome of 'the sit down' that Domino had talked about. If he ever did manage to do what he had come to do and get back alive, there was a sit-down of his own organization scheduled, The Convocation, and that was very much on Sai's mind, too.

The others would be there: Athena, Mir, Caleb, Libo, Luxor, all of the MOONrats, with their amazing skills - mathematics, genetics, coding, chemistry, logistics - and himself, with his absurd penchant for reading. At first, he had been useful: his near-photographic memory for the written word had enabled him to read the books the others wanted to read and to dictate to them what he had read, usually without understanding it. But the others had understood, and they had learned for themselves. Now, he was all but useless to the organization: obsolete, pointless. The journey to the rainforest, this mission, had been an attempt to find a purpose, to bring something of value to MOON.

Caleb had convened The Convocation, but he had not said why or what it would be about. Still, it would be a chance to see the others, to explain his plan for the rainforest, to get their help, to work together. All the MOONrats would be there, arriving from all the corners of the world where they had dispersed so that the humans who were hunting them could not find them all and kill them or experiment on them, again, as they surely wanted to. But as Mir had pointed out many times now, their coming together was dangerous: not just because all of them would be in the same place at the same time, but because the act of bringing them together left signs that could be followed, no matter how carefully Mir worked. 'Digital pawprints,' he called them.

Sai closed his eyes, remembering Caleb's response to his suggestion, his plan.

"*You*? Go to the rainforest? What on earth for? You belong in a library, not in a rainforest. And you are hardly the ideal physique for such a mission, are you?"

Sai felt – again – Caleb's scorn in the jibe about his weight.

"Reading does not prepare you for the wild places of the world, Sai."

"Maybe not. But it is good for something. You know what's happening, don't you? Humans are cutting down the rainforests."

"I know. For timber. And to make room for farmland for growing soy and raising cattle."

"Yes. Do you know the word *'gavisti'*?"

"No."

"It's Sanskrit for 'war'. Do you know what it translates as?"
"Enlighten me."

"'The desire for more cattle'."

"And what do you propose?"

"To go there. To meet with the animals' leaders. To work together – them and us. To stop the destruction."

"How?

"My plan."

His plan was all predicated on one idea: something that Caleb did not understand about humans.

"Care to explain this plan?" said Domus.

"No. I want your trust and support, and our resources."

"Very well. Tell Mir what you want."

And now here he was.

There was a rustle of leaves, and Domino landed lithely on the branch.

"Still there, Sai? You good?"

"I think so," said Sai, "as long as I don't look down."

Domino laughed.

"Has the... erm... 'sit-down' happened yet?" Sai asked.

Domino shook his head.

"Nah. Later for that."

"Can you tell me about who will be there?"

"Sure. Carlo. Mauro. Emilio. And the heads of the other Five Families: Dante Aligatori, Mario Puma, Fat Paulie Capybara an' Enzo Coypu an' Mickey Boa an' Vipero Scacchi. An' they'll have their *consiglieres* too.

"But Carlo runs the forest."

"Yeah. Sure. For now."

Sai looked at Domino.

"What's going to happen, do you think?" he asked.

Domino laughed.

"What's gonna happen? Someone's gonna get whacked. That's what's gonna happen."

EMILIO

It had been Emilio who had originally approached Carlo about co-operation between the ground and the air. He would not have made a deal with anybody else. Snakes do not cut deals with anyone they do not respect, but they respected Carlo. Carlo took orders from no-one, enjoyed his freedom, took no liberties and showed every single living thing *respect*, which was what came back to him. From the tiniest mite to the mightiest cat. From a billion ants. From burrowers and climbers, herbivores and predators. From wings, scales, feathers and fur. From the forest floor and the riverside, from the air and the treetops. From every hide, hive, nest, den, tunnel, hole, sette, colony and eyrie. Respect.

And why? Because nobody but Carlo could have brought about such an enduring peace and held the strings of the billion different dances that made up the life of the rainforest. Nobody else could have been so respectful, so unassuming and yet so concerned about those under his protection. For the smaller animals, he was a guardian; for the mighty animals an equal. Emilio had seen the subtlety of the sloth — his fair-clawed distribution of power and influence in the forest — and understood why it had been accepted. The sloth never broke his word, never refused a favor, never called those favors debts, never exacted tributes. And he always smiled. Respect sown, respect reaped. And then, business took care of itself.

So, if Don Carlo moved slowly, reflected his *consigliere,* it was only because he didn't have to move for anyone. But working for him was both an honor and a burden and being sensitive had its drawbacks. Only days ago, the extent of Emilio's responsibilities had felt like a greater load than any snake should ever have to bear. As he lay coiled at Carlo's side and listened to the pleas and the tears of the animals under the Don's protection, as he watched the wrung paws and limp miserable tails, as he tasted on his flickering tongue-tip the distress of the dispossessed, Emilio wanted to cry: listening to the animals was breaking his heart.

"Don Carlo, it does not stop. Every day, they come nearer, and there are animals running, birds flying before them, as if from fire. With their saws and axes and their machines, they destroy our homes. What will we do, *padrone*?" A macaque, her eyelashes tangled with weeping.

"Ay, *compare*... my eggs... all dead, all dead..." A fish-eagle, bright-eyed with the effort of holding back his tears, never making eye contact because the eagles had their own rigid codes of dignity. In the eagle's bowed posture Emilio saw one with a bellyful of torment that he himself was only sipping.

"Don Carlo, I do not know how many friends I have lost and we will not see their kind again..." A crested lizard comes to put the case of the smaller animals, the floor-dwellers.

"What will my children eat, *padrone*? Where will they live? Must a mother see this?" An old chameleon, changed for mourning, her skin all black.

"They come, and they take *padrone*. And I mean they take everything, and then they go, leaving nothing behind for anything to live on. They call us *animali* and laugh as they take our world from us..." A tough-looking fer de lance, quick and poisonous, who only a few short months ago was working his way up through the ranks of Vipero Scacchi's family, the *capo di rione* of a clever, thriving waterfront gang, now disbanded. "Our part of the river is poison. We have no living. Where can we go, Don?"

So many animals, thought Emilio, *and always the same plea:*

"Help us, Don Carlo."

He had listened and watched as the animals pleaded and sobbed. Carlo had smiled and nodded and the animals went away with lighter hearts because they knew their Don had heard and would act. But when they were gone, Emilio turned to his Don and asked,

"What will we do about these tree-thievesss, Don Carlo?"

And the Don's reply left him
feeling cold.

"I don't know."

And when he turned in shock to look at his Don, he saw that Carlo was no longer smiling.

"Call a meeting of the Families," he said quietly.

DOMINO

Domino brought food - delicious fruits that he called *cupuacu, acai,* and *cocona* – and shared them with Sai. Sai relished them somewhat guiltily: he had always liked his food a little too much. Almost as much as he loved reading. Actually, more.

As they ate in silence, Sai reflected. From what he heard from Domino, he was forming a picture of the organization of the rainforest, its leaders and its players. His own organization, the MOONrats, was different: it was one 'family', not five, and no individual was considered above any other. It had always been that way, ever since their escape from the laboratory and their coming together, each with their new, astonishing gifts.

Sai chewed the succulent, sweet *acai* and thought again about the Convocation. It could not happen until Sai returned: all attended; it was the rule. Plans would be discussed, votes cast, and actions could then be taken. If Sai could meet this Carlo, if he could convince him to accept his plan, his organisation could help. All Sai had to do was survive. And Carlo, too, he supposed. From what Domino had told him, though, there might be a change in leadership. *The Sit-down,* thought Sai - their form of Convocation. Only in their world, disagreement could get you killed. That, at least, did not happen in his.

"Can you tell me how Carlo came to be in charge, Domino?" asked Sai. "And who exactly is Mauro?"

19

Domino sat back against the treetrunk and began:

"Mauro, he's the boss's eyes and ears. He does the movin'. All day, every day, messages to an' from Carlo. Mario handles contact between the families. He's quick, he's smart, he keeps his bill shut. An' he never stops, he's at it all day long, hoverin' long-beak-deep in Carlo's or Fat Paulie's or whoever's ear, beatin' his wings for the background hum jus' so he's sure nothin' else can catch what the word is. He's got his own family business to be about, sure — birdy stuff — but it ain't nothin' the Don won't hear about, cuz Mauro, if he moves at all, it's for Carlo. Never lands, snatches quick shots o' nectar for the buzz he gets off it, gettin' around."

"And Carlo trusts him?"

"Oh, yeah. Probably couldn't even operate without him. Mauro an' Carlo go back, as far back as it goes. I mean, they grew up in the 'hood together, playin' aroun' the same tree… Mauro was such a wiseass he could actually fly *backward*, an' Carlo moved one foot, maybe two feet in a mornin'. But even then, you could see it was Carlo who had the smarts. Mauro, for all his speed, never seemed to get as far as Carlo. It's like the sloth can see under things, ya know? Or maybe it all makes sense if you look at it upside-down. I dunno. How's a guy with only a little smarts like me supposed to figure out the guy with a treeful? But when Carlo started tradin' with the other families an' communities on the information Mauro was gettin' passed to him from birds from every part of the jungle… they were made. It was beautiful. Carlo was a genius. One time — I'm talkin' a long time back, ya' understand — word of a big storm comin' gets passed down from one o' the condors an' lands in Mauro's ear. So he takes it to Carlo, thinkin' it'd be a courtesy o' the Don's to tip off the crocs, whatever, but the Don says, 'Crocodiles don't drown. Tell the ants.' The ants were, like, layin'. Well, they get the word from the bird in time an' start movin' the eggs out o' danger: Carlo saved a couple o' colonies. The ants? They couldn't even *think* how to thank him, an' when those guys put their heads together, it adds up to a very smart animal indeed, lemme tell ya. Another time, the colonies come to Carlo with a beef about some soldier ants from outta the 'hood musclin' in big-time on their operation. What does Slothi do? He tips off the anteaters an' the antbears. They go in, tongues blazin' — they never ate so good! The ants' top guy, Formiccino, and the anteaters' guy, Slerpio, they ask the boss what they could do for him — like they felt they owed. Carlo tells 'em, "One day, I'll need a favor. I'll call."

Now, do you figure on anybody else gettin' those guys to sit down together? Ants 'n' anteaters? Ants would never do that normally; they're too proud. An' like, those anteaters? They look down their noses at'cha, an' it breaks your balls a little, even if they're only little like an ant's. But cuz it was Carlo, the ants said 'yes' to a sit-down with the noseguys. An' everybody heard about it. Do you know how much respect Carlo got for that? An' it grew, too — word in, word out — 'til everybody sees that Carlo's way is the juice. I mean, it was perfect! One of the birds spots a dead deer in the woods. Get the word to the bird. Mauro puts it out to the Don, and the Don puts it out to wherever he thinks it fits... like maybe the big cats, or maybe the vultures or the ants if it stinks a bit. Doesn't matter: it's all food in someone's belly.

Carlo's way, everybody got a piece of the action; everybody got cut in, all the families. Luca Crocodili got the river, Vipero Scacchi and Mickey Boa got the jungle floor, long as they kept things sweet with the big cats. Fat Paulie Capybara got the waterfront with Enzo Coypu, an' Santino Jagi got a big piece of the trees. 'Cept no-one was listenin' to them no more, cuz now Carlo was the one to go to. None of the animals wanted to go to nobody else when they needed somethin' done or figured they got somethin' somebody oughta know. An' then Carlo was runnin' things, like the whole operation."

"It sounds… perfect," said Sai

"It was. Except for one thing. It put Luca C's jaws outta whack."

CHAPTER 2

Luca's Vendetta

CARLO

Don Carlo's power was based on information and on the control of the means of its acquisition. He, alone among the Dons of the Five Families, had his sources of information truly organized. That gave him the lead on his opponents every time. Nothing happened in the jungle that Carlo didn't know about, so ultimately, the other families had to come to him to get advice on and approval for any new business.

One day, several years earlier, the river Don, Luca Crocodili, had come to Carlo with a business proposition. The proposal was offensive: to put burrowing animals to work digging gold, which Crocodili's crew would trade with men.

"We buy them off, Don Carlo. If we give them gold, they will leave us in peace," Luca assured Carlo and asked for permission. Mindful of the crocodile's vanity and touchiness and careful not to offend, Carlo made a show of thinking about the offer. He simply hung in silence, as Crocodili would expect him to. There was no question of accommodating the reptile: dealings with the tunnel-dwellers were peaceful, so there was no conflict of interest. If he allowed Crocodili's soldiers to go into their territory to take slaves for gold-digging, he would lose all respect. And to lose respect would be to lose power. The animals would see it like that. Carlo could never allow such a venture: it was bad for everything, set a dangerous precedent and sent the message that any animal could be used for profit. This would make the animals very insecure make things very unstable, which was bad

24

for everyone. And besides, the burrowers, like everyone else, had the right to expect from Carlo the respect that they showed him.

What the river Don was asking was preposterous. Obviously, Crocodili had been listening to his *consigliere* again, the gecko. This idea had the lizard's stink about it. Rosario Gecko made no bones about his admiration for the humans' way of doing business. *Slaves* thought Carlo. *Only a cold-blooded animal could want such a thing. I wonder if the crocodile knows that the gecko has sharper teeth than his Don?*

Finally, after a very long silence, Carlo gave his decision.

"Luca, you have your river, and I have my treetops — our interests do not clash. But this gold... it would also bring men, and then we would lose control of our business."

"Why would it bring men?" said the crocodile. "Are you suggesting that I will not be able to run such an operation? I tell you, Don Carlo, out there on that river, what I say goes."

"You guarantee that your animals won't let slip the source of all this gold?"

"Yes."

"You trust all your *caporegimes* and soldiers? There's no-one you think might sell you out?"

"They wouldn't dare."

Carlo shrugged affably.

"It wouldn't even have to be anybody selling you out. Someone might just let it slip in friendly conversation. Word gets out on anything, eventually."

The crocodile was getting angry.

"Nobody knows my business except for what I choose to tell them."

Carlo said nothing. As usual, he had the drop on the reptile: Crocodili's tick-bird was in the sloth's loop, tight with Mauro, and Carlo had some information that he could use. The difficulty lay in letting Luca know that he had something on him without it sounding like a threat and without giving away the source. Carlo thought about both problems. Again, there was nothing unusual in the length of time he took to mull things over, as far as Luca was concerned. When he spoke, it was very, very slow.

"Luca, I would like to be accommodating, but I must tell you that my answer is no. Your proposition will bring men too close. I do not think that they will be satisfied with what you bring them. They will want it all. They will seek out its origin. This is what men do: they want. And then they find things out. And take."

Carlo paused before adding quietly, "You and your wife and your nine children will live well enough without their help."

Carlo felt the crocodile stiffen. That Luca's wife had recently laid a clutch of nine eggs was not common knowledge. A delicate moment, as the reptile stared at him speechlessly and then looked away.

"*Salute*, Don Carlo," he said.

Then he turned away and went back to the river, wondering once more how the sloth got his information.

As Carlo watched Luca disappear into the forest, he knew that the crocodile would not forgive this refusal. Carlo had both crushed the reptile's greedy, callous scheme and shown him that if information was power, then Carlo had more of both than the river capo.

Expect trouble, thought Carlo.

He sent for Mauro the hummingbird, knowing exactly what he was going to do about Luca. While he waited, he thought about the value of information, something he had learned as a very young sloth. Understanding had come to him one dawn as he was about to go to sleep at the end of a busy night spent eating leaves slowly. Although he was tired, he found the twittering of the waking birds too shrill to fall asleep and so hung from his branch and listened. Separate all the cheepings, chirrupings, squawkings and cawings from each other, and it was possible to make out the different conversations. A din he had previously resented for cheating him out of well-earned sleep was, in fact, the sound of tens of thousands of lives: birds telling each other their dreams and cracking jokes, discussing feeding places, how so-and-so's eggs were doing. As Carlo listened, it occurred to him that of all the animals in the jungle, the birds were the most talkative, the most far-traveled, the most seeing and knowing. They knew when rain was coming, or jaguars. They had families a thousand miles away that they thought nothing of visiting, and they talked to everyone. And as he fell asleep that morning, he had already decided that if he couldn't actually see all of the rainforest himself, he could certainly get the birds to tell him about it. *And of course*, thought Carlo now, with Luca very much on his mind, *I can also ask birds to send messages*. In this case, to a certain seabird, and his very dangerous lady-friend.

DOMINO

"So, y'see, Sai, it wuz me tipped off Mauro about the hit on Carlo. Hey, no big deal: right place, right time, right? I wuz jus' down by the river when Luca came back from the sit-down with the sloth. Mauro's done me a lotta favours, so when I heard the croc hissin' big time all kinds of blue murder, I figured that the boss needed to hear about it. An' not jus' the nasty things Luca was hissin' neither, but Rosario too, whisperin' inna croc's ear about how it was *time*. Now, ya gotta remember this was the early days: Mauro an' the sloth had jus' suddenly come from nowhere to runnin' things, an' there'd been no beef from the animals cuz they didn't step on nobody's toes. So there'd been no war. I figure Luca took this as a sign that the sloth wasn' up to it. I mean, the sloth an' the hummingbird didn't exactly *look* like bad guys, not like Luca. Luca 'The Teeth'? Hey, that scaly scumbag had *eaten* all o' his rivals along the river. How the hell else was he gonna figure the next step? The crocodile set out t' whack the sloth.

Luca Crocodili

When Luca Crocodili declared war on Carlo, he did not target any of Carlo's family or friends or any of the associates of the sloth's operation. Nor did he seek an extensive or drawn-out conflict. Because firstly, to have done so would have been to force the animals of the rainforest to take sides, and in this, the crocodile knew he would run a poor second to the sloth; and secondly, because a limited conflict would enable Crocodili to claim that the war was simply a matter of business, and nothing personal. In the sit-down that would inevitably have to follow such a move, he had to be able to present to the heads of the other families the face of a reasonable crocodile — a reptile with all the families' interests at heart — and he would have the promise of gold with which to charm the other capos. Crocodili was smart enough to know that he would get only one chance to rub out the sloth and that he could not do it himself. He looked for an assassin instead and called on the services of a murderer known as Scorpionne.

It was a good choice. Scorpionne came from the deserts far to the north and was little known, but he already had a chilling record. There seemed to be no-one he couldn't get at with his death sting. One touch, they said of him, and you would know long agony and beg for death. Falcone, an idealistic bird of prey who had been making things difficult for certain business concerns, ceased to be a problem after a visit from Scorpionne. Up till then, everybody had assumed Falcone was untouchable.

Crocodili guaranteed the fee, summoned the poisoner, and dispatched a vulture to fly the assassin in. Scorpionne would do the job in his own time. Luca waited for the news of Carlo's passing, daydreaming about what he would do with the absolute power that would become his when he became the *capo de tutti capi*.

CARLO

Carlo knew about the hit within hours of its being called in, a tribute to Mauro's information-gathering networks. But a visit from a strange-looking bird was the first in a chain of events that even Mauro, right next to the Don throughout, could not piece together until it was over. The white bird arrived in the forest one evening and came to Mauro first out of respect. This was a bird-to-bird protocol that could not be ignored. He announced himself as Al and told Mauro he had come at Don Carlo's request and with information of great concern to Carlo besides. Mauro had never seen anything like him. There was that look in his eye of one who has flown around the world. His wings were enormous. With the exception of Giorgio Condor, he was the biggest bird Mauro had ever seen.

Mauro did his duty as a go-between and set up a meet at the top of Carlo's tree. The bird and the Don talked for a while, and then the great white stranger left. Carlo said nothing after the bird's departure, and Mauro knew better than to ask. He went about his normal business as the Don expected him to.

That night, as Carlo and his wife and children were having dinner high up in the branches of their tree, Mauro noticed a tiny movement at the base of the trunk. It was no more than the turning of a blade of grass, but sharp-eyed Mauro spotted it. He stayed motionless and unseen in his nest and watched as a scorpion found a foothole in the bark and started the long climb to the top. Sting raised high over his back, a bloated bulb of venom quivering with malice, the intruder scuttled up the tree purposefully and quickly. Mauro launched and buzzed with desperate speed to warn the Don. He found Carlo at the tip of a branch, which was bowing rather perilously under his weight. The lulling, gentle sway and bounce of the branch seemed — impossibly — to have further relaxed his unflappable boss.

"Carlo..." began Mauro breathlessly, hovering near.

"There is a scorpion climbing up my tree. He wants to kill me. I know," said Carlo.

Mauro's beak fell open.

"How...?" he began but obeyed immediately as the sloth first put a claw to his lips, then pointed. The scorpion was on the branch, edging forward down the arcing bough. Mauro hovered. He was no bigger than the scorpion, and while he had the edge over the killer for speed, he was not armed for anything more violent than sucking nectar. *Maybe I can flip the scorpion off the branch with my bill*, he thought desperately. *As for Carlo*... immobile on a swaying branch high above the jungle floor... *I'll die before I let him touch Carlo*, thought Mauro.

Perhaps three feet away now, the scorpion was smiling, the tip of his sting weeping a single moonlit tear of poison. He spoke, his voice a dry rustle, like dead, dry leaves underfoot.

"Don Carlo, I bring greetings..."

"...from Luca Crocodili. Hello, Scorpionne."

Scorpionne stopped in his tracks. Then he smiled. Information was no protection now for the sloth. *I've got the poisonous sting and this hairy chump is helpless, caught between the sting and the drop, and his hummingbird has nothing to fight with. This is the easiest job ever.*

Scorpionne stepped forward, thinking that he would drop onto the sloth's belly and walk up the body to the head, then get in the sloth's face, spit in that face, and go for the nose. That was the best place to put the death sting — it'd take longer to kill... Then he'd stick around, watch him die. Scorpionne stepped over the foreclaws and looked down over the edge of the branch into Carlo's eyes. And he was still wondering *Why is this hairy chump smiling?* when Carlo let go of his branch. The branch whipped up, and Scorpionne found himself first flying up and away from the tree, then spinning in mid-air, then, sickeningly, plummeting. He crashed to the ground, balled-up in his hard armour, and immediately sprang to his feet, unhurt, just angrier. He cursed himself for wasting his chance and focused his mind on the job.

No hesitation this time, just kill, he told himself. The sloth would be even more immobile on the ground. *So,* he thought with chilly glee, *I get a second chance.*

He looked around for the sloth. He was not on the ground. He glanced up. Carlo was hanging by three claws from a branch only a few feet off the ground, trying to get the other nine claws on the job. Scorpionne moved for the tree. Mauro caught the movement, and hissed, "He's there!" and Carlo called in a favour, with a whistle. The ground around the base of the tree suddenly burst into crackling life as a hundred thousand red ants poured from their tunnels and engulfed the assassin like a flood of blood. As they washed over Scorpionne, Carlo heard a scream and looked down to see a desperate sting arch high and plunge down onto the back of its wielder. Within seconds, the ants were gone, and so was Scorpionne.

Mauro hovered, watching.

"Ya gonna do something nasty to the croc, boss?"

"It's already happened," replied Carlo, and started the long climb back up his tree.

The following morning, a patch of crocodile hide, nibbled by ants into the shape of a human being's boot, was delivered to the rock beneath which Rosario Gecko lived. It was a message from Carlo: 'He who would walk with men will need shoes.'

Rosario Gecko misunderstood the message and took it to mean that he needed to find another crocodile to work for: an even bigger one. Luca's vendetta against Carlo was Rosario's now, and Rosario swore he would find someone to see it through all the way to the end.

MAURO

At first, Mauro couldn't see how Carlo had gotten to the croc. Luca got whacked in the river, underwater, which meant that either it had to be Shiv the narwhal or Turtelini who made the hit. Except Turtelini was strictly saltwater jobs, and the narwhal didn't clip things anymore. Mauro couldn't figure it. And Carlo said nothing so Mauro never asked him directly. But he listened out for word on the thing, and finally, he got word from an associate downriver, a shore-wader. And the word was a big, pale-grey fin had been seen headed upriver, then later again downriver to the sea, the same night as the Luca thing. Mauro remembered the stranger and put the white seabird in the frame. Then the truth fell like a big ripe fruit: the white bird was the seabird Don, Al Batrossi. And the fin was his friend, Bianca Sharki.

Luca C. versus Bianca, thought Mauro.

And he tried to imagine how Crocodili felt when he was bitten in two, right outside his own front door, where he'd been waiting for news of somebody else's death.

CHAPTER 3

The Sit Down

CARLO

So, the affairs of humans have come to affect us, Thought Carlo, and sighed. When there were only the forest-dwellers' demands on the jungle, there was no problem. They took only what they needed and showed respect. They knew that the forest was big enough for everyone. Not so the humans, who used earthmovers and fire to dip theirs. And they came closer every day. One day, the forest would no longer be there.

And what can I do? thought Carlo.

Nothing.

How could I ever make them see reason?

How could I even *talk* to them?

EMILIO

Emilio arrived early for the meeting of the families, and waited at the bottom of Carlo's tree for the Don to climb down. It took a very long time. Slothi did not hurry. Hugging the tree, he moved claw under claw with measure and absolute calm. When he put a claw on the ground, he took the other nine off the tree and flopped gracelessly onto the floor, then spent a long time righting himself. Emilio thought about how vulnerable Carlo looked on the ground, but Carlo himself seemed unconcerned, claws folded over his hairy tummy, wiggling his bottom, stretching out his hind legs, waggling his toes.

"Aaah," he said, smiling.

He greeted Emilio and commented on his worried appearance.

"Change your expression, Emilio. Smile. That way, the Dons and their *consiglieri* will not know what you are thinking."

Emilio tried a smile. It ached.

"Then at least lose the frown, my friend," suggested Carlo.

Emilio could keep quiet no longer:

"Carlo, go back up your tree! Addressss the Donssss from there. I can protect you if you are in your tree. On the ground, you're vulnerable. You are in real danger."

Carlo replied simply:

"Then I'm where I should be. In danger."

Emilio shook his head and started to disagree, but Carlo continued, "The forest — and everything in it — is in danger. How can I know what I should do if I do not share that danger?"

"If there isss treachery, where will it come from?"

Slothi pondered for a very long time. Emilio was patient. The longer the Don thought, the smaller the snake's anxieties became. The sloth finally answered.

"I'm not sure. Yet. The *consiglieri* are the ones who wield the real power in their families. The Dons are shrewd but vain, and their greed is the greed of snatching monkeys. Hunger, talent and will took them so far, and when they saw that they had reached their peaks, they were wise enough to hire others to do their thinking for them. This is one way to lead: to be a face. But thinking takes place behind the face — so behind the face is where you find the thinkers."

"Rosssario and Sssalvatori," said Emilio.

"Yes. The gecko and the vulture are very clever. Once the Dons had established their power, it was essential to consolidate it. So they took on new blood, as I said, animals to bring in new ideas, apply new knowledge to old problems, and correct the wrong-headedness of these old ones. They ran their businesses, and we have had peace. But now they have become lazy and they let their *consiglieri* do the work. These advisers now have their eyes on the Dons' places. It would not be natural for them not to. Today there will be treachery, be sure of it. There is too much at stake."

"Who do you sssuspect?" asked Emilio.

Carlo paused, looking away across the trees. He shrugged.

"The puma and the alligator believe they have the most to gain," he said finally.

Then, with a buzz that Emilio had only just registered on his tongue-tip, Mauro arrived.

"Hi, boss. Hi, Emilio. Guess who I've just flown over?"

At that moment, a monkey bellowed.

It was a signal.

The other Dons had arrived.

After Domino left, Sai began to feel drowsy. The entire forest had gone quiet. Sai walked along the branch to where it met the trunk, and in that nook he lay down, closed his eyes and fell asleep. He woke to find Domino on the branch, grinning at him.

"Cheez, how the hell can you sleep? Biggest day in the forest we ever had an' you take a nap?"

"Is the Sit-down over?" asked Sai.

"Oh yeah… an' you ain't gonna believe what happened."

"It's over?" asked Sai. "You were there?"

"It's over."

"And what happened?"

"What happened?"

Domino laughed.

"What I said would happen. A lotta guys got whacked."

"And who is in charge now?"

"Carlo. Aw, Sai, you shouldda seen it — all the heads o' the families comin' through the forest to Carlo's place for the big meet. Everything, I mean *everything*, inna jungle jus' shuddup. The birds first, then everythin' else, then some monkey lets rip widda "Oooh-oooh-oooh-aaah-aaah-a!" which means, "Monkeys, get the hell outta

38

here!". Then nothin'. Zip. Diddley. Bupkis. Pal, *the trees* wuz holdin' their breath.

I wuz watchin' from a tree an' I dint say nothin', cuz down there wuz the most powerful animals inna jungle. They wouldn't think nothin' o' havin' me whacked for bein' a wiseass an' I know I shouldn't have been there but... hey, let all the other monkeys split, not Domino: I wanna know.

So I'm inna tree, an' the forest is *silent* but for the Dons comin' through... silent like never before. Luca Crocodili's – the guy that got whacked I told you about... his nephew, Dante Alligatorio, was leadin' the way, with Rosario, his lowlife gecko, ridin' on his back. Dante... dumb enough to think jus' cuz he was feared he wuz respected when they ain't the same thing: That pond-life jus' got cruelty... that is one sick reptile:y' know what he did on the night he took over from his dead dumb uncle Luca? Ate his uncle's loyal tickbird. Shouldda left a trail of slime wherever he went was what he shouldda done.

Next up was Mario Puma, runnin' a bit of the floor an' a bit of the trees now that Santino Jagi was dead. He looked good. Mario did. I gotta give him that. Very strong. You could tell he'd been workin' out. Probably spent a day lickin' himself so he could look good ta the other Dons. Yeah, an' there wuz his guy Salvatore Vultura.

Now, I couldn't hear too good, but I can see okay an' I can smell jus' fine an' Salvatore stank. I mean, what can ya say about a guy who pees down his own legs to keep 'em clean when he's steppin' through stiffs — stiffs he then eats? Yeech. Those two figured. Everyone knew the black cat was real unlucky to be around, an' with the vulture I rest my case already.

Then there was Fat Paulie Capybara and Enzo Coypu, still runnin' things along the waterfront. Then the floor guys, Micky Boa and Vipero Scacchi, slitherin' in last but not least. Pal, if I live to be a hunnert, I ain't gonna see nothin' like what I saw then. I'm tellin' ya,

I could get fatter then *Paulie* jus' lunchin' out on the story I got. An' if I'm lyin', this ain't *maracuya*... it's a poison treefrog."

CARLO

The heads of the families gathered round the tree and faced Carlo, propped against the trunk, with Emilio coiled at his Don's side and Mauro hovering above them.

Carlo turned to greet them in turn, right to left, Emilio noticed.

"Dante. Rosario. Welcome."

The alligator returned the greeting with a grating throaty rumble. The gecko nodded.

"Paulie. Enzo."

The enormous capybara, smelling of river weed and mud, waddled forward to kiss Carlo on the cheek.

"Don Carlo," he said.

His coypu did the same. They seemed well-disposed, but Carlo took nothing at face value.

"Mario. Salvatore."

The puma purred, "I'm honoured, Don Carlo."

The vulture hopped forward with a rustle of stained feathers to extend his veiny, wrinkled, thin neck to kiss Carlo on the cheek.

Carlo grinned through the smell. Salvatore nodded to Mauro, the bird-to-bird thing.

"Vipero. Michele."

Micky Boa and Vipero Scacchi rose up from out of their coils and hissed their respects. They nodded to Emilio and coiled back up.

Everyone waited for Carlo to speak.

And waited, in silence, but for the buzz of Mauro's wings.

The unnatural quiet of the forest was disturbing some of the guests. Carlo was enjoying it. Puma unfurled his tail, sat back on his haunches and sighed quietly. Dante straightened his armored tail. Then, silence again.

Carlo still did not speak. Boa's and Scacchi's tongues were reading the air for signals, just like Emilio's. Finally, Carlo cleared his throat, a claw politely over his mouth.

"Welcome to my tree. I have called you here today to discuss matters which concern us all, and I want to thank you for coming. As you came here today through the jungle, you noticed the quiet. A mark of respect to animals of power. Each one of you is a capo of your own kind and of the territories where they live. This is power. We have it. We took it because we saw that it was there for the taking. We were strong enough to act and become the animals we are today and wise enough to know that strength must continually seek more strength. We took on wise counselors to help us remain strong. And so we remained. Nothing can harm us. This means we can do what we want, and nothing — no animal, no law — can touch us. This would be freedom if we did not have animals under us who are not so strong."

Carlo paused. He had still given nothing away about the matters in hand. Emilio thought, *When Carlo showsss his mind, ssso will the other Dons.*

"Strength," continued Carlo, "is why we are respected."

The others were listening intently, watching Carlo. To Mauro, hovering above Carlo's ear, Puma looked bored and Dante edgy, but then Dante was being asked to think, and that was not a strong point with the alligator. Emilio was watching the consiglieri to see what they reacted to. A start, a facial tic, might signal intentions.

"And where does this strength come from? From our might? From our poison teeth?" Carlo was saying, "I do not think so. I think the respect which the animals confer on us is the source of our power. Our individual talents are not enough to have achieved what we have. I mean," he said, with a modest gesture of his claws, "look at me."

Polite laughter from all, but from the waterfront Don and his *consigliere*, Enzo Coypu, laughter that was just a little too loud.

Emilio caught it, and wondered, *Would these rodentsss dare attack usss?*

Carlo continued, "A few days ago, I invited to my tree any animal who wished to speak to me. More came than I could see, but it was always the same story — humans with fire and machines, destroying the forest, leaving only charred floor behind them. Now, they will say it's nothing personal, it's just business. But every day, our territories get smaller, and we do nothing, and worse, we are seen to do nothing. We are losing territory. We are losing respect. We are going to lose our power and we will deserve to. We run the forest because the animals think we do. When they stop thinking it, we stop running it. I say that we must join forces to save the forest, to do everything possible to stop humans cutting

42

down our lives. That is what I wished to say to you." Carlo folded his claws back over his stomach and waited for the Dons to speak. The *consiglieri* were now at their bosses' ears, whispers mixing together with winks, turned claws, nods, indecipherable gestures.

Sssignalsss, thought Emilio, *which I cannot interpret. Watch the consssiglieri*, he told himself.

Then, there was a light touch along his flank. Don Carlo leaned down to him and said in his softest voice, "The cat."

And indeed, when Emilio glanced at Mario, he noticed that the cat's tail was moving slowly from side to side: never a good sign.

DOMINO

"... I mean, I could *see* what wuz happnin' but I couldn' *hear* an' I wuz thinkin' that anythin' so big the Dons gotta come across the jungle to hear it is gonna touch me too. So I figure I kinda gotta right to listen, no? So there I am, makin' my way real quiet through the branches, tryna get within earshot of the Dons, but like without bein' seen. I gotta reputation for havin' big ears an' prob'ly the Dons didn' want no-one listenin' in on the sit-down, so I figured that when I got near enough to hear things... that was near enough. Anybody sees me, I'm gonna make with the three wiseass monkeys routine: ain't seen nothin', ain't heard nothin' and hey, whaddyaknow, my mouth stopped workin' too. Turns out I didn' have to. 'Cept for the fact I get there about halfway through, I heard it all, I seen it all — the only guy inna jungle, not a Don who did. Me — I swear on my kids' tails."

EMILIO

Emilio watched the cat as he stood up to speak. Mario Puma was unquestionably the strongest of the Dons. He had learned well from his Uncle Santino and taken over the running of the cats' share of the forest very capably after Jagi's death. He was getting good advice, too. In Salvatore Vultura, he had a formidable *consigliere*: anybody who waded through pus to have lunch was going to harbor very few illusions about the business of the forest. The anaconda found that he had stiffened thinking about Salvatore, his muscles tensing instinctively as if before a threat. But Carlo had told him to watch the puma.

Fine, thought Emilio. *I'll watch Mario to sssee if he is the danger. But what about the alligator? Who'sss watching him?*

CARLO

Mario had a good argument, Carlo had to concede. He spoke well. Mario had learned a lot from his uncle, wily old Santino Jagi. Probably took a few lessons from Salvatore into the bargain. The other Dons all looked very impressed. Mario was very handsome; nice white teeth in that dark face. *Nice speaking voice, too*, thought Carlo.

MARIO

"Don Carlo," began the cat, "you are respected for your power and admired for your reason. What you say about the animals is true: their respect keeps us powerful. But can we respect animals who hand over their lives to the more powerful so willingly? Should we respect animals too weak to govern their own existences?"

Mario looked at all the Dons in turn, before continuing.

"I agree with you again, Don Carlo, when you say that it is not our individual strengths that make us what we are, but co-operation with each other. Co-operation is good. We cats have a saying: if we all pull in opposite directions, the carcass is torn apart — then we get pieces, not the whole. I say that if we are to best serve the needs of the animals under our protection, we need to co-operate with men, who, let us be honest, are ultimately responsible for the rainforest. Let us talk to their capos, make a deal over the forest and drink at the same river. They call themselves reasonable. Is not one of their great boasts that they are the only animal which reasons? Now, we know this is not true. We, too, can be rational. And I believe, Don Slothi, that with the respect you command, you could reason with them."

Mario sat down.

Flattery indeed, thought Carlo. *Nice words. Reason, respect.*

But we sloths have a saying, too: Never snatch a compliment. It shows where you are weak.

MAURO

Mauro was not convinced by the cat. The silky purr he delivered his speech in had a way of building up to a roar when the cat felt like it. The Don knew that. Emilio would be on the cat's case, too. But the other animals looked sort of convinced. Vipero and The Mickster had a big stake in this. So, too did Fat Paulie and Enzo. Dante was so dumb he'd be thinking about Luca and a way to get even with the sloth and nothing but. Rosario would have seen to that. Splay-toed, pop-eyed and still, Rosario listened. Of all the *consiglieri*, he had the greatest influence on his Don, though he had said nothing from his position behind Dante Alligatori's ear.

I got you, gecko, thought Mauro, thinking of Scorpionne.

Then he noticed how twitchy the alligator was getting.

DANTE

Dante was getting sick of the speeches. He had eighty teeth, and he was armored, and he found words irksome. He also had very small ears and a tiny reptile brain, so listening and thinking were not strong points either, but he had Rosario for that. Rosario did all the thinking and told Dante what to say. That way it left him free to think about the big things, like alligatorettes. And ruling the jungle: that was Dante's main thing in life.

So when Mario Puma had come to him one day and suggested that the forest would be better off in their claws than in the sloth's, Dante had listened. He especially liked the bit about playing with Carlo before he died. He told Rosario. The gecko came up with a better idea, which Dante liked even better than the cat's, which had used the word 'we'.

"Just play along," said Rosario, and Dante had.

But now the game was dragging on. It was getting boring. He was getting hungry. It was time to either get wet with blood or go back to the river. It was time to make Rosario's play.

DOMINO

"… an' after Mario sat down it jus' went quiet again like there wuz only eye contact an' muttering I didn' get between the consiglieri an' their Dons. An' I thought, *I don't know what's happnin' but they sure as hell do, so if I stay up here in the tree I'm gonna get it all — all the whats an' whys.* Well, I didn't get the whys at the time — we only got that when Emilio put the squeeze on Salvatore afterward — but I got the whats. *What* happened? Like, the impossible happened — twice: Dante had an idea. An' the sloth flew."

CARLO

Men like cats, thought Carlo. *You cannot burn or chop down a river. Mario and Dante. The most ambitious; the most to gain. Which will it be?*

He closed his eyes on the Dons and their silence and let himself drift down into the calmest part of his mind.

Myself. My mate. Our children. Our kind. We who call ourselves Ai. Our ancestors lived on the ground and weighed more than a fallen tree. It was necessary to adapt. We adapted. Over hundreds of thousands of years we swapped tails for claws and made the trees our home. We have no such time to adapt to life back on the ground.

When he opened his eyes again, his gaze was on the traitor, who was looking straight back at him. He saw it there in the yellowy slits, and Dante knew he did. Then the reptile's stubby feet were pushing against the ground, kicking up dirt, his huge tail whipping for extra boost, and Rosario was leaping from the alligator's back. A pair of crushing jaws were opening on him, and to save his life and that of the forest, Slothi drew on everything he had in his being — and jumped.

DOMINO

"I'm tellin' you, Sai, I nearly fell outta tha tree! Like my jaw droppin' wuz gonna pull me with it when I saw the alligator go for Carlo. Of course, it was all arranged that that wuz gonna be Mario's privilege, 'cept Dante'd been a spoilt brat since he had his eggtooth, couldn't stand the thought o' somebody else gettin' what he wanted. So he goes for the sloth — like, the glory's gotta be all his — an' the puma sees that the action's started without him an' he comes in, like, a quarter second after, but it don't matter now cuz Emilio's on it too an' cuz Carlo ain't where he wuz. Like, he jumped! Did I say 'flew'? Hey, get real, this is a sloth we're talkin' about here. He grabbed Dante's... nose, face, beak, whatever the hell you call the snappy bit on a croc... an' cuz it was openin' up Carlo jus' kinda got a hold an' vaulted over onto Dante's head, makin' this little noise, *aiiiiii!* He lands on Dante's neck, *like he turns in mid-air,* an' slips a claws into his eye-socket an' rips out this little object with a horrible SCHPLOP! an' Dante goes belly up. Yeech! Nasty, huh? Hey, at least it was quick. The cat shouldda been so lucky...."

EMILIO

As soon as Dante moved, Emilio went for the cat because, out of the corner of his eye, he'd already seen Carlo reaching out a claw to the alligator's upper jaw, looking to use the vertical lift to get him out of the way of the eighty teeth. The Don was all right against the alligator so far but the cat was moving on him too. Emilio uncoiled as fast as the cat sprang, and met him head-on.

DOMINO

"There wuz all these sounds, like the cat's miaouw was risin' from his throat, y'know, *raaaaaaaaaaarr!* the way it does when kitties think o' killin'. Then Mario's pouncin' an' then there's this sound like a coconut fallin' onna rock, an' it's the snake an' the cat smackin' heads, but *hard.* Like, I could see the kitty was goin' for Carlo, but he was too slow cuz the snake's headbutt an' prob'ly Dante lyin' there like the skin-thieves got him, musta put him off. Anyways, he's too slow, and Emilio keeps movin' forward after the knock, gettin' busy wrapping himself round

Mauro, keepin' his head away from Mario's jaws, tryna get a collar roun' the kitty's neck. Mario's kinda dazed-lookin', but he ain't so dazed he don't know the snake's got a grip. An' now he starts lashin' out widda claws, whippin' his head round tryna get a bite o' the snake, but he's got, like, Emilio's tail roun' his throat, an' Emilio's got his teeth over the cat's family jewels, ya know whaddim sayin'?

Like, *ouch*.

Loudest noise in the jungle, pal — snakes eatin' hairballs.

Buddy, *the whole damn jungle* put its hand over it."

Emilio kept his body out of the way of Mario's teeth and quickly coiled himself round the cat. When he reached the rear, he saw the dark, furry, heavy, round fruit hanging in front of him and bit as hard as he could.

Mario — now screaming, emptying, toppling.

Here, kitty, kitty, thought Emilio, and he tightened his grip.

Mario — encoiled, thrashing, weakening.

And Emilio squeezed harder..

Mario tried to hold out, staking his strength against Emilio's. So, for a moment, because he had time to kill, Emilio thought about how it felt to hold your breath as he did when he went swimming underwater. For a while, the oxygen feels as if it will last forever because you have never known its lack. Then it starts to feel used-up, and you, stifled. Your lungs start to ache. Soon, the ache is a heat and you have to exhale and breathe again. But what if you can't? What if there is no oxygen? The ache becomes a pain, the air inside you now fetid like a cave lived in too long. The pain becomes unbearable, sparks dance over your eyes,

and a white fire in your chest, which only cool air will put out, rises up into your mouth. At the price of your life, you exhale because you cannot... not.

Mario's strength finally gave out, and his chest caved in as he tried desperately to snatch another breath, another moment of life, but Emilio was ready. When the cat sagged and his lungs emptied, Emilio tightened, breathed deeply, and put on the full crush. Through the mewing and the useless flailing of paws, Emilio squeezed: through the muffled crack of the ribs going, through the weakening twitches, to a final sigh. When Mario was dead, Emilio uncoiled and looked around for his Don.

Carlo was already heading back up his tree.

DOMINO

"S'pose you're wonderin' where the gecko got to, huh? Rosario? The little sucker wi' the little suckers? Well, Rosario soon figured out it was time he was gone, so he starts makin' it through the jungle lookin' for a rock to hide unner, ya know? Things ain't lookin' so great for him back there, what with boss Dante lookin' so floppy lyin' there belly up an' his old pal the kitty all set to disappear down Emilio's mouth... Anyway, all that's happening, an' who's got their eye on the little guy? Mauro. Mauro got him. Hey, he don't look like much but he's *quick*. I'm watchin' the sloth examinin' Dante's little brain on the end of a claw an' Emilio doin' his bit on Mario, an' the hummingbird jus' takes off after the gecko, *zzzuum*! What with the jumpin' sloth, the floppy croc, the snake with the crush on the puma an' the vulture flappin' round squawkin' with piss runnin' down his legs, I don't see it. But get this: I heard it. There's this, like, *squidoiing!* an' like, a vibration goes up my tree. I look down an' there's Mauro, offa the ground, only his wings ain't movin'. Swear — he wuz stuck inna tree with Rosario skewered onna end o' his beak! Hey, I'm so happy, I jus' start laughin', makin' my way downa tree ta lend a paw. I get down. I'm laughin' so hard I can't getta hold of the bill t' yank 'im out. Mauro's buzzin' all mad. Finally I pull him out, wipe a few bits of Rosario off his beak 'n' tell him, "Hey, Mauro, ya got a bent beak!" Y'know what he says?

"Id nod fuddy, doo shoopid fuggin nunky!"

Domino bellowed with laughter, slapping his thighs.

"Ah, Sai... ain't every day things go so right. Anyways, I put a word in for ya with Mauro. Carlo says he'll meet. Says if you really can help, he'll hear ya out."

"When?" asked Sai.

"Now. Let's go. Here... get in my paw. C'mon. Carlo's waiting."

PART 2

THE BIG MIAOUW

CHAPTER V

The Square

Sai walked into the room. The cat-flap closed behind him, and he took in the apartment. Apart from the fact that it smelled a little of cat, it was perfect. The owners were away, and they'd taken the cat. It could not have been more different from the place he had just come from, but it was what he was used to, and Sai liked it immediately: for a rat of his very sybaritic tastes – food, comfort and books - it was ideal. Light filled the elegant quarters, flooding in through four sides of windows that framed the room. He sniffed the air and sighed with pleasure. Looking around, he noticed the spray of flowers – orchids, instantly reminding him of the lush jungle he had just returned from - that had been placed in a vase on the small table by one window. Step-ladders had been provided for ease of access to the sofa and chairs, the reading desk, the bed and dining table of the empty human room, and most importantly, to the bookshelves.

Dwarfed by the room's dimensions, Sai thought of Gulliver as he climbed a ladder and hauled himself onto the table. He lifted his head to sniff the flowers and to admire the pastel shades of their delicate petals. He turned and looked out of the broad window behind him. The view gave onto a large plaza teeming with human and animal activity. The plaza was a great square, a fountain at its center, bordered on all sides by elegant five-storey apartment blocks, with arches and columns skirting the whole.

Through the glass on the other three sides, Sai had a vista of the mountains behind the city, and a panorama of the vast urban sprawl sloping down to the port and the sea that marked the

56

beginning or end of the city, depending on which direction you were travelling in.

Sai came down the ladder and made his way across the room. Again, a little clumsily, Sai scaled another ladder to a low table by the sea-view window where food had been thoughtfully laid out: dishes of seeds and nuts and a shallow silver bowl of water glinting in the sunlight. Exhausted by the journey, Sai sat down and ate greedily some pecan nuts and dried apricots. He was hungry. Not as good as acai, Thought, or camu camu, or maracuya, or cupuacu or kimbu, the new fruits he had eaten in the rainforest. The place was worth saving for that alone, he thought, grinning. Wish I had some now.

But other memories still burned with warm fondness, real pleasure. I survived! thought Sai. Carlo agreed to my plan, because I showed him how he could talk to humans and what to say. And as the Don, Carlo had agreed to do it. Sai had said thank you and goodbye to Domino, and Carlo ordered someone very important to carry him back to his cage. Griselda, a harpie eagle, terrifying to look at, took him in in one of her claws and held him as safely and gently as she would have one of her own eggs, and he had flown in an eagle's talons over the world. This time, he watched without fear and marvelled at the beauty of the forest. Yes. It was right to fight to save it.

She had left him by the cage. He had climbed back in and shut the door, and knew that he was once again safe.

Well, now, at least, he thought, I will have something for the others to pay attention to. Maybe – just for once - I'll even get a little Respect.

Carlo had given him hope, and in return Sai had given guarantees that had given Carlo hope. But I will need all of the others' help in this, all of them, thought Sai.

The travel arrangements on his return from the jungle had been executed without the slightest hitch or delay: once he had found his way back to his cage and reactivated the GPS tracker, the same driver working for differentjungles had found him and returned him from the jungle and delivered him to the airstrip. That plane took him to another. Other hands took care of the cage. Then, it was time to disappear. Extra security measures came in: Sai was not delivered to this place by differentjungles. That focused too much activity on the one place they would all be. So it was a slower way by which he travelled: someone was paid to leave the cage door open; Sai found a way to get beneath the airport, where a rat-drawn sled waited for him, trundling in darkness for miles. Then, a dash in broad daylight to where a car was waiting to take him to the city. The car's human driver was wholly unaware of the sling beneath the chassis bearing Sai and his bodyguard. The bodyguard was silent; the journey very noisy, long, unpleasant and unsettling, but necessary. When the car reached the outskirts of the city, Sai and his bodyguard abandoned it disappeared down a drain again to be once again carried to this place by another rat-sled. There, rats had met him to bring him through the innards of the building, here, to this room, and he had arrived in the appointed place exactly on time.

He looked out of the window again, onto the plaza, at the people strolling. His thoughts drifted. He had moved around so many times now he did not care to remember. One didn't question the order 'leave now' when it came. One left, or one died. A single certainty came with being a MOONrat: men are hunting you, men will always be hunting you, and they will kill you if they find you. Or worse.

Of twelve MOONrats only eight still lived: perhaps the very number of the humans who knew about MOON and wanted to kill them. The collective mind and reach of the MOONrats matched mankind's. It was not MOON's doing, but men's. They sought to vastly accelerate their intelligence. They created a

58

formula. They tested it on rats. It worked. The rats escaped. They fled. They hid. Very rapidly, they came to understand what a human brain could *do*. Memorise. Speculate. Piece together. Learn. Adapt. Create. They could all remember the time of the injections decades ago: bright lights and cages, and the name of the program: M.O.O.N. Ordinary rats now obeyed them without question. Ordinary rats believed them to be beings from another world gave themselves as labour for their schemes. MOON rose, and humans knew nothing about it, except the handful: *the men who created us then, the men who hunt us now*.

Eventually, made sleepy by food and the soft perfume of the orchids as much as by the long, long journey, Sai came down the ladder and headed for the bedroom. There was a full bookcase on the way. Sai browsed for a while.

There was a gentle rattle of claws at the door behind him. Sai turned back into the room and said, "Come in."

A brown rat stepped into the room.

"Good afternoon, Lord Sai."

The rat standing before him was large, heavy-set and strong-looking, with taut muscles visible beneath dark fur. He held his claws in front of him, slightly curled, as if ready to use them. The claws looked sharp and strong.

"Good afternoon," replied Sai.

"My lord. I am Max. I am security advisor to King Marcus, in whose city you are a guest. I put myself and my services at your disposal."

Max seemed to find the words difficult as if he had had to rehearse them and was still uncomfortable with his lines: this wasn't how he normally spoke. Sai thanked him, but the rat seemed as unconcerned with niceties as he was unused to speaking. He excused himself with a final message.

"I have been asked to inform you that the Preliminary Convocation will take place tonight after dark. You will, of course, be taken to the appointed place in a suitable mode of transport when the time comes. It is not far."

Sai had questions.

"Where are the others being accommodated?"

Max hesitated.

"My lord, for reasons of security, I am not permitted to tell you where except to say that they are being quartered comfortably in other apartments around the plaza."

Max excused himself without waiting to see if Sai had further questions. As Max slipped out of the door, Sai caught a glimpse of the two rats standing to attention in Max's presence. The two guards stiffened as Max passed, then relaxed visibly when he was gone, looking relieved.

Sai turned to the bedroom, thinking of the huge soft bed that waited for him. Really, the apartment was delightful, catering to all of Sai's appetites. He climbed onto a pillow curled up, thinking that a long nap was all he needed to be ready for the auspicious meeting he was to attend. It would be good to see so many old friends.

"For reasons of security..." the rat had said. *Hmmm... security being the MOONrat obsession... but "not permitted"?*

Sai was not used to hearing "not permitted". Sai was used to hearing "Yes, sir".

He fell asleep, and when he awoke, it was dark.

ERR

I heard it on The Big Miaouw — the hear-it-and-pass-it-on set-up that ran across the city like a wire stretched tight from the port to the mountains. The Miaouw was a shout that went out whenever a cat got wind of somethin' somebody oughtta know. If it was small-time the yowl didn't travel so far; cats didn't miss a lick or look up. But if it was a shout about a restaurant throwin' out grungey fish-heads an' chicken bones or a little old lady puttin' out saucers of milk, it traveled pretty far, even deeper into the city if it was the shout on a heap o' boats landin' catches down at the docks.

Everybody listened out for The Miaouw, even if it was only the street cats who depended on it because they didn't have nobody bringin' 'em food whenever they did the figure-of-eight-around-the-ankles *I love you* fake-ass shuffle.

Sometimes The Big Miaouw was real important: dead fish bellied-up in the river — *don't eat 'em, don't drink here*; cat flu in the neighbourhood — *stay away*; cats disappearin' in the night - men with nets roustin' cats with no collars like they were no better 'n' dogs — *stay out of sight*; killer dog — *stay up on the walls*. Sometimes it was good news: rats' nest — *paaar-ty! Come along, bring a friend*. Sometimes it was routine bad news like a road death, or other times real spooky, like a human losin' it like plenty do in the city an' puttin' out poisoned fish. Sometimes, it was a shout about a cat-gang turf rumble, and sometimes, it put out straight good news, like so-and-so's kittens were born an' doin' fine an' were goin' to good homes, not down to the river in a pillowcase with a couple of rocks for company.

61

When the miaouw was big-time it went across the city like ripples go across the pond when you make a grab for the stupid fish. That was how the cats passed it all along, an' the bigger the yowl, the more cats heard. That was how I heard about the canary: a miaouw that came out not even medium-size from one of the alleys that lead in an' outta the square — scuzzy under-paw trash-rich windin' narrow streets, five floors up on either side, not much light, lottsa bad smells, turf-marker piss-stinks hustlin' to be the one taken seriously. All the shout said was, *Dead bird in the plaza!* Most cats mussta figured it wasn't worth a look cos by the time they got there the tweetie'd be gone.

I had my face in a trash-can when I heard it. I thought, *plaza*, and started runnin'. I didn't look up at the faces at the top of the shoes I was dodgin', I just kept close to the wall like you got to, and made my way through to the plaza without gettin' kicked or cornered and without nobody I didn't know tryin' to stroke me. The plaza was as much my territory as any other cat's, an' I was runnin' cos I didn't like the shout: a dead bird. Yeah, but who? Pigeons I didn't care about, sparrows I didn't care about, an' if one of the parrots that'd bust outta the cage an' set up in the trees in the plaza had done the big squawk, I didn't care either. I didn't talk to the birds much, didn't eat 'em, didn't even chase 'em. But I knew what it was that took me to the plaza lookin' for a dead bird.

I came into the plaza from one of the back alleys, scoped the place for dogs in general and one in particular, saw a couple poodles an' little yappy Yorkies, but they're nothin', no threat. There were bigger dogs, but probably that time of night they'd eaten, and besides, they were on leashes, bein' walked like good dumb dogs. Plus, the plaza had lots of trees I could make for if I had to quick-scoot out of harm's way.

The square was full of people strollin' or sittin' drinkin' at the tables laid out underneath the arches that skirted the plaza — usual stuff for a warm summer night. There were cats and dogs queuein' up behind dirty people for the bin-bag bonanza. There was lots of noise — singin', shoutin', laughter, music, barkin', sirens, cars — comin' in from all over the city like a cloud and rainin' on the plaza. I made a circuit, lookin' for the cat who put out the shout, but I didn't see nobody.

I padded round real nonchalant, checkin' out the pigeons peckin' around in the square and roostin' on the ledges above, makin' sure none of them didn't drop on me what they like droppin' on everything else: black and white crap in my fur that I'd have to lick off. That would've given me good reason to get real mad at the pigeon who did it. I figured they knew that. I strolled nice an' slow round the square, lookin' for the dead bird, scopin' the gutter, under tables, behind shoes and between chair legs, thinkin' that I should check the fountain and the bins in case the bird got drowned and maybe scooped up an' bin-bagged already.

Then, somethin' in a far corner of the square, a little flash of color caught my eye, and my heart started racing. I started runnin' because the color was right, right enough to stir it all up again... And as I got nearer, I had to tell myself that it *couldn't* be *her*, she was long gone. Then I got there, and it wasn't her, but she was a dead ringer, an' that was enough. Female canary — young, yellow. Bite marks on the back of her neck.

My fur stood up. My ears went back against my head. A noise came out of me, an angry one, stronger than the part of me that tries to never let anythin' show. It wasn't my canary lyin' there dead, but it might have been. And I knew what had done this to her, even if that only narrowed the suspects down to a couple of million. I split before someone saw a dead bird

and a cat put two and two together and got it all wrong, and before the cops could collar me for it.

When the door shut behind him, the first thing Sai did was try to vomit the fruit he had consumed earlier. But he couldn't. He leaned against a table-leg heaving unproductively. He snatched shallow breaths, closed his eyes against the dizziness that scrambled his mind, told himself to fight, to regain control of his thoughts. He opened his eyes, rose shakily and staggered weakly to the window. The arguments at the Convocation were a cacophony in his mind:

"And we see what they will do to the planet if left unchecked..."

"We have no right!"

"When they would do it to us? They hunt us! They murder... US!"

"The consequences... unpredictable, but perhaps..."

"They threaten all life on the planet, it is true..."

"And *your* plan? What life will remain after *that*?"

"We need them. We feed off them."

"WE need not be parasites!"

"We must control their numbers…"

"And my plan to save the forest? What about that?"

And Caleb's final statement:

"Pointless, Sai. No longer necessary. With my plan, the rainforests will be saved, all of them, because there won't be any humans left to destroy them. We simply have to wipe them out. I have the weapon. Shall we deploy it?"

It was no longer men that MOON had to fear. Or, it was no longer *only* men that MOON had to fear. It now had MOON to fear. And the rat kingdom.

Sai's mind boiled. In the course of a single night he had seen friends corrupted with the promise of power. And he himself had stood silently by, like a coward, when Marcus ordered the bird murdered. Poor canary. What could she have told anybody? Sai forced himself to assess the situation calmly. Four of MOON had opposed Domus' proposition. Three had seconded it, and also a ninth rat, not of MOON but a ruling rat nonetheless, a host-king consequently entitled to vote; a king who could not hide his glee at the prospect of mass slaughter: King Marcus.

Now Sai knew two things:

We cannot let him have the power Caleb is offering. We must say 'no' to this.

And if we do, they will kill us.

My choices are mass murder or suicide.

Outside, at the mountain's summit, pink clouds flocked to the sun, color on the frayed edges of the night. Light and dark began to merge. *Chiaroscuro* thought Sai — the blending of darkness and light. *Which is stronger in MOON? Where once we embodied the best of man and the best of rat, some of us have now cast aside both to embrace the horror in the deepest chasms of the rat and the human heart.*

Another wave of sickness washed through him. Had he been poisoned? He fought the paralyzing nausea, now recognizing it for what it was: fear. The fear he had learned in his journey into the forest: fear for his lown ife, and fear for the lives of those others who opposed Caleb.

"Beware, Sai," Libo had whispered as they dispersed after the long arguing. "Caleb will not be thwarted. We must, all four of us, cast our vote. Do not take food, Sai. I fear poison."

Sai shivered. Libo was right: should one of them fail to cast a vote, the Proposition would carry. There was no doubt which way Marcus would vote. Libo saw clearly, too, what Sai had guessed: Caleb was prepared to murder. The life of one of his companions was nothing compared to the prize he had set his mind on. Sai looked around the apartment.

This is where I will be for the next two days and nights, he thought.

I cannot speak to those who share my view or to those who oppose it.

Security, I am told.

The lovely apartment no longer seems so welcoming.

Caleb is insane.

My courteous host is a monster, his Head of Security a killer.

This guest-room is a cell, my protectors are my gaolers.

A canary is dangerous.

Black is white.

MOON is half in darkness.

In this place, where I must do my clearest thinking, nothing is what it seems.

Caleb's plan left Sai dazed by its completeness and ferocity.

Caleb has thought of everything.

He turned toward the window and saw his reflection looking back at him.

Two of me thought Sai. *And we both look scared.*

LOUIE

Louie sniffed the air, and it made him gag. If there was a worse smell in the city, well, he didn't know of it or want to, and he was not an over-particular type of rat, just very, very unlucky. A black rat's day-to-day life was to be crap-out-of-luck every time, every time. Black cats didn't know what bad luck was: they served it up didn't have to live off it like a black rat did.

Louie in the sewer. His recent above-ground luck stank like the air down there: figure an enforced three-day sewer vacation as the crappiest-luck thing that could happen to a black rat just *had* to come true.

Louie listened for the sound of sniffing and scuttling, claws on the slimy floor below but heard only the gurgling of the turgid river. He didn't look out: no point. Zero light, solid darkness out there, with no way of telling whether it was day or night aboveground. Besides, he was too scared of being spotted: sewer guys see fine.

They don't know where I am, and nor do I: the plaza's above, that's all I know, thought Louie.

His eyes were only slowly adapting to the dark. The walls of the fissure he'd found were close, bent his whiskers on either side. The hole was narrow but deep. He couldn't see the river or riverbanks from the back of the crack and was counting on that working two ways.

Louie shivered though it wasn't cold in the sewer — the stinking river seemed to warm the air even as it turned it foul. He shivered because he had the yips, real bad. On a good day, Louie rated as one of the least popular guys in the city, one who routinely looked over his shoulder every ten paces because there was always someone out there who wanted to rip him off or rip him to pieces, and that was on a good day. Today rated as extra bad. Like last night. Like the next few days, too.

Louie was scared, but Louie was smart: smart like a guy who has to chisel and scam and sneak and thieve to keep from getting thin. Louie tried to work angles. His brain was working things over faster than was good, boiling in the fever air of the sewer. Keeping to the very back of the crevice, he tried to piece it all together:

Marcus' crews would be looking for him by now. And 'crews' could mean anything up to two million rats. They were out looking and sniffing for him. All the high places, probably, all the obvious places: anywhere black rats could climb where the brown rats couldn't. It'd be slow work because the climbing would put them off, but not for ever. Brown rats always worked something out in the end: they were smart, they'd figure it — wall cavities, vent shafts, plumbing, garbage chutes, cable trays, wiring ducts... all ways UP.

Three days, remembered Louie. *Three days and then it happens, and it won't matter what you heard because then everything's dead.* Three days hiding out in a sewer where the brown rats would never think to look for him, where there was no light to see by, where the stink was so bad your own couldn't give you away. Louie thought about the smells on him: nothing strong, nothing that would shout above the stink of human and brown rat shit and piss.

Nothing *on* him, then, but something *in* him — brown rats could smell Fear. Fear was what might give him away.

Think Nice Things, Louie, he told himself. *Think about all the Nice Things that will happen again when you get out.*

Not 'if'. 'When.'

Nice Things to lull the fear.

Fear was good sometimes: it kept you alert, which kept you alive. But other times, it crippled you — it could be your worst enemy — and the fear was always there. Being smart was bad luck. Big problem with being smart *and* scared? You could always imagine the worst... especially while you were huddled in a hole, praying it wouldn't come true. There was a little voice in Louie squeaking the worst thing. Louie wished it would shut up because it was going to wake up his fear.

The worst thing? What brown rats did to black rats.

Louie shivered, gritted his teeth, stuck real close to the back of the crevice, thought Nice Things: up on the roofs with Sax, singing... looking at the moon, planning on the day he'd go there and make The Big Cheese his turf.

The Voice came back:

No, Louie: by the time you get there, the rats from the moon will have eaten it all.

Figures thought Louie. *Crap-luck life.*

SCHAEFFER

The goddamn partner was driving Schaeffer nuts. Schaeffer helped him out, but the two-legs couldn't do squat to help him because he was two-legged and dumb and slow and didn't know dog-dick about the job. He drove the car and fixed Schaeffer's chow when they clocked off — they shared an apartment — and that, basically, was the partnership. They had the same beat but very different jobs, and Schaeffer wasn't about to put in for a transfer, so he was stuck with Fatso.

His partner didn't talk to him much, which suited Schaeffer just fine: he had his kind of police work, and Fatso had another kind. The two-legs moved the winos and the smellier beggars on from where the clean people sat and drank, and he occasionally chased a thief or, more likely, shouted into the radio on his belt and then made Schaeffer go get 'em. Schaeffer would go do the dangerous bit, Fatso would get the collar, and Schaeffer would get a pat on the head, thinking someone should slap blueboy's fat butt for a change and make him run after the bad guys.

The partnership stank, and the chain of command was round Schaeffer's neck, choke on. But when he wasn't doing the two-legs' job for him, Schaeffer could do his own: keeping an eye on the plaza, keeping track of all the dogs, cats and birds, and making damn sure the rats stayed behind drain-bars, down in the sewer where they belonged. Schaeffer wandered around nice and visible, so everybody knew he was there, a full-on police presence. He was nice to all the two-leg kiddies, letting them pull his ears while making sure that no wiseass-coming-on-badass dogs bit their soccer balls. He told the pigeons to be nice and not crap where everybody ate, so between him and the guy on the other end of the leash, the arches and the plaza were covered.

Schaeffer knew every inch of the square and everything in it by smell. He had a nose for police work. He knew the scents of every barker and howler, every bin-bag ripper and turd-artist; of all the snatch 'n' dash sausage-blaggers hanging around waiting for an opportunity to make a thief out of a bum. He watchdogged the wannabee bad guys who thought they owned the place just because they once took a pee there; kept tabs on every lamp-post lingerer, leg-humper, flea-bitten mongrel loser and cheap-date trash-can gourmet. He knew the street mutts in the back alleys, the family pets, the barfly pooches and guide dogs, the scruffy, the dirty, the hungry and the lost, the hardball terriers and the shivery little chihuahuas. He knew the perfumed, ribboned, straight-from-the-beauty-parlour high-class poodles and pekes and the different tartans of a dozen cissy-dog waistcoats, and he kept the plaza safe for them. Or from them. Depending on which side of the good dog/bad dog line they left their paw prints.

He knew them, and they all knew him: he was Schaeffer, the top cop dog, police training college graduate with honours. Three generations of cop in his family, police-dogging in his blood, a cop to his German bones. His authority was stamped on the badge on his collar — *Schaeffer, BCPD: PD 647* — and he'd made a lot of collars in his time. Everyone knew the plaza was Schaeffer's beat, and nobody messed because dog mess was *verboten* on his patch. He could follow you forever on a scent you didn't know you'd left, and he never gave up, never forgot a smell. He had a big bark he backed up with bite when he had to, and the only chance an offender had was to be very quick and to never, ever come back to the plaza. Schaeffer knew that the only time there would ever be an animal crime on his beat was when he had to go do his partner's damn job for him.

Occasionally Schaeffer had to leave the plaza, sometimes for days at a stretch, helping Fatso again. That was when he was at his edgiest: when procedure demanded he leave the beat, get in the car and go get caught up in some case across town. That was when the wise-asses whooped it up. Turds appeared all over the square, tourists had steaks heisted straight from their plates, footballs got bitten and punctured and little kiddies bawled, legs got humped, bins got turned over, mongrels tried it on with high-class dogs, and no lamp-post or column was safe. And Schaeffer couldn't do a damn thing about it.

Sometimes the department was so screwed up he could have howled. The partner was the pits. Schaeffer did his job for him, and at the end of the shift, they'd go back to the apartment. While all Schaeffer could think of was being out on the beat doing his duty, letting the innocent just-out-for-a-walkers and mangy punks alike know that the law was there, the blue blob would park his lazy ass on the sofa, turn on the television and slob out with a can of beer balanced on his gut, stroking his gun or scratching his ass. Schaeffer would have been pawing and whining at the door if he'd thought it would get him out into the street and not just a smack on the ear.

So he'd just have to get in his basket use the time to think about procedure, methodology, smells and the law. Sometimes, he'd think of putting in for a transfer, except he knew he'd miss the beat too much, and the only other assignments were the ball games and the Metro — dull dog-house postings. Narcotics had juice for a career-minded dog, except it sounded better than it really was: working the airport, sniffing suitcases all day in too-clean surroundings, lots of waiting around and working with people – a bum job. Then he'd think, *What the hell? I do my job,*

Fatso does his. They were two sides of the same Police Department, both sworn to Protect and Serve. And no matter how dumb the partner was, no matter how dumb procedure was, it didn't stop Schaeffer from getting the job done. At the end of the day, Partner slobbed, watched television and let the job go. Schaeffer lay in his basket, thought about real police work and licked his balls. It beat television.

RR

I slunk out of the plaza like a murderer, and probably that was what I looked like to any passer-by who didn't know me — didn't know about me an' canaries. I left the canary unburied. I didn't like leavin' her out there with a thousand pairs of feet trampin' by, but I couldn't carry her away without takin' her in my jaws and havin' to run a gauntlet of hissin' humans. Some of 'em would've figured she was maybe still alive because even they know that birds will try an' trick a cat an' maybe bluff one last chance t' get on the wing by playing dead. I'd have been cornered and hauled up by the scruff and smacked around the head 'til I let go, and then I'd be blamed for killin' her and probably gotten another slapping... So I went back to the alleys an' prowled awhile, thinking about the Jane Doe, but mainly about another canary, remindin' myself that the promise I made her was good for all canaries if it was to mean anythin' at all. I found a passageway, got off the street, crawled under a gate, found a quiet yard, an' sat there, alone, rememberin'.

I guess it was love, but it ain't easy for a cat to love a canary in the right way, an' I used to wonder whether that was what she was singin' about there in the cage: 'bout how close we was, 'bout

73

the day I was a young stray cat cruisin' the rooftops an' I saw her for the first time, an' I went to it thinkin' *food*... an' then, I heard her sing and time froze. We just looked at each other, her probably picturin' me with feathers round my mouth... but she was wrong. I wanted t' hear more song *soooo* bad I rolled on the floor an' miaouwed, beggin' for it. She mustta seen I was a sucker for a toon.

I went back every day, fell in love with the music an' the canary, told myself she loved me and told her no cat was ever gonna touch her cos baaaad ginger Frankie Frr was the cat they gotta get past t' do it. It was love, the real thing, from the heart, so true it ached. The songs were so beautiful. I couldn't make out the words. Songs from the old country, I guess. Maybe she was singin' a toon for me. I never knew. I still don't. I never will. Sometimes, the songs were so sad they broke my heart with notes sharp as claws laying me open to my soul, makin' my fur stand on end so I'd want to yowl. Those songs were easy enough to understand: they were about how she couldn't get out of the damn cage an' about how I couldn't help, an' maybe about how even if I could, it wouldn't have worked for us.

She saw birds flyin' by all day every day, an' though they weren't as pretty as her, they was free an' she was behind bars... Some old dame lived on the fifth floor, didn't walk too good, didn't have a family, or least if she did, she didn't see them much... gotta have a bird in a cage, like that's gonna make it all better. Shouldda had a dog an' kept it in a trashcan.

Now I know what she was singin' about. It wasn't me, wasn't the diva an' the alley cat, it wasn't love she was singin' about: it was freedom, an' how life ain't nothin' without it. When I came to see it that way, I took it so bad after a while, I couldn't be near her for long; had to make an excuse about a case or a contact or a lead an' split. But I could hear her song all over the 'hood, an' it was like cold water on my fur. Me! Mean, big, tough

Frankie Frr, keepin' it together in a tough world, the ginger cat you didn't stroke the wrong way unless you was real tough... An' then I'd hear the song floatin' on the breeze, meltin' me, makin' me a kitten. She'd sing an' somethin' real big, real deep inside me would move an' I'd try to make it go away, but she'd just keep singin' an' the song would float across the city night clear as the moon, an' find me out an' tell me my heart. Maybe so's I wouldn't forget. Maybe so's I couldn't forget. The songs were like butterflies you couldn't box away. Songs about freedom an' songs about how you gonna give your heart to somethin', or someone, like it or not. The canary — she had my heart: it was there right next to her in the cage.

One day I went back to the little bit of terrace on the fifth where the old dame put the cage, determined to spring her. I knew somethin' was wrong when I was approachin' an' I didn't hear no song. I got closer. Then I saw why. The old dame was dead — had been for a couple days judgin' by the smell. Nobody'd cared enough to have found out. The city can do that to you. Poor old lady. Nobody cared that she was dead except me, an' that was for another reason anyway. I cared because if somebody'd bothered enough to look in on the old dame, maybe she wouldn't've been dead, an' the canary would have been fed.

Bottom of the cage: yellow feathers, grey grit, her head under her wing. Something died in me then — make that eight lives left. Tears in my eyes, I blamed myself and promised a dead bird I'd protect all the canaries. I got out through a window and scratched at a neighbour's door 'til someone came, then I miaouwed at the old dame's door 'til one of the neighbours realised that the old dame needed attention and I split before the cops arrived.

That was what I was thinking about in the yard. That, and the bite marks in the Jane Doe's neck. All of a sudden I wanted to hear birdsong again, a canary hittin' a note that could break a glass

75

heart, an' holdin' it 'til tears came to my eyes and my fur crackled down my spine.

I miss her. I miss the music. I got my toons from other birds now, but they were never as good. An' anyway, Zoot Jackdaw and his Rooftop Swing Combo weren't playin' that night.

Sai tried to think one step ahead of Caleb. He accepted the food that was brought to him but ate none of it. Hunger was the least of Sai's concerns: he had spare flesh, he would not fade. There was no leaving the apartment and no slackening of vigilance from the guards at the door. There would be no visits from the others. Were they being fed poison? Had they been convinced or coerced into joining Caleb's party? Had, conversely, a miracle occurred: one of the pro-Caleb faction had experienced a change of heart? There was no way of knowing.

With only anxieties for company, Sai knew it would not be long before he started to experience despair, his thoughts spiralling down into catastrophic pessimism. Was that part of Caleb's plan? To isolate opposition to his twisted dreams of power, and thus weaken it? Sai thought of his old friends Dorothea, Priscillian, Spero and Nestor: all dead now, all hunted down by the very humans who had made the MOONrats what they were. Sai missed them badly — they all would have wholly deplored Caleb's scheme, means and ends alike. And yet the scheme was not ridiculous: that was the worst thing. The idea was all too feasible and looked well within the realms of possibility. He had tcreated he weapon, had planned its deployment, its timing, and he had carefully calculated its effects. He had thought about it as a human, not as a rat, but no plan devised by humans ever went perfectly. There was always human error.

Sai shuddered.

Two days to go until the Convocation.

Hope depended on finding an error in a brilliant plan.

I need time. I need information. I need to get through this and concentrate on helping Carlo, and I need all of MOON's skills to do that.

He waddled over to the bookcase and found a book that had caught his eye on his arrival: *Florence, 1320-1480.*

Sai heaved up the ladder, hooked the top of the book's spine with a claw, and tugged it 'til it toppled to the floor with a thump. The door was immediately opened. One of the guards came in, alarmed.

"My lord, noise may alert humans to our presence here."

Sai fixed him with a piercing pink stare and ordered him to take the book to the reading table by the plaza-side window. He watched the team of rats the guard fetched move the book to where he had told them. Then Sai dismissed them curtly.

"Leave me."

He opened the book and started reading.

SCHAEFFER

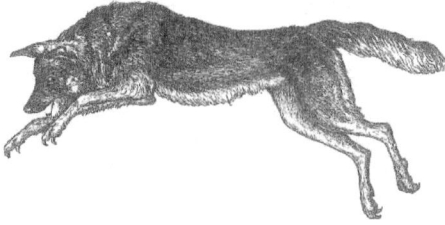

Out of sight, out of mind... *In a cat's ass*, thought Schaeffer with grim satisfaction as he sat in the back of the car and Partner took them across town, back to the plaza.

The mid-town midday traffic was agonisingly slow: Schaeffer barked at Partner to put the siren on and got a smack on the ear for it. He gave up and let the idiot take charge. Vehicles wheezed like fat old dogs through the city. Humans growled at traffic lights and worked car-horns the way a dog barks when it's been cooped up in a flat on the fifth floor for two days and needs a crap.

Schaeffer's week so far: a temporary posting to Narco, a day spent away from the plaza rooting around a trailer park across town, sniffing for powder. It was a spaniel-job, and it should have gone to a rookie —- he was too damn good to waste on a routine sniff-out. But the assignment went Schaeffer's way anyway. Usual procedure: the cop dog did the police work while his two-legs bitched at the top of the lead and took lots of coffee-breaks. The two-legs all stank heaps worse than the load the dog was sniffing for, and this being a case where the two-legs would be getting the credit when the dog dug up the stash, it was all being done by the book — the dumbest way, in a grid-search pattern. Visuals, because two-legs couldn't smell for shit. 'Procedure'. They should have let the expert off the leash. He would have tossed the trailer-park in an hour tops and had the bag out of the ground before the second box of donuts was even opened.

Schaeffer found the load even though it was wrapped tight in three layers of plastic, and buried. Whoever put it there had eaten pastrami before he buried it, and that was how Schaeffer found the bag. Even if the bag hadn't stunk like meat, the soil smelled all dug-up and fresh, and Schaeffer had been sniffing for that first thing. The guy must have been real dumb to eat a sandwich that stank so strong and then bury the bag smelling of it in a place where you *never* smelled pastrami. Any good cop dog knew that if you wanted to hide something, you thought about smell first. Did it fit in, blend, sit natural with everything around it? Schaeffer could remember his first class at training college — OD 101: Olfactory Deduction — with a departmental legend dishing detail to the rookies: Captain Sam Gold, 'The Retriever', the most decorated Narco dog in BCPD history.

"Where do you stash a steak when you boost a butcher's? Answer: in his trashcan. Where do rats live? Answer: where it smells worst.

Why do cats wash so much? Answer: 'cause they got somethin' to hide.

A good cop dog thinks with his nose. If the human you're lookin' for smokes, what do the butts smell like? If it's dogs you're lookin' for, ditto..."

They pulled into the plaza and took a long, slow circuit around, Fatso looking for dames to park next to. Schaeffer looked through the window, and saw some dogs who really should have known better than to be on his patch — a couple of bin-bag-worriers and Scotty McDougall, looking respectable in a tartan waistcoat and fooling everyone but Schaeffer. Schaeffer had Scotty fitted out with a snitch jacket.

Scotty McDougall, aka 'Smokie McDog', but an aka from waaaay back. Schaeffer had Scotty's smell filed in his memory next to his record: the white terrier was a one-time ankle-worrier who used to run with the Westies, a distraction guy. He grabbed

79

hold of the two-legs' trouser-bottoms and drew all the looks with his comedy growling while the real crime went off — a hot steak or chop heist straight from the plate in broad daylight. The gang had gotten fat on it, running the scam all over town. They got cocky and did it on Schaeffer's patch while he was on duty. Schaeffer had lost the jaws-guy because he was real fast, but he picked up his smell and went back for Scotty, who was sauntering around, making like he wanted to be in the plaza and not at the hide-out divvying up the loot. It took Schaeffer about five seconds to bark the little guy's protests down to a whimper, another five before he rolled over and gave up the name of Zippo Whippet. Schaeffer memorised Zippo and said, "I see you again, I'll tear your throat out." He figured Zippo would know to stay gone. And Scotty'd snitched: now he was Schaeffer's.

Fatso let Schaeffer out of the car. He stretched low and long, lengthening his muscles to drive the cramp out, breathing deep to get the smell of Fatso and the car out of his head. He barked at Scotty.

"Mac! Get your butt here!"

The westie's tail dropped. He slunk over, looking at the floor.

Schaeffer glowered at him, kept the growl down low, but let the small guy know it was there, with the big bite sitting right behind it.

"I been away, Scotty. Just a couple of days. Don't tell me you figured it was a transfer and decided to get the gang together again."

The little westie shook his head.

"Och, no, Officer Schaeffer. Ah'm a gud dug so ah am."

Schaeffer growled, "Oh yeah?"

And frisked him anyway, sniffing head to tail for steak smells. Scotty stank but not of anything incriminating.

"You stink, Scotty. But legally, you're clean. Better keep it that way, too."

"Aye, aye, Officer. Likesay, ah'm no a bad dug."

"You seen Zippo lately?"

Scotty shook his head looked down, probably remembering how scared he'd been of Schaeffer when he'd been turned snitch.

"Seen anybody new in the plaza?"

"New dugs? Nay new dugs, but there's been rats oot 'n' aboot the night."

"Doing what?" growled Schaeffer.

"Askin' fae rat, Louie. Thass funny tha' is... Louie's no broon an' these wus broon rats."

"Yeah, yeah. So what else?"

Scotty shuffled.

"A big gingey cat's bin snootin' aboot. Askin' questions an' that."

"Questions about what?"

"Aboot a wee bird. A dead bird."

Schaeffer's ears pricked up.

"What does he look like?"

"She. Yelly fairthers..."

"The cat! Ya mutt."

"Oh. Likesay, gingey. 'N' bits ay white 'n 'is fur 'n' that."

"Did you chase him?"

"Och no, Officer, likesay ah'm..."

"Yeah, yeah. A good dog. I heard ya the other times. 'Cept, I wouldn't have cared if you *had* chased him, Scotty. Dogs chase cats, right? It's natural. So why didn't you?"

The little white dog nipped at a flea, uncomfortable.

"Well, ah'm no a big dug like, an ah..."

"... figured he'd shred your sorry ass?" Schaeffer offered.

Scotty looked away, a long-distance stare back to better times when he'd run with the westies. Nobody messed with him then: he'd been big-time, a three-steaks-a-day top-dog, bitches all over him. Now he begged at tables by day and nights he followed drunks home, hoping they'd throw up.

Schaeffer looked down at the little dog and his grimy, dumb waistcoat.

"Beat it. I'm gonna give you ten seconds, and then you'd better be gone from the plaza. *Smokie*."

The little dog yelped,

"Ah cannae run that fast, it'll take mair'n ten seconds tae..."

"Nine... eight..."

"Ah'm no built fae't! Ye cannae run that fast if ye havnae got long legs!"

"...seven, six..."

Schaeffer watched as Scotty scarpered.

Schaeffer chewed the snitch-meat over. A dead bird in the plaza. Brown rats looking for a black rat. A ginger cat asking questions. His hackles prickled slightly. He figured he knew who the ginger cat might be. And if *he* was snooping round the plaza, Schaeffer wanted to know why.

Fatso whistled. Schaeffer came to heel, wanting to bite.

LOUIE

Out of sight, out of mind, thought Louie, curled tight at the back of his hole. If only. The brown rats hadn't seen so much as a whisker of Louie since he overheard the MOONrats and Marcus on the terrace, and the longer it stayed that way, the better because if they found him, they'd kill him. Twice. That was the way it was between the brown rats and the black rats: brown rats ran the city and didn't allow any competition. They went more or less anywhere they wanted and helped themselves to whatever they found. They robbed and killed whoever got in the way, and tribute and kickbacks went upstairs to Marcus. Make that downstairs: King Marcus lived deep down in the dark heart of the sewer. The city belonged to the brown rats and had done for as long as anyone could remember. Black rats hid from brown. Black rats were too small and too few. Brown rats were bigger, nastier, hungrier, and there were millions of them. Black rats hid from brown like they hid from everything else. There were scattered communities of black rats left, always hidden, high up, where the brown ones couldn't climb.

Louie flinched in the dark: the communities were in so much danger. He had to get out and tell them, warn them. *The old death is coming back. We will be blamed, hunted down, destroyed...* But he couldn't move: he couldn't go further into the underworld, nor up into the plaza. By day or night, the plaza had a thousand eyes — dogs', cats', humans' — all hostile: everything wanted to kill him. Wherever he ran, he would be hunted. He had no friends to turn to up there except one, and Sax would be southbound by now if he was smart.

No, he wouldn't: Sax wasn't afraid, not like Louie. Sax was cool, and Sax was fly. Sax had his voice and that made him Great, but Sax wasn't afraid enough. Louie'd warned him, told him, "Get out of the city, Sax, things're gonna get nasty," but Sax had just looked blank, and Louie hadn't had time to spell it out to him. How could he? Only a rat would have truly understood.

He'd had to get off the roof, lose his pursuers. He'd came up with the crazy idea of hiding right under their noses where the smell was so bad it leveled the odds. Louie had nowhere else to go: anybody suspected of helping him would make an enemy of the brown rats, and that was the very worst enemy you could have. Any bolthole he might have had would be watched. Only here, in a hole in a wall near where the sewer met the world, did Louie think he was safe.

But it wouldn't last forever: he was hungry and thirsty, and the air felt like mild poison, building up.

Sitting at his reading desk in the apartment that had been prepared for his brief stay in the city, Sai found that he was too distracted to concentrate on the book before him.

In the rat's mind, the shrill imagining of slaughter and destruction was a din over which he could barely hear himself think. He could not read. He looked out of the window, down onto the plaza. He saw complacent humans walking in the sunshine, unaware their lives would become pure horror in a matter of days. He saw a policeman with a police dog — representatives of human authority that would soon be obsolete.

Caleb wants to take over the world, to build tyranny on the foundations of death. Caleb is planning to unleash a death, which, by its very nature, has no limits. Pasteurella pestis. *This death, this ancient, terrible power; its origins uncertain, its lifespan... indefinite? Who would wish for its reappearance?* Sai wondered.

Yet he knew the answer: somebody who had imagined how to harness its power to his own ends.

Caleb thought Sai: o*nce I admired him. Now I fear him.*

He returned to the bookcase, his mind a little clearer, his will a little stronger. He felt pangs of hunger but ignored them, just like he ignored the food that had been brought to him. Other deliciousness awaited: on the bookshelf before him was Boccaccio's *Decameron*, and a description of Florence in the grip of the Black Death.

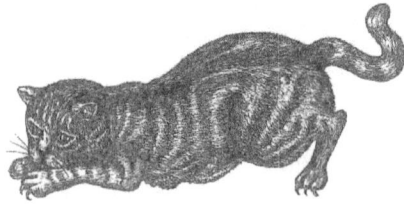

ERR

The bite marks bothered me, because I'd seen that kind of bite before, though only ever on a pigeon, never a canary. The bites weren't post-mortem as the beak was open. She'd died screamin'. They weren't bite marks a cat would have left: the punctures were on the back of the neck, curvin' inwards like a cat's teeth do, but the holes weren't circles. They were fine slits, two of them, and so close together they looked like one wound. But I looked real close and I could see that the middle of the gash was ragged, and the wound profiles were for sharp, squared-off flat teeth, not round. Incisors, not fangs. Only one animal could have done that: a rodent. And I figured it wasn't no hamster or mouse. Which put a rat in the frame. Motive? Hell, who knows anythin' about rats and their motives? Food wasn't a dead cert because I'd found the canary and she hadn't been bitten about the body: no attempt had been made to eat her. A lot of rats like to kill for the hell of it; a lot of cats too. I seen some frenzied killings in my time — dogs doin' it to cats, cats doin' it to birds an' rats, rats doin' it to anything small enough or, if there was enough of them, takin' down the bigger guy. This was no frenzy. The bites were quick and clean. I turned it over in my head, trying to see all the angles.

So what was she doing on the plaza floor and not in the cage? If she was out of the cage, why didn't she fly? I couldn't figure anythin' out, so I went back to the corner of the plaza where I'd found the bird. She'd been taken away. I looked up at the building she'd lived in. I'd need to take a prowl up there, and soon, but there were things I could do down on the ground.

I started askin' questions. Cats I talked to — the ones who lived around the square and who I saw every day — had all heard The Miaouw, and most of them remembered what they were

doin' on the night. Nobody knew anythin' about the bird, though. Some hadn't even known there was a canary on the fifth floor in that corner of the plaza. A couple of cats gave the impression that if they had known, there wouldn't have been any evidence of a crime. Hell, they wouldn't even have seen it as a crime, just what you gotta do when you gotta eat. I could see it in their eyes. I could see they were thinking, *A bird lives, a bird dies: what's it to you?*

I guess I'm a pretty strange cat for the thing I got about canaries.

I never tell cats what put it there.

I made my way round the plaza, and the pigeons got out of my way, flappin' off and givin' me the bird-eye, which means, *Watch your fur when I'm in the air, pal!* The pigeons weren't to know I was strictly a fish kind of cat, an' I wasn't about to tell them in case they started getting fresh. They're slow an' pretty easy to catch, leastways in the city they are: probably all drowsy cos there's always plenty to eat scattered round the plaza floor an' it's nice an' warm. Maybe it's breathin' traffic-fumes in the sun makes 'em so dopey. Whatever, lottsa cats lunch out that way, so there wasn't a whole lotta love lost between fur and feathers. I figured nobody on the ground had seen anythin', so I was lookin' for anybody who maybe'd been up on the roof or in the air about the time the canary got murdered. Which meant I gotta talk to the birds if I couldn't find a cat who got somethin' for me to go on. I prowled, headin' out of the plaza into the alleys around it.

All I wanted was the name of the cat who put out the shout on the dead canary, but cats is cats and cagey about sayin' too much. I asked trash-canners and a couple of house-cats from the neighbourhood. No-one remembered exactly who the shout came up from, or if they did, they weren't about to just let it go without a paw gettin' greased.

It took me most of the rest of the night to get the name: ol' Blue Eyes, Siamese Chi, honked it up. Sam. I should have known. I should have gone to him first.

Sam was a big Persian who lived in an alley off the plaza, fat an' jolly an' comfortable, with a big family around him. He was dark grey, double-fluffy, an' a lot of cats had made the mistake of thinkin' they could walk all over him cos he looked like a rug. Big mistake: his fur wasn't so thick that insults just bounced off it, and flat-faced Sam had a southpaw that came out of nowhere. His best street-fightin' years were over, but you could still see the occasional cat from his past, a quarter of an ear lighter for not havin' watched out for Sam's left hook. He owned a couple of humans, which meant his address was basically Cream Street, but he still got around.

In his day, he'd been tough, charmed a lotta ladies, an' proved he was cat enough to defend his own. Sam was gooood company: lots of times, we'd prowled together up to the roofs to hear Zoot an' the crew croon. He knew what my thing about canaries was, even if I didn't ever tell him why. When I found him, he looked as if he'd been expectin' me. When I came down his alley, he stopped lickin', shooed a coupla grandkittens off to play and got up to greet me.

"Frankie..."

"Hey, Sam."

We rubbed noses. Sam sat back.

"Figured I'd see you soon enough. Ya heard about the canary on The Miaouw, right?"

I couldn't jive Sam. I nodded. He scowled. He respected me even if he thought the canary thing I had was weird for a cat.

"This a case? Is there, like, any fish in this for you?"

I shrugged.

"No, I didn't think so. Not witchoo. It's purr-sonal, ain't it?"

He shook his head. I felt defensive. I said, "Just curious,"

Sam looked me real hard in the eye, a reminder of what every cat gets taught before he even gets off the tit: what curiosity does to cats.

I said, "I hear ya, Sam."

Sam lightened up batted me gently round the chops with a paw.

"Funny kinda cat you are, Frankie."

He told me what he'd seen. He was sidlin' roun' the plaza after a day spent nappin' when a canary dropped to the ground a few paces ahead of him like a gift. He didn't touch it, though. Figured it was another cat's supper.

"Did you look at her, Sam?" I asked.

"Hell, no. Somebody'd've thrown a shoe at me if they'd seen me next to a dead birdie."

I told him what I'd seen; what there'd been on the tweetie's neck. I told him to let other cats know but not to put it out on The Miaouw. He told me to be careful. I prowled.

I didn't have a whole lot to go on, and, to tell the truth, I didn't even know why I was lookin' into the canary's murder. A rat killed her. There were about two million rats in the city, and my contacts in Ratsville were zero. Odds of makin' the case? Same as meetin' a dog with nice breath. Or a nice rat. I was thinkin', *Why do I wanna get any nearer to rats than I have to?*

I'll tell you how it is with cats and rats. Cats teach their kits: *Never hesitate. Never play with a rat: it ain't no mouse. Just kill it.* That is it. That is how it is and always was. No way can they be allowed to even dream about sharing territory with us: any alleyway encounter gets bloody. Cats start kits off with mice, just practice for the real thing... then take 'em out into the alley one night when they're big enough, show them what they gotta do and teach 'em: Leave the body in the street, that way, the rats get the message. I came across plenty of rats in the alley late at night, did what a cat gotta do. Rat an' cat, paw to paw? Rat got no chance. Rats in numbers is when you find out how tough you are.

One time, by the port, I got jumped by five ship rats. Rats jump you, the only way Out is In — no hesitation. I did the first two with teeth, opened up the third with claws, red-striped the fourth with a longshot swipe as he hauled tail, and missed the last one. But these were black rats, little guys compared to the brown rats down in the sewers. Brown rats are tough. Sewer rat's life gotta be ugly, an' it makes them mean an' tough an', most of all, hungry. Stick your face in a trashcan without sniffin' first, you could find a full-crew rat pack. Four, maybe even jus' three of them, an' you could lose your whole nine at once for just a quarter second's thinkin' about what you need to do instead of just doin' it... an' y'ain't permitted to run. Just thinkin' about them made me want to wash.

I couldn't see how I could get the bird's killer, but I kept on lookin'. I went to the building with the balcony that the canary fell off. I waited in the alley for someone to come out and then I slipped in the door as she closed it and made my way up the stairs. When I got to the fifth, I found just one door. I pushed against it, but it didn't budge. I sniffed under the door caught a strange perfume, sweet like flowers but none I'd smelled before, and a tiny whiff of rat. If it hadn't been what I'd sort of expected, I'd've put it down to the fact that pretty much anywhere you can smell rat. They get everywhere, and the smell lingers. I looked around for a window that would let me onto the balcony, but they were all shut. Dead end. I went back down, no questions answered.

SCHAEFFER

BCPD policy towards rats was to chase, apprehend and question any rodent wiseass enough to show its pointy face aboveground. Schaeffer's inclination was to bite on sight, one he only just held in check: rats meant the underworld, and the underworld meant Marcus. Marcus was any cop dog's Most Wanted guy. Figure the sewer rats as a gang of millions, with Marcus right at the top, and you had the name of a guy who ordered robberies, thefts and murders all over the city. Based on BCPD estimations, a quarter of the city's stored foods were stolen by rats every year, with a ten percent kickback ending up in Marcus's larder.

Schaeffer wanted Marcus more than he wanted anything. Problem was, nobody ratted on him. Schaeffer couldn't get solid evidence, and even if he'd had it, he could hardly go down into the underworld and arrest him.

As he walked at Partner's side around the plaza, he looked down at the drain covers, half expecting to see shining eyes gleaming back up at him, but the drains were just storm drains. The sewer, where the rats lived, was beneath the plaza.

"Rats in the plaza," Scotty had said. Brown rats looking for one Louie, who was a black rat. Schaeffer had already run the name by other police dogs down at the station but there were no outstanding warrants against anybody called Louie, so it looked as if the rodent was clean. As for the dead bird, it turned out that while Schaeffer had been away on sniffer detail, another police dog had been on patrol in the plaza: patrol dog Berger had discovered the body and done a preliminary forensic sniff-over of the victim and crime scene. Then he'd peed against a pillar to mark the area out as a crime scene off-limits to dogs.

Berger said he'd smelled rat all over the bird, but cat all over the crime scene, and couldn't say which one struck him most likely as the killer. Schaeffer asked if he had any ID on the cat smell, but Berger nixed it — the plaza fill-in job was a first for the younger cop. Berger was still cutting his teeth on Metro Patrol, hadn't had much experience with the street and wouldn't have a patch aboveground until, in the eyes of the Department, he'd made his bones. When Schaeffer pumped the rookie for wound profiles, he complained that his partner had been radioed before he could do the sniff-over thoroughly, and he'd been pulled off the job. Schaeffer snarled silently at the chain of command. He pushed for more. Berger couldn't say what made the wound on the back of the neck, but they were not post-mortem: there was blood on the neck feathers.

Schaeffer chewed it over as he cruised the plaza: rats, a dead canary, and a cat asking questions...

He padded along, worrying it over in his head, trying to find possible links. Fatso stopped to talk to a dame, all smiles and cap-touching politeness. Schaeffer waited, stayed vigilant, faked bored. He sighed, sat, noticed that the storm drain next to him was blocked: bunged up with paper and trash. Then he saw a cat come into the plaza from a side alley, making for the corner where the canary was found. Schaeffer stiffened, stared, made the ID. Ginger and white male, white paws: Frankie Frr.

He watched as the cat headed for the door to the building, sat and started washing, looking natural. Then the door opened, and Schaeffer saw the cat stop licking, look round quickly, then slip into the building as the door closed.

Schaeffer ticked off questions he wanted to ask the cat, then stood up and set off to do some police work. He got one pace before the leash pulled him up, and Fatso hauled him back. It was the nearest Schaeffer had ever come to cocking a leg to the chain of command. He felt like chewing Fatso out for his rank-pulling but knew he couldn't — insubordination meant back to training college. Schaeffer let it go. He licked his ass and made a mental note to lick Fatso later, right on the lips.

I knew things were gonna hot up when I saw Schaeffer eyein' me from the other side of the plaza. I didn't know if he knew I was wise to the surveillance. When I saw him tuckin' his head down an' tuckin' in, I didn't know if he was fakin' natural or doin' it because he couldn't help himself. But that didn't really figure for me, not with Schaeffer. Most cop dogs were pretty dumb — none of them had been born on the street. They had procedure, trainin' an' discipline where they shouldda had instinct an' a nose. An' they went round with humans, which I figured did for good police-doggin' what a leash would do for a cat.

It was a big city, but I covered a lot of it in those days. I knew a few BCPD dogs, an' I reckoned Schaeffer was better than all of them. Schaeffer kept the plaza in order, even cats gave him that, an' he didn't do it by sittin' on his ass growlin' at pigeon poop. He worked the plaza thorough as a cat, sniffed around, following up leads an' gettin' collars. Problem was, he didn't like me or my kind of cat.

Waitin' to get in the buildin', I watched him from the corner of my eye while I washed, seein' him clear watchin' me. I couldn't work out whose case he was on — mine or the canary's. And then I found myself thinkin', just for a moment, that if I had my eyes and his nose, I'd have a whole lot better chance of trackin' down the killer. I let it go.

I didn't feel like I had any leads worth chasin'. The apartment was where I wanted to look next but I had to figure a way to get in. I decided to take some time and think on it. I figured, go down the port, do some fishin', clear my head, get away from the alleys, go breathe some fresh air.

It was a sunny day. I felt good. I trotted over to Fat Sam's to see if he wanted to come along. When I got there, he was teachin' some of his grandkittens how to box, jabbin' out a paw and showin' them guard an' slash combos. He shooed them off to play when he saw me comin' down the alley. They tumbled off, laughin' an' whappin' each other round the head.

"Frankie."

"Hey, Sam."

"Still on that case?"

"Not today. Wanna come down the port, sit in the sun, maybe hook a fish?"

Sam nodded, got up, said he could do with a day away from the noise, an' a snooze. He'd been up all night. "Goddam rats all over the place," he said.

LOUIE

Louie was asleep, or Louie was awake. Asleep, awake, asleep, awake... He couldn't understand why he was sleeping so much, but he dozed off in darkness and woke up in it, and the only colour in his life was in his dreams — golden cheese wheel suns and creamy stars, blue sky, clouds, red brick, green leaves and the dazzle of shimmering emerald neck feathers against the grey plumage of the world's best singer and friend.

Dreaming of Sax brought it all back... The terror: Louie crying and shaking and Sax throwing a hug around him, the only living thing other than another black rat who would, and telling him, "Don' cry, lil buddy. Dr Toons is gon' sing all that bad shit away: scoo bee doo..."

Louie wanted to stay with Sax as much as he needed to take his next breath, but THEY would come for Sax, too, and they could kill birds when they wanted to. Louie begged Sax to fly away but knew he wouldn't, not with Zoot's next show so soon. He knew he couldn't make him understand. Louie told him why he'd miss the gig where he'd be. Sax looked like he'd have given him his wings, and hugged him.

"Be dancin' lucky, Louie. Don' know what this big death shit yo talkin' up is, but it ain' gon' happen in Sax's city, y'hear me?"

Louie hadn't looked back when he ran off along the rooftops.

Now, he kept his eyes closed, sniffed very quietly, and shuddered.

The air down here, said the Voice again. *It's bad....*

If there had been rats, he would have heard them. There were none. He felt relief and anguish at the same time: he was still undiscovered, but the waiting was horrible.

ERRR

I hit the night alleys. I had spent the day by the port jawin' with Sam. We fished awhile, caught nix, got splashed, hated it, gave up, an' dozed. After a nap, I asked Sam about action around the plaza — in particular, anything on the canary. An' what was all this about rats coming out of the sewers? Sam gave me the lowdown on the night before: more rats out in the streets than he'd ever seen. Fight night: a long night spent marking out territory in red. Sam was slit-eyed with tiredness.

"Funny thing was," he said, "the rats didn't seem like they was out for a fight. More like they were lookin' for somethin'. Something's goin' on, Frankie. I'm tellin' ya..."

Sam wondered off home. I hit the streets an' made for the plaza, dogged by a nagging sense of things not comin' together, of something bein' off. I decided to try take a look at the balcony. I had a kind of fur-rubbed-the-wrong-way type feelin', an' I wanted to run to burn it out. But I strolled: a runnin' cat attracts attention, an' I was tryna keep out of Schaeffer's way. But the balcony kept drawing me, like her song used to....

When I made the plaza, my luck must've turned: there was no dog on duty. An' when I got to the apartment block where the canary'd lived, I was just in time to slip in past a guy with a bag of groceries in his arms, pushin' the door in with his back. I got round him an' scooted up the stairs to the fourth, my footfalls covered by the guy crashin' doors and startin' the lift. I crept up the last flight nice an' quiet.

Nothin' had changed: the door and window were still shut. From under the door, inside the apartment, I caught the same flowers, the lingerin' stink of rat. I turned to go, disappointed again. I was halfway down, between the fifth an' the fourth, when the lift stopped on the fourth. The door swung open, the guy stepped out, put his groceries on the floor, went for his keys. I could smell fish in the bag and tried to rate my chances. Then the guy pushed his door open, an' I got a better break than fish: an open window givin' onto the balcony, an' a table beneath it. I saw my chance. I ran inside, leapt up onto the table, jumped onto the sill, clambered outside an' jumped onto his balcony, one floor down from the canary's last known address. The guy shouted at me, then shut the window. His terrace was tiled red an' was big enough for any cat. Nice an' private too. High walls on two sides — you couldn't see the neighbours.

On the plaza side there was a low wall with tall, pointed iron railings. The view of the plaza was good, but it felt like you were lookin' out of a cage. The guy had a table and chairs, though, an' I hopped up onto the table, leapt up for the top of the wall. I came up short but I got my claws into cracks, scrabbled with my back legs, an' hauled myself up. I looked across a line of walls an' terraces. Where I was had the same layout as on the other side of the wall, but the humans had it different: no furniture this time, just a cleaned-out bird-cage standin' empty in a corner of the terrace, door closed. The cage was at the top of a stand mounted on a round base, an' it was cat-proof. I figured the cage had been moved. A few feet away there was a ring where the city dirt hadn't reached, same size as the cage-base.

I jumped down an' padded over an' put my nose to the stand. I smelled cold metal, canary an' rat. I ran my nose up, sniffing rat-canary-rat-canary all the way. I followed my nose down the stand onto the terrace floor, let the smells lead me to the plaza-facing wall, up it, an' along it. I followed it 'til it came to the high adjoinin' wall. I stood up as tall as I could on my back legs, but the scents went up further than I did. I looked around for a way onto the wall. There was nothin' I could climb on. I sat down angry, swatted at a fly. The scent led to the next terrace. I needed to take a look, but I had no way of gettin' there from where I was. I climbed the wall and jumped down back onto the neighbour's terrace, and saw that my timin' was still out. The guy had shut his window. I was spendin' the night under the stars unless I did somethin'.

There was only one thing I could do: I put aside my pride an' miaouwed to be let back in through the window. He opened up eventually, but before he let me out he made me drink a saucer of milk, stroked me without bein' asked, made dumb noises an' tried to pick me up. I hated it. Finally he opened the door an' I ran downstairs, my dignity rattled. I felt like I'd just swallowed a hairball, but another cat's. I wrote the day off as a loser. Nothing new learned, no feet forward. Then I got to the bottom of the stairs, slipped through the door an' stepped out into the plaza, an' walked slap bang into the square's favourite crime hound, peein' against a wall.

SCHAEFFER

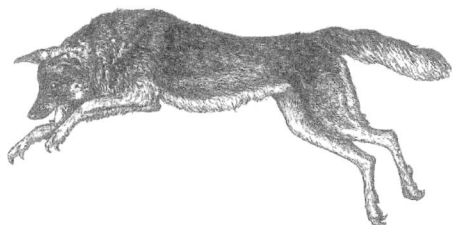

Schaeffer knew Frr and didn't like him. Frr was trouble: the Moggytown private dick had no licence from the city PD and conducted his investigations with a complete disregard for the law. That he'd tracked down cat-killers and apprehended a kitten-snatcher got him respect in the alleys and made him popular with the ladies, but it didn't make him a saint in Schaeffer's eyes. Canaries went missing in his neighbourhood — cage doors popped by night and the tweeties gone... No feathers, no blood — but still....

At best, Schaeffer had Frr down as a trash-can vigilante with no respect for the law. What stuck most in Schaeffer's craw, though, was that the cat had no chain of command round his neck and wasn't worried by procedure. Nor did he have a dumb, fat-ass partner.

In Schaeffer's book, 'feline' and 'felon' were close enough, and Frr was both. To Schaeffer's knowledge, Frr had committed assault and cat-burglary and had once boosted a store for sausages with which to bribe a night watchdog into turning a blind eye to a Breaking and Entering. It was Schaeffer who'd busted the bent dog, and he'd wanted Frr too, but Frr disappeared. Schaeffer knew he couldn't make squat of the bribery and B&E testimonies now, but the canary thing was Murder One, and Frr was always ears-deep in something. So Schaeffer had had the apartment door under surveillance from the moment he'd come on duty. Partner was with him, but he was talking to dames again and wasn't bothering to patrol the square, which, for once, was what Schaeffer wanted. He needed to sniff the scene out; toss it for evidence that might link the cat to the canary.

Schaeffer whimpered for a pee. Two-legs let him off the leash. He ran right across the plaza to the spot where Berger had discovered the canary's body and sniffed the scene out to try and fill in the missing details from Berger's report but got nothing. It was two days old and the scent was faded, buried beneath a hundred everyday plaza smells.

Schaeffer went round a corner, out of view of Partner, cocked a leg against a wall, was still going when the apartment block door swung outwards, and Frankie Frr appeared. Schaeffer tried to stop peeing but couldn't, even with somebody watching.

Frr grinned.

"Been drinkin' on duty again?"

And Schaeffer saw red. The cat laughed and made to saunter away just as Schaeffer was finishing up. Schaeffer went after him headed him off.

"Hold it a second, Frr."

The cat stopped, smiled and licked a paw.

"Why? Ya forgot t' shake it, by the way."

Frr played Cool-cat kept licking his paw.

"Thinkin' about gettin' a home, Frr?"

"Just out for a stroll on a warm night, Officer. No law against that."

Eye contact: no fear in the cat's eyes. Schaeffer bristled.

"True enough. 'Cept this is an official police crime scene, Frr. Or can't you smell?"

The cat wise-assed him, "Cat don't smell as good as a dog, Schaeffer. Or as bad."

Schaeffer lost it.

"Against the wall, Frr!"

"I'm clean."

Schaeffer sniffed him down for canary, got nothing, but still couldn't hold back. *Shake him down*, he thought.

"Two nights ago, Frr, there was a murder in the plaza. A little bird was bitten through the back of the neck. She lived in the buildin' you just came out of, Frr, an' you're a cat... I'm takin' you in."

The cat laughed at him.

"What?! Kiss my pink-eye!"

Schaeffer showed teeth, growled,

"You're under arrest, Frr."

Frr dropped the cool hissed, "Arrest me for what?"

"You're a murder suspect!" Schaeffer barked back.

"No chance, dog breath! You got no evidence, no witnesses! You don't even have Probable Cause. This is ratshit an' you know it!"

Schaeffer barked him down.

"So what were you doin' in the building, Frr? Checkin' to see if she's been replaced? What, you figure they opened a take-away up there?"

Keep nipping, thought Schaeffer. He could see he had the cat rattled.

"Where were you two nights ago, Frr?"

The kitty punched back, spat,

"Where the hell were you, Schaeffer? Cos I didn't see you in the plaza that night. Whaddya do? Stay in to lick your butt?

"I..."

"It's on your breath cos you're talkin' it, Schaeffer! Did you see the body? Did you see the damn bites?"

Schaeffer backed down some.

"Another officer reported..."

The cat cut him out.

"I saw him. He was a pup. Dumb too: he saw a dead canary, took a piss, secured the scene against nothin', an' never once even looked up. Ya know, many canaries like t' hang around on the ground?"
"I..."

"D'y'even know what floor she lived on?"

Schaeffer shook his head, dog tag tinkling.

"Know what sort of bites they were in her neck?"

"It ain't hard to figure..."

"So what did it?"

"A cat, obviously..."

"A rat! Dumb-ass dog. They were rat-bites! I saw them, you didn't. An' your second-hand source didn't even know what he saw. You been here at night when the rats come out to play, Schaeffer? Lately, there's been more rats than any cat has ever seen. Rats lookin' for somethin'. Where were you when we drove 'em back into the sewers? I didn't see you on pest control."

Frr's tone changed: contempt.

"You think you know the plaza? I wouldn't bet my next hairball you're gonna crack this before you get pensioned off. BCPD don't care about a canary! How much time have ya put in on this case? How many dogs ya got workin' it? Ya gonna bury it as an Unsolved, maybe dig it up for somethin' to do when ya retire?"

Schaeffer wagged tongue, trying to cool down to think. The cat had aced him. Frr nodded to the other side of the plaza: two-legs was whistling.

"Time for walkies, huh? Gotta go. Still, maybe you can be back on the case sometime next month, hey, Schaeff?"

Schaeffer flinched. Frr got in his face.

"The canary — I didn't do it. I want who did an' I'm gonna keep lookin'. I know what I got, an' now I know what you got: nothin'."

Frr got nose to nose.

"The only lead you got is waitin' for you on the other side of the plaza. Go walkies, Schaeffer. There's a good dog."

Then he turned and walked off, tail in the air as a mark of respect to the BCPD.

Schaeffer whined, torn. He looked at Fatso on the other side of the square, going purple whistling. He looked at Frr slipping into the darkness of the alley, pink-eye visible like a target. He looked back at the partner, saw the chain of command as a leash around his neck, looked at freedom disappearing into the alley. He thought about the two-legs' kind of police work, and his own, and figured at worst he'd be busted to the Metro... dereliction of duty... Just a couple of days off to do some real police work... yeaaah.

The Metro wasn't so bad.

It was better than swallowing a cat's contempt.

"Hey, Frr," he shouted down the alleyway, "I know what the rats're lookin' for!"

He ran after the cat, into the darkness.

LOUIE

Louie took a deep breath and regretted it. The air smelled foul and felt thin, like you could pant in it all day long and never feel you'd taken a breath. He knew it was working on him, slow but building up. He felt sick in his guts — bitter hollowness and stinging stomach. He'd eaten poison before like every rat had, but Louie listened to The Voice and ate smart: *Sample. Wait. Let your body tell you if it's good...* and taken only a few of the pellets. They were green grains, new to him. He knew within minutes, rode out the cramps and the shivers behind a fridge, learned a new danger.

Now, he was learning about another danger:

The air down here said The Voice.

Louie knew. He felt it in the tiredness that overtook him even though he'd not long woken up, saw it in the images that flickered in his mind — that the air, too, was slow poison, was making him sick.

Fear building: *think Nice Things to keep it back, ignore The Voice.*

The Voice was saying, *Time, luck...* The Voice was saying that it was kind of funny that Louie should lay low in Brown Rat Central but spin the joke out too long and...

The Voice whispered about a bite in the back of the neck like the canary got for just *maybe* having heard... and the other thing they did to make rats who knew things talk — rats who knew about Marcus taking over the city, rats who knew where the black rat communities hid, rats who knew the god-rats were real, who'd actually seen the MOONrats in the flesh. Louie'd always thought they were a myth, a mommy-rat bedtime story for little black rats going to sleep hungry, again, these rats from the moon who built machines and palaces underground, who understood anything men could. The rats who were going to come down one day and end the war between black and brown lead them all up into the moonlight to dance.

Yeah, right, thought Louie.

Fat chance.

Turns out they were fat rats split 50-50 on wiping out the city.

The Voice, urgent. *Three days.*

Three days until... what did he call it? *Convocation.*

The scene replayed in Louie's head, burned in there, unforgettable.

Their voices. Growly, "Thus the proposition: that we use *Pasteurella pestis* to gain control of the city, King Marcus to assume all executive powers after the... transition."

Squeaky, no hesitation. "The bacillus?! I oppose! I utterly oppose... Lunacy! You think you can use the plague to...?!"

Squeaky, shrill, weak-sounding. "... Domus... all of you..."

Growly, "Vote, all."

Silence.

Squeaky. "WHAT?!"

Growly — hear the smile bending his voice, "Four to four. Preliminary Convocation inconclusive. Three days, then. You disappoint me, Sai. Forever the cloister and your dry books? Have you no stomach for your destiny? Eat well, Sai."

Black rat shit-out luck, wrong place, right time. Louie JUST out for a night-crawl, a bit of scavenging but mainly moon-gazing, thinking, *Can't wait for Zoot's next gig, maybe I'll go see Sax tonight*, strolling along on a plaza-side roof. Stopped when he heard scurrying, rat voices, he got curious... Even cats knew better than that.

Edge of the roof. Louie kept his head down, listened, heard it all.

Growly MOONrat saying: "Marcus for king." "We can fix it for you".

Marcus hot for it. "Can we pin it on the black rats?"

Lots of voices.

Long talking.

Louie heard it all.

The equal split, the No-No Squeaky guy sounding flaky... "Three days, then."

Then, *"Cheep!"*

Growly, no smile, "What was that?"

Marcus. "Hey, a little birdie. Birds sing. SECURITY?"

Silence.

Long time.

Looong time.

Then, "Chee..."

Louie took a peek down at the terrace and saw... the miracle rats, King Marcus...

And... there's the BIG rat, mouth full on the balcony edge below, going crazy pointing. "LOOK! There!"

Bird drops from his mouth falls out of sight like a stone.

"GET THAT BLACK RAT!"

Louie. *Fear BIG — can't move.* Rats peeling off and coming for him. Then Louie running faster than he'd ever run, wondering where the hell he could hide in a city where you were never more than fifteen feet from a rat: rats that wanted to kill you....

After they ask their questions, said The Voice.

Louie, down in the sewer, fever head, slow poison, weak and getting weaker, falling into sleep, falling into dreams, not wanting to.

Warm air in the sewer.

Louie, shivering at the back of the crack, scared, cold.

The dreams kept turning bad.

CHAPTER 5

Prowling

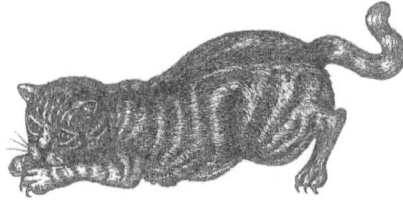

FRR

I wasn't surprised Schaeffer asked me to be his partner — damn dog can't do a damn thing on his own, always gotta have someone t' run with. But dogs, ya know, got a real powerful sense o' smell, much better than any cat's. We can see in the dark, but a dog can go by smell — that's how good a nose a dog got. Dog can smell like a cat can see. So, apart from wonderin' how they can stand to get so close, ya gotta figure that when they do that nose-to-butthole thing they do, they get to know each other pretty well. Schaeffer knew a lot of dogs. Dogs got big ears. Dogs get around. And I needed help. Just as long as he didn't pull rank on me, I figured I could work with him: Schaeffer could help get things moving. It looked like I was getting a partner. But I mean — a dog, ya know?

I could hear the alley whispers already.

"Frankie Frr teamed up with a dog*!?"*

"A police dog, cat!"

"Oh my good golly! Gimme fleas, p-lease!"

"I mean, what's a cat if it ain't got its independence?"

"Where is that cat's prrrride?"

I'd have to live with it, I guessed.

Schaeffer caught up with me in the alleyway. He said, "Tell me what you know, an' I'll tell you what the rats are lookin' for."

I told him, "Uh, uh, down, boy. You first."

He said he needed me to tell him everythin' so he could add it to his snitch's stuff to see if it fit. I said I'd rather leave a turd unburied than spill first. He said,

"I'll go this far for some of what you got: the rats ain't lookin' for a what, they're lookin' for a who. Your turn."

I told him I'd been up to the apartment above where the canary lived an' tried to take a look around, but couldn't get inside. I told him I'd smelled rat there. I'd been to the balcony terrace on the fourth and checked out the canary's cage, an' it smelled of rat. The wall next to the cage smelled of rat, so I figured the rat came down from the floor above crawled along the wall 'til he could make a jump for the cage. Then he climbed round to the door, got in, did it. He came down the stand an' hit the ground. I figured with the bird in his mouth: I smelled rat *and* canary on the floor.

Schaeffer said, "Brown an' black rats don't smell the same."

An' I said, "Both stink."

He asked what I thought she was doin' in the plaza an' not in the cage, an' I told him that probably the rat was gonna eat her an' wanted to do it away from the roof in case a cat came across them. That maybe he had her in his jaws an' got buzzed by a bird, or chased by a bigger rat, an' had to drop her. Who could say?

Schaeffer took that in, then asked, "Who climbs better? A black rat or a brown rat?" An' I told him, "Black rat, no contest: brown rat's too heavy to hang on for long. Maybe a strong one could climb a bit, but not much. Black rat can do five storeys no sweat."

All the time, Schaeffer's noddin'. He was gettin' answers to his questions, but I'd given up enough without gettin' anything back. I told him I wanted his angle there and then, or else I was down the alley an' gone. Schaeffer dropped it: the brown rats were lookin' for a black rat.

"Name?" I asked.

He said, "Louie."

I said, "Hot damn! I know Louie, he's Sax's friend!"

An' Schaeffer said, "Yeah? Well, I make him for the canary snuff."

"No way, dog!" I replied.

But Schaeffer said, "He's a rat who climbs: I think he did the bird."

I wasn't listenin'. I was thinkin' of Sax, shooby-doober for Zoot Jackdaw. If anyone knew where Louie was, he did.

"We should split up," I said. "I'll do the alleys. You do Dogsville."

Schaeffer nodded. "I'll meet you back here at the end of the night."

I asked him, "What're you gonna do?"

He said he would go look up some Houndtown connections — dogs he thought could help — and squeeze whatever juice he could out of it. What was I gonna do?

I told him. "I'm gonna ask around, try an' find Louie."

I watched Schaeffer pound away.

I headed for Sam's. He didn't look so pleased to see me this time. He wanted to know what I was doin', smellin' of dog. I told him about the case said I needed to speak to Sax Pigeon. Sam told me that Zoot an' the Combo were playin' that night.

"Why don't we just go on up there an' listen, try to get a word with the bird after the gig?" he suggested.

Then I told him why I wanted to speak to Sax.

Sam said, "Sax won't sing: he ain't no stoolie."

An' I said, "Then I'll have to make him."

Sam came up with the old one about what nasty things to expect from hangin' round with dogs. I was wonderin' how my favourite singer would feel when I killed his best friend.

I told Sam fleas were the last thing on my mind.

Really — the least of my worries.

Caleb had said he would use fleas. Tiny, almost undetectable, they were perfect disease carriers. They would bite the warm-blooded, and the bacillus would do the rest. The humans had antibiotics, but they had weakened with reckless use, and the bacillus had ways of spreading itself. It caused explosive, wracking, bloody coughs that sprayed it into the air, passing on to anybody who breathed it in. Caleb would have to get it into the human environment first; into their homes. Dogs and cats were obvious vectors. Rats, too.

Domus doesn't draw the line between species, thought Sai. *He just sees what stands in his way.*

It wasn't only the masters of the overworld who were going to die. Rats were going to die in great numbers, too. It was with argument that Sai hoped to use to move the pro-Caleb faction and Marcus. Marcus had subjects and, therefore, he had responsibilities. Even Marcus could see that a king ruled over nothing if his subjects were all dead, and surely even he had a conscience to which Sai could appeal. Or could he? Plague historians filled their accounts with statistics of human fatalities, but there was nothing at all about rats.

Yet the plague killed rats, too. It even killed *Xenopsylla cheopsis*, its favoured fleas. Infected humans could expect excruciating lymphatic swelling on their necks, groins and armpits, subcutaneous haemorrhages and nervous system failure before they died. While the plague raged, their society would crumble under its blows. In the past, in plague times, famine, war and turmoil fed on each other. Latent insanities bubbled to the surface — superstition, ignorance — producing terror, scapegoats, persecutions and pogroms. It would not be so very different now. History repeated itself.

The pandemics had been recorded. The first in Athens, then Arabia, reaching Egypt in 542. It spread to Rome and ravaged the Empire of Justinian, ushering in Rome's fall. It moved to England, became known as the Plague of Cadwalader's Time. It spread to Ireland by 664, where it scythed through the population. Then it went to ground. In 1347, it returned and took three years to kill one-third of the population of Europe. It went to ground again for three hundred years, just long enough to be forgotten. It reappeared in London 1665. The city reeled under the stink of corpses and the mass graves at Black Heath and Graves End. Then, again, the plague vanished. Finally, in 1892, it surfaced in Yunnan Province in China. It reached Bombay in 1896: in India, it killed six million.

The world staggered in its wake. Countries shivered, spasmed.

The plague travelled the world in the belly of a flea and the fur of a rat — though not exclusively a rat. The archaeologist Chwolson traced the plague back to 1338-9, to Lake Issyk-Koul in Semiriechinsk, Central Asia, an endemic zone, where the Manchurian marmot, the jerboa and the sislik played host to the fleas. Yet the plague was associated with rats in man's mind: an outbreak of plague would usher in a campaign of extermination as if the rats were responsible for the bacillus and not just another victim. And how many dead? The seafarers would be blamed, of course: the ship rats, the black rats, the followers of the Crusaders who brought the plague to Europe. They would feel the awesome wrath of the grief-stricken, decimated brown rats.

Sai blinked. He knew he did not yet fully understand all of Caleb's plan.

He looked out of the window at the people in the plaza. Soon to be dead. *What can I do?* he asked himself again.

Believe, he told himself.

Believe you can win.

Believe in the others.

Believe in the plan for Carlo.

LOUIE

His eyes had adjusted to the sewer gloom, but he kept them shut: either he was asleep, or he couldn't bear to look. *It's night*, he thought. *Rats at work.* He could hear them: lots of activity, breathless scampering along both banks of the sewer, two-way traffic. Rats stopped to talk and trade gossip / info / schmooze / insults. Louie kept catching:

"...black rat..."

and

"...Marcus..."

and

"... Max..."

Louie, tucked-up scared, thinking Nice Thoughts so his fear wouldn't smell: moonlight, cheese, Zoot, birdsong —

"Cheep!"

Tuck up even tighter, screw eyes shut, breathe shallow and fast...

"Quietly!" said the Voice.

Tiredness coming on... dreams getting worse... dreams of eating, being eaten — both torture... dreaming of being afraid of being afraid... fear-sweat smell, sniffed out = snuffed out.

NO, DONT WAKE THE FEAR UP! THINK ABOUT... THINK ABOUT... THINK ABOUT...

Sax! Sax's beautiful voice. Hear it in your memory, your mind.

Hold onto it.

It's a lullaby in hell.

Sam an' me trotted through the alleys on the way to watch Zoot an' the Combo. Zoot's place was a free house, an' the gigs were a speakeasy: you left your grudges, gripes, an' appetite down on the ground floor. Zoot'd put together a great crew, everybody knew that, an' it would've been a real shame if some cat figured they was just a musical interlude before dinner. Lotsa cats like to eat birds, but just as many don't, an' pretty much all cats like a toon. For this reason, every cat in the city had agreed not to eat any of the band, or any of their boyfriends or girlfriends. Zoot an' the crew made lots of folk happy, so no way were they gonna be some fatcat's dinner. I could never have eaten a bird — the music meant too much to me. Guess it's just as well mice can't sing or I'd've starved a long time ago.

We got to the wall that was the first step up to Zoot's rooftop. We ran along the wall, came to a busted-out building, half of it knocked down. We climbed it, jumped from there onto a balcony, went into the building, used the stairs, got to the very top, jumped through a window, an' there we were: at the gig.

We'd got there towards the end. I could tell because Zoot was doin' his blow-the-walls-in big last number, 'It Ain't Over ('Til The Fat Birdie Sings)', an' when me an' Sam turned the corner, we saw a whole crowd of birds, cats, bats an' even a couple of rats, dancin' in the moonlight.

The place was jumpin'. 'Nipped-up hepcats were jivin' paw to paw, yowlin'. Rats were reelin' an' squealin', rollin' an' squeakin' along with the vibe, boppin' side-by-side with cats. There were puffed-up pigeons struttin' around, doin' The Flap, chests puffed, heads goin' peck to the beat, cooin' along with the music. Bats was hangin' around, a big line of smiles upside-down along the roof, swayin' in time an' clappin' webby wings together. Maybe they couldn't see what was happenin' but they had a sense for the beat like nobody else. Ol' Joe Crow was on the roof, croakin' along way outta toon, but nobody cared — the music was too good. The band had *steeeam* comin' off of it. My fur fizzed. Sam sat back, a smile on his chops like a week of cream, his eyes slitty with bliss, his tail pounding the tiles in time with the toon, his purring intense, deep and even.

Bobby 'Rockin Red' Robin cheepin' "Breep deeby" in alto counterpoint to Zoot's raspy-like-a-cat's-tongue "Sha-za-za-zum." Beautiful Diana Paloma was doin' backin', cooin' "Prrooo, prrooo, prrooo, prrooo," an' right out front was Angel Nightingale, holdin' notes clear an' beautiful as the stars. An' shoo-boppin' at the back was Mr Fixit himself, Sax Pigeon, keepin' the whole structure together with "Re-bop a doo-wop ah-shooby doo-wah!", poppin' his neck an' hoppin' from foot to foot, and I wondered if he was protectin' a killer.

An' then the toon built up to a crescendo: five birdsongs comin' together so you couldn't see the join, five voices in total harmony, holdin' out the note 'til there wasn't nothin' on the roof not hummin', 'til with a

"Sha...za...za..zzzuuummm...skiddly   biddly...   bo diddly...YEAH!!!"

Zoot rought the house down.

      The crowd went wild. I was on my feet yowlin' for more as the birds lined up wingtip to wingtip, took a bow and went off to the birdbath for a drink, everythin' around them still cheerin'.

"Damn," said Sam, gettin' up, "we shouldda come earlier."

      I told him I was gonna try t' speak t' Sax. Sam said he was bushed an' he was goin' home. I watched him go, then looked over to the birdbath where Zoot and the crew were washin' and drinkin' an' started to make my way over. The second I did, though, the band-members started flappin', lookin' jumpy.

"Aw, hey," I said, "that was a great show. You're great, Zoot. All o' ya. Hey, Sax, can I talk to you for a couple o' seconds?"

I was too pushy. Sax had a couple o' hens with him, cooin' at him what a great guy he was and strokin' his wings. Sax gave me the bird-eye. I thought about makin' a jump for him but gave that up as a bad idea and tried a desperate longshot.

"Say, Sax, do you know where I can find Louie? I got somethin' for him."

 Sax turned away, tight beak. He hopped up onto the edge of the building.

"Hey Sax!" I said. "Where ya goin'?"

Sax jumped an' flew away.

SCHAEFFER

Schaeffer met Frr back in the alley by the plaza as the night was ending. They swapped what they'd got: Frr's fluffed play for Sax, Schaeffer's Houndtown skinny. Schaeffer reckoned Sax had flown the coop by now, but Frr said no: Sax was too much of a hen-fancier, and here in the city, he was famous. He was a big name, so where else was Sax gonna go? Become a wood pigeon? No: they should figure Sax was still in the city. His ego wouldn't have let him leave.

Frr asked Schaeffer what he'd got: a bit on Sax. He liked to hang out in another plaza, a smaller one across town. Then something struck Frr.

"Where d' you say Sax hangs out?"

Schaeffer told him.

"You still wanna talk with the pigeon?" asked the dog.

Frr nodded.

"That ain't gonna be easy," observed Schaeffer.

Frr told him he had a friend might just be able to help them get a word with Sax.

120

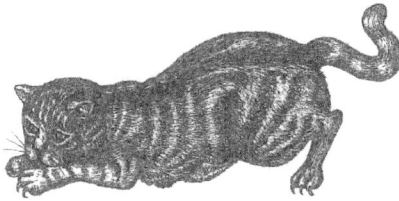

FRR

Priscilla Pigeon was young an' cute, pretty by pigeon standards — hey, not that hard, I know — an' she owed me one cos I'd once saved her life. It happened not long after my canary died, an' I was on a mission to help birds out: I figured that meant more than just not eatin' them. I was away from the plaza one night, prowlin' the streets, when I noticed an old smelly-coat two-legs rummagin' in a trashcan. On the floor by the trash, a pigeon was peckin' crumbs. She wasn't payin' the two-legs any mind an' to tell the truth, nor was I. She looked real old, an' I reckoned she wouldn't see the winter out. I was wrong: it was a scam. The old lady was all bent over an' shabby an' hobbling, but she was crafty like a cat. She faked engrossed in the trashcan. The pigeon ignored her, pecked crumbs. The two-legs shuffled nearer. The pigeon kept on pecking at the ground. Then a hand lashed out fast as any cat's paw, grabbed the pigeon, an' tried to stuff her into a pocket. Luckily, I was on it. I ran over, jumped at the hand, an' scratched real deep an' made the old two-legs shriek. She took her hand out of her pocket to make a grab for me too, an' the pigeon scrambled out an' flew off. Later, she found me and thanked me, gave me her name, an' said, "Anything I can do for you..."

So Priscilla owed me one, an' I'd never had a need to call it in, or least, never thought of a way she could help me out. Like, what favours can a pigeon do for a cat, y'know, 'cept for not poop on him? Turns out, she was exactly what I needed. I told Schaeffer what I had in mind. He said he didn't like it:

"That's entrapment, Frr."

I said, "Whatever gets the job done."

121

SCHAEFFER

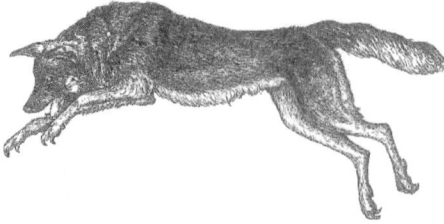

Schaeffer and Frr took different paths to the little plaza where Sax was reported to hang out because they couldn't be seen together. That was Frr's thinking, anyway. Frr's thinking: the cat was devious, Schaeffer had to give him that: an entrapment ploy followed by some serious strong-paw stuff with Schaeffer standing by to jump in with the good-cop routine post-snitch.

"Not nice," said Frr, "just workable."

Schaeffer got to the square before Frr, as they'd planned.

The square was just like the main plaza — big pigeon turf with buildings high up on all four sides, miles of ledges, trees scattered around, two-legs wandering through with happy, tail-wagging, law-abiding pooches on leads — but no bars, no shops. *Soft beat*, thought Schaeffer, *a pre-retirement posting... Look at that, would ya? That old two-leg bitch carrying — I mean, carrying! That scrawnyass, pampered... sheeez...*

He'd come trotting in off the street and positioned himself more or less right in the middle, in the sun, nice and visible. At first, all the pigeons pecking around flew away when Schaeffer sidled up. They made for the buildings surrounding the square and gave him the bird-eye from their perches. Once Schaeffer rolled over onto his side, though, went floppy like he was going to have a doze, a few of them came down to the ground again, too hungry to put off breakfast. Schaeffer lay on his side, faking yawns, eyes slitty, but that was a fake too: he was watching everything, and what he couldn't see he'd hear, or smell. He looked at Frr slinking in the shadows and waited for the tail flick, the signal that the pigeon had landed.

Schaeffer had reservations about Frr's plan, the most obvious being what if Sax didn't show? Then there was what if Sax didn't go for the lady and flap, eyes shut, into the trap? What if he saw Frr and split? Finally, what if it all went right, and he still wouldn't sing?

Frr'd told him to take it easy, it'd work. Sax was a musician, a toonhead. He had a two-track mind: music and groupies. Schaeffer grunted, not being a big off-duty music fan. He didn't feel too convinced about it. *Surely*, Schaeffer was thinking, *Sax wouldn't be* that *easy.*

There were lots of pigeons now, ignoring him but still wary. More were coming down to feed. Schaeffer lay on his side and looked through the pigeons. Across the plaza, Frr's tail lashed once, and the cat went belly-to-floor, tense.

Make that Sax, then.

Schaeffer pricked his ears up slooooow.

Sax Pigeon

Sax didn't even peck at the corn scattered in the plaza: not hungry. Worried. Gizzard knotted up tight. Worried about Louie. Louie: gone now for how long? Gone down there, into the darkness and the dirty shit-stink, the bowels of the city: the sewer.

He's gonna die down there, thought Sax.

And then a cat was on him, pinning him down.

No, thought Sax. *It's me who's dead.*

SCHAEFFER

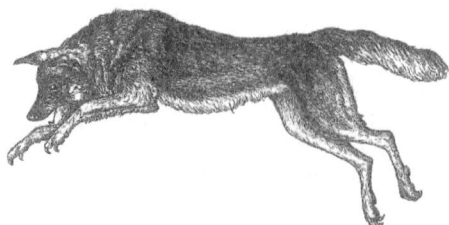

Sax was so caught up in the loony-toon world inside his head he never heard Frr's footfalls behind him: Schaeffer and Priscilla sucked up all the pigeon's attention as Frr crept up on him from behind, just as they'd planned. Priscilla saw it was time for her to be gone now that she'd paid back Frr for saving her life, having very good reasons for not wanting the connection between her and Frr known.

Frr was slinking across the square, getting nearer. When Sax was within range and when he saw Priscilla bending at the knee to jump, he sprang. Around Schaeffer, hundreds of pigeons suddenly panicked, and jumped into the air, deafening him with their flapping, obscuring his view with their sheer number. When the cloud had lifted, and the pigeons were flying away or back to their window-ledge perches, Schaeffer saw Sax flattened out, face down on the ground, wings pinned: Frr's plan had worked. Schaeffer could hear the pigeon's heart thumping, he reckoned not entirely on account of Priscilla: Frr's jaws were in his face.

"Hi, Sax. Y'know, y'really shouldda spoken to me last night. Then I wouldn't've had to come all the way across town t' see you, an' I wouldn't be so hungry. Where's Louie?"

"Whooooooooo?"

"Louie. Your friend, the black rat. You know the one - likes music, likes climbing. Likes canaries."

"Don' know what ya sayin' to me, cat. Don' know no Louie."

"Tell it to the birds, Sax. I seen him at Zoot's shows, I seen you talkin' to him. Word is, you two're real tight."

"Don' know what ya talkin' 'bout, cat."

Schaeffer listened in, waiting for his cue. Frr growled, "Sax, either I leave here knowin' where I can find Louie, or I leave here with feathers round my mouth."

Sax shivered but kept his beak shut.

"Spill it, Sax."

"Damn cat wanna get me a snitch jacket! You know what happens to bird-snitches?"

Frr knew. It was the big thing he had on Sax. It wasn't nice.

When it was known that a bird had ratted another bird out, it got the peck treatment. One bird at first would peck hard on the snitch's back, fake an apology, *Oh, sorry, pal, thought it was a fly,* then another bird would do it, and another and another. Once someone drew blood every bird who passed would have a peck. The snitch had one chance, and that was to get away. But if blood had been drawn, the cut usually went nasty in the filthy city, and death came long and slow, up on a ledge all on your own.

Frr pushed it as far as it could go.

"Sax. I'm gonna find Louie with or without your help..."

"So do it, fish-breath!"

"... an' when I do, I'm gonna scoop out his heart an' leave it in the plaza t' get trodden on. Then I'm gonna put it out that you told me where to find him..."

And Sax folded.

"No! Louie ain't done nothin' to no-one, cat! Leave'm alone!"

"He snuffed my friend, Sax, a little canary in a cage."

"No..."

"YES!"

"NO!! Louie didn' kill no-one, fool! He just saw who did! Louie ain't no killer."

"Convince me."

"He's hidin' from them that did kill the bird: Marcus' mob. He told me."

"What if I heard different?"

"Then chump cat don't know shit."

Then Frr froze, a late take on *that* name.

"*Marcus* did the canary?"

"Not Marcus, fool! One o' his rats. Lemme go, dammit!"

"No. Where's Louie now?"

"Take a swim, hairball! Y'all stone crazy jus' wanna kill somethin'."

"Not me, Sax."

"Huh."

"Hey, thing's change. I'm tellin' you, Louie ain't my guy now. But I gotta talk to him."

"How am gonna know you won't kill 'im?"

"Cos you say he didn't do it. Cos you say someone else did. An' Louie's gonna tell me who did, an' I'm gonna kill that rat instead. So tell me, or I'll kill you."

Sax sang. It came out choked, lump-in-the-throat tight.

"He's in a sewer. Underneath the plaza."

Schaeffer took his cue, leapt up.

"Freeze! Undercover police dog!"

Frr jumped up, back arching, hissing. Sax saw his chance, and flew off.

They watched him fade to a tiny dot and disappear.

"Nice work, Frr," said Schaeffer. "Y'got what we wanted."

"Yeah," drawled Frr. "I told you it'd work. I told you he'd stool."

Schaeffer was grinning.

"Yeah, y'must have had him pretty scared, Frr, I gotta hand it to ya. So scared he stooled twice."

"Huh?"

Schaeffer was showing teeth, smiling. Frr looked down — black and white, in his belly fur.

"Aw, sh…"

Schaeffer was barking with laughter. Cats' MO — they have to be clean, but they won't touch water. If dirt gets in their fur, they lick it off. They can't help it. They lick it off, whatever it is. And then they swallow it.

Schaeffer started howling.

FRR

Better ice-water than that. I wished I didn't have a cat's touchiness about bein' the butt of the joke. Schaeffer had a big grin on, a lollin' tongue floppin' out of it. He was still chucklin'. He was real happy: his tail was waggin'. It was killin' me. I was thinkin', *Carry on, dog, an' I'm gonna do the impossible an' make you uglier.* I tried to look dignified as I bent to lick it off, an' I tried not t' think about how it was gonna taste.

"Shit-eatin' grin, huh?" said Schaeffer, and rolled on the floor.

I sprang claws. Butt-breath gloated.

"No point in cleanin' up yet, Frr. You heard where the rat is: that's where we gotta go."

Wrong, dog, I thought. On two counts.

"You figure on me goin' down a sewer, Schaeffer?"

"Well..."

The grin had widened. Schaeffer looked dopier than ever.

"Ain't gonna happen."

Schaeffer sat down. Came over reasonable.

"Hey, Frr, wait a minute. That's where Louie is, an' he knows who killed the canary. You wanna crack this case, you gotta go down there."

"Why not you?"

"I'm too big to get down a drain."

"And I'm not? Uh uh, you got the hots to go down a sewer, go find a main entrance. There's one down by the port — ya can't miss it: it's where the prawns like t' hang out. Get in that way. Dogs eat shit - don't see why ya can't step in it. I mean, it ain't like everybody else don't gotta on account o' dogs... Knowhaddimean, huh, Schaeffer?"

I turned to go.

Schaeffer whined, hangdog expression.

"Frr, ya can't just leave it..."

"Can too, Schaeff."

I turned my back and gave him the pink-eye goodbye.

"Dammit, Frr! Come back here!"

I stopped, turned round, gave him the real reason.

"If Louie's been hidin' in a sewer for two nights, he's dead cos that is brown rat world. He's been sniffed out, been bitten through the neck, an' his brain's been eaten. Except that can't have been a very good meal considerin' how dumb Louie was. Black rat hidin' out in brown rat territory's smart like a cat tryna break up a dogfight. Louie's dead, Schaeffer. Go home."

LOUIE

Louie woke from a nightmare to squeals, and the squeals told him the nightmare had come true. They'd found him.

Voices: rats jubilant, thinking *Reward*.

Squeals / words:

"We've found him! The black rat! He's in there! Smell him!"

Sounds: *Sniff sniff. Sniff sniff.*

And "Yes!"

Louie didn't dare look. There were lots of rats down there — the squeaking was intensifying with each passing second. More rats arriving all the time, making more noise, bringing more rats... each one bigger and stronger than Louie. The din said We are thousands.

The Voice said, *Be brave*.

They said, "Smell his fear! Smell his fear!"

Louie'd wet himself. He started crying softly — couldn't help it. Fat warm tears spilled over and rolled down his nose. He sobbed, once. They heard it.

Laughter — with teeth.

"Heeheeheeh! Come on down, little black rat. We want to play with you!"

"Boohoo! Boohoo!"

"Crybaby! Crybaby!"

Fear paralysed Louie, but froze his tears, made him lucid.

He heard claws scrabbling at the walls, vainly trying to climb up to him.

The Voice: *Be brave. You have to climb out of the sewer.*

Fear: **No!**

Them: "We know where you aa-re!"

The Voice: *Look at them!*

Fear: **NO!**

Them: "Cissy-fur! Pissy-fur!"

Louie shuffled to the opening of the crevice took a peek. There was either enough light, or else his eyes had fully adapted. On both sides of the effluent, the floor writhed a shapeless, vast furry beast. Louie cried in his throat. Every head turned up towards him, thousands of noses twitching and sniffing: gasps of shock turned to hate — hisses rose up from the boiling river of rats. Rats threw themselves at the sides, their claws in stonework slick with slime that'd crawled out of the waters and was half-way up the wall.

Failing, falling rats climbed on each other's shoulders; ladders of rats reaching up the wall. They couldn't hold it, toppled, fell into the brown river, splashed and laughed like play-time, long tails only distinguishing them from the fat brown tubes floating alongside.

A chorus started up.

"Get him!"

"Bite him!"

"Hold his head under!"

Louie ducked back in the hole hid his head in his paws to shut the sight out. But the squeals... he couldn't shut them out. All the hate and incisor-sharp laughter.

Them: "Crybaby, crybaby, we're going to eat your head!

Black rat, scaredy-rat, don't cry — you'll soon be dead!"

The Voice: *Look! Down the tunnel...*

Fear: **Head back IN!**

The Voice: *Look!*

Louie, frozen, eyes sparkling, staring in unblinking terror.

There! Down the tunnel!

A single ray of light.

Outside, the sun had hit the plaza.

The Voice said, *Now!*

SCHAEFFER

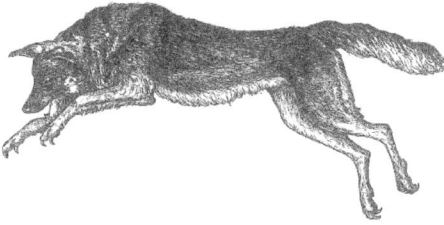

Schaeffer sprinted through the last of the night, damned if he was going to give up. He tore along the streets dodging the pre-dawn walkers and cars, ignoring the storm of smells, the city's business floating on the ether. He took stock: partnerless, his only chance to crack the case was finding a black rat in the sewers.

I *shouldn't have ribbed Frr so hard*, he told himself, *shouldn't have tugged his whiskers: cats are a lot more sensitive than dogs, though only when it comes to themselves and their pride. Damn cat*, growled Schaeffer to himself. Too prissy: he could dish it out, but he couldn't take it. *Adios, Partner*.

Schaeffer thought about what Frr was doing right then, grinned, told himself the cat was gonna eat some more when he brought Louie in. He pounded on, heading for the plaza, counting on his official partner being somewhere else: he didn't need to see Fatso right now. Back at the station, Schaeffer supposed, he was on a charge. Insubordination? Dereliction of duty? At the very *least,* he'd be busted back to training college, and that was if the Chief was in a good mood. Worst case, the Chief would have his badge.

Schaeffer ran on, a swift, easy lope, drumming paw-falls, tongue billowing out of his mouth, ticking off probable scenarios in his mind.

One. Busted: lose the pension and the retirement home. Have to take a security job: round-the-clock junk-yard watchdog, a dish-a-day loser chained to a shabby kennel, all mean an' oily, barking through a wire fence at anything that moved because the job was a full-time whine, all the while knowing your back legs are going while you wait to die.

Two. The Chief decides you've gone rogue. Why not? Cop dogs did, often enough. The badge got to you, and you figured you deserved a little more for your sacrifice than the Department would toss you. Schaeffer had seen it happen. When he was in training at the Academy, a cop dog had tried to shake down a butcher's dog for protection, payable in scraps, figuring the meat-house mutt for a soft touch. But the butcher's dog knew scraps wouldn't wag the cop dog's tail for long and that the demands would soon hike up to Best Cuts. He nixed. The cop threatened teeth, but the patsy was fitter than he looked and chewed the cop dog's ears off then reported him. The cop dog was now a lifer in the Pound, cooped-up twenty-three out of twenty-four with nothing to do, hard-timed by the other cons. The Department was real big on Discipline, real hard on cops taking kickbacks and living off the gravy. The thought of the Pound kept most dogs straight. At its hardest, the department had sent dogs for The Big Sleep — lethal injection for biting two-legs.

Three. Find Louie, question him, and find out what Marcus's mob had to do with the canary snuff.

And then what?

Any which way the stick flew, it landed in cack — splat! AWOL with a street cat felon; moonlighting your own case one thing, but eating police time another, deserting your partner another, the case Zero-priority in the eyes of the Department — yet another.

Splat! Splat! Splat!

Maybe I should have toed the line, thought Schaeffer, *stayed heel-side with my deadweight two-legs, cos there's no way back on The Force after this....*

The plaza was near now. Schaeffer panted and caught its smell on the air: drains, trash, old booze, butts... and another smell, faint but getting bigger. A smell Schaeffer didn't like one bit.

Rats.

LOUIE

The brown rats howled, but there was nothing they could do. Louie had his head out of the crack and was reaching up and round for a hold in the wall-face.

"He's getting away! He's getting away!"

They kept trying to scale the walls, rumps-on-shoulders rat-ladders, but the sides were slimy, and they couldn't hold on. But that didn't stop them trying.

They won't stop, said the Voice. *Go, or stay here to hear them taunt you as you starve to death.*

Louie hauled himself out of the hole and climbed upwards and along, limbs spread wide against the wall, claws digging in. He was above the slime-line, clinging on perpendicular to the seething mass of fur and teeth. He saw them at a strange angle: rats stretching, claws extended towards him down a gentle dip, reaching nearer, nearer, and then suddenly yanked back by some invisible force.

Keep going, said the Voice.

Louie's heart throbbed. He snatched uneven, ragged breaths, closed his eyes against dizziness, clung. He tried to remember the journey in: one bend? Two? He opened his eyes and saw that the brown rats had come up with another idea. Ahead, where the tunnel curved away, on the banks of the river, rats were simply standing on top of each other. Furious invention, desperate quick-thinking. Piled high, inclining down to the water's edge for solidity, the mound reached halfway up the wall, almost to the slime-line. As rats lost footing and tumbled into the effluent, others clambered up to take their place.

Louie started off again, not even needing the Voice to tell him that if the pile of rats got high enough, some of them might be able to climb on the dry, rough rock above the wall-ooze. Might be able to cut him off... He shortened his reach, going for quicker.

"He's getting away!"

Beneath him, rats jumped up, nipped at the air, hissed, flailed claws, gnashed. Frustration bred more invention. It started behind him but spread like a ripple through the rats: a song of hate.

"FALL! FALL! FALL! FALL! DIE! DIE! DIE! DIE!"

Individual voices pierced the din:

"Eat your balls, cissy!"

"Scream an' scream, die for days..."

"Bite through your skull an' *suck*!"

The Voice: *They're trying to break your strength! They're going to seal off the wall and force you to climb across the roof.*

Fear: I'm not strong enough.

Them: "DIE! DIE! DIE! DIE!"

*   *   *

SCHAEFFER

Schaeffer hit the plaza and pelted to the corner where the canary had been found. The sun was climbing fast over the mountain, throwing out its light, spilling orange over the rooftops, spreading warmth. Schaeffer didn't stop to look. He sniffed hard for where the rat stink was strongest — over in the far corner.

Procedure: bark into every drain, let Louie know he was a protected witness, convince him to give himself up.

Instinct: go where the rats are.

Schaeffer did it by the book. Hoping no-one would see him, he barked, "Louie! BCPD, we want to help!" into the drain.

Nothing. He dashed to the next.

"Louie! BCPD. Come out. We can protect you!"

Nothing. Next.

137

"Louie!"

Schaeffer sprinted to the corner drain barked into it. As never before, he could feel the seismic tremble of massed rats surging around down in the sewer. Their squealing was a high, constant whistle, a shrieking din that shivered through the plaza floor beneath Schaeffer's feet. The squealing was alarm. Anyone could hear that. Intruder! Attacker!

Or fugitive, escapee, thought Schaeffer.

"Louie! You are a protected witness. Come out!"

He ran to the next drain down.

Barked: "Louie!"

Look up. Daytime. The plaza getting steadily busier. Two-legs, dogs, pigeons — all looking at me gone-out.

He crept on, every step like he was carrying a rat on his back. His eyes were half-shut with the effort, and his lungs burned as he gasped for foul air. The muscles of his legs felt stretched; his bones ached to the core felt split. He had no feeling in his claws: a sure-thing bad sign of coming cramps.

Beneath him, against the wall, the rat-mountain had crept higher. It had passed the slime-line. The first summit-rats had taken to the wall. The incline stopped them: they rolled down the hill, splashed into the water, climbed out sodden and streaked with darker brown, started up the hill again, shit-caked, seething and hate-filled, never giving up.

Louie hauled himself up to the apex, where suddenly, the pull became massive as if the river of shit below him was sucking him. Upside-down down was up, up was down. Louie was hanging on with everything he had, trying not to fly upwards into the river, into the shit and the waiting claws and jaws.

The Voice: *Be ROCK, Louie... sniff! Clean air... do you feel it...*

Fear: I CAN'T HOLD ON!

Them: "DIE! DIE! DIE! DIE!"

And something else, faint, coming through the tunnel from behind:

"Rooooooouuuuuuuuuiiiiieeeee!"

Louie hauled on, feeling like his tail was holding a string of rats.

The roof arched up on the other side of the sludge river. Louie tacked across. Limbs spread, claws numbly finding their way into cracks. The hate behind him faltered for an instant, like a shock running through the mob.

Someone said, "We can't stop him..."

Someone else said, "Marcus will be angry..."

Dismay. Shuffling feet. Tails dragging.

 "We were never here..."

"Never here..."

"Didn't see..."

"Disappear..."

Louie turned the bend and saw a fat beam of light up ahead, spilling in through the basin pipe beneath the drain bars. Louie's heart leaped.

The Voice said, *Daylight outside.*

He kept moving.

Fear said: Daylight!

Louie kept moving.

They said, "..."

Then that voice again:

"Rooooouieeee!"

It's not real, Louie.

Louie watched the rats heading away beneath him, heads-down floor-sniffing. No insults now because they didn't dare admit they'd seen him and let him get away. Ahead, the light burned his eyes. It looked hard, solid. It looked as if you could walk up it. Louie reached a claw out, got a hold in the pipe, and scrambled up with his last strength. He sat in the trash-choked basin, looking at the drain bars above him and beyond them to the sky.

The Voice said, *Daylight. Be soooo careful. Keep to the gutter...*

Fear said, Don't go out here! Get out of here!

Louie gripped the basin side and heaved himself upwards, running on empty. The stench below was still choking him, and the sunshine made him blind-giddy. He shut his eyes, but the spinning didn't stop. Sick-dizzy, boneless-weak, he reached a claw around the bar, clung, hauled himself up, threw his other front leg over, hauled again, scrabbling, and flopped into the plaza, gasping.

"Rouie?"

It's not real.

IT IS!

Louie opened an eye to gaping jaws, huge teeth and hot dog breath.

Black rat shit out of luck.

Louie passed out cold from sheer terror.

GRR

    I cleaned up, went back to the alleys behind the plaza, an' prowled like a cat's supposed to.

    I had Schaeffer on my mind, an' how he'd rubbed me up the wrong way with his jokes. Most cats would've said, *Way to go, cat. Don't take none from a dog — it ain't as if they can get away with braggin' about cleanliness.* But still, some little voice of conscience told me I'd put pride before what was practical, an' there was a queasy feelin' in my guts that didn't have nothin' to do with what I'd had for breakfast.

    I prowled no appetite for company or food. I hadn't had a good nap in days but I didn't feel like sleep. One word — Marcus — kept makin' me twitch. Marcus. Like splashes of water on me.

The King Rat. Cats dream of it: gettin' the King Rat an' rippin' out his liver.

Marcus had had the canary killed, I knew that now. An' it would've been on a whim, an' it would've been for fun because this guy had a million others bringin' him food. Marcus was my guy now. An' I knew I would never touch him, never even see him, an' it messed with my sleep an' my appetite.

I crept around the backstreets. Alley cats avoided me, wouldn't look me in the eye, slipped away. I'd teamed up with a dog, which meant, as far as any cat was concerned, I had fleas, whether I had 'em or not. (Which I didn't.) Didn't matter, though — my rep on the street was officially lousy, an' it was going to take a long time to regain the respect I used t' have. There was a sour taste in my mouth like old fish heads — again, not entirely of Sax's makin'. Normally, I got no pangs of conscience from what I did: I live on the street, it's tough — a cat gotta do what a cat gotta do. Right then, though, a little voice was tellin' me I'd given up on Louie before I knew for sure, an' that ain't thorough, that ain't right. I was havin' a hard time convincin' myself I did it for the right reasons an' not just to get away from Schaeffer cos he was cockin' a leg over my pride an' laughin' at me. I knew the voice would go on. There wouldn't be no place in the sun to relax cos Louie'd be on my mind an' my conscience. Not a great weight, but there was my canary, too.

I made for the plaza. I sauntered, thinkin' about a canary in a rat's jaws. The thought made me shiver. I hated to think of her bein' my canary, an' I hated the voice in me that said starvin' was a slower dyin' than bein' bitten by rats.

I thought about Schaeffer's sense of duty, his obedience to some code he had in his head, an' about me walkin' away from mine.

I'd broken the promise I'd made to the bird I truly loved.

142

I strolled. Dog-turds littered the alleyways, fillin' the air with their stink. I wondered about how much worse it was in the sewer than even the street an' reminded myself that at least I didn't have dogshit in my fur — the very lowest a cat can go. I turned the alley into the plaza. Then there was a flash of black an' brown an' a collision that knocked the breath outta me an' sent me rollin' down the alley. I rolled for yards, feelin' every single goddam squelch beneath me, then my balance came back almost as soon as it'd gone, an' I was back on my feet.

Clamberin' up from the ground was Schaeffer, lookin' dazed, a dumbdog *hey, what!?* whine in his throat, head to one side. I didn't even have to look to know that I had more dog poop on me than even Schaeffer had in him — which was plenty — an' I waited for the howls of hilarity. But Schaeffer couldn't speak. There was a rat in his mouth. I thought, *Louie?*

He put the rat down, real gentle. I could see the rat's ribs fannin', knew he was alive, an' I'd been wrong. I was about to swallow somethin' much worse than doodoo: my pride.

An' a dog was gonna be feedin' me it.

I flinched, knowin' how bad it was gonna taste goin' down.

Then a miracle came out of the crap.

Schaeffer apologised.

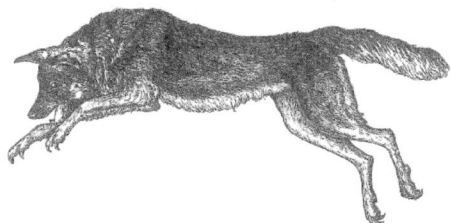

SCHAEFFER

Schaeffer put Louie on the floor softly. The little rat didn't stir.

Schaeffer said what he wanted to say. Frr didn't reply, just nodded.

"That Louie?"

"Yeah. I guess."

"You *guess*?"

"There was about a million of 'em, Frr!"

The apology had cost Schaeffer nothing. He had some personal pride, but nothing like as much as a cat does. The best thing about dogs is that they can laugh at themselves, and even though police dog training beat the softer side out of a dog — the ball-chasing, play-fighting side — and replaced it with discipline, Schaeffer didn't have pride so much as a sense of duty, and pride in the execution of that duty. Bringing Louie in alive was enough for Schaeffer to be feeling good: good enough to give Frr's ego a little stroke.

He didn't mention the mess in Frr's fur, didn't tell him who it belonged to and what he'd had for dinner like he could have, and Louie hadn't come round and made any wise-ass remarks either. Fat chance: no rat ever lipped a cat and got away with it.

Frr said, "Let's get out of the city."

Schaeffer picked up Louie and trotted after Frr.

They went down to the port, and Frr went down the quayside stoop and sat himself on the bottom step by the ocean. Dabbing at the waves as if they were scalding, flinching and occasionally hissing, he washed himself from nose to tail with seawater. When he was finished, he looked more like a hedgehog than a cat.

Louie came round while he was doing it, and, for a moment, panicked when he couldn't understand why he was by the sunlit ocean, breathing sea air and not sewer-gas. He turned to the dog, whose breath, now, somehow, he associated with safety.

"Am I dreaming?" he squeaked.

The dog said, "No," with a puff of sweet dog breath.

A miracle from shit, thought Louie.

Then he heard *a cat* say,

"Louie? Nice t' meetcha."

Make that two.

Louie didn't do it. Sax had already said as much, but I didn't automatically believe a toonhead pigeon before my cat's instinct. I was havin' a hard time believin' what I was hearin' and seein', but I guess it was a time to put aside everythin' I believed impossible and possible an' accept that anythin' could happen.

Such as: a cat with a couple of dead canaries hauntin' him teams up with a police dog an' winds up listenin' to a little black roof rat tell a story about Bossrat Marcus and MOONrats from space plannin' to turn the world on its head and put rats at the top of the pile.

The canary was killed because she might — might — have heard.

There'd been a snuff-shout out on Louie, too, for what he'd heard.

It was all impossible. It had all happened.

The sun was hot on my back, an' my fur was steamin'. There wasn't a cloud in the sky, an' tonight would be beautiful. We'd see the moon real clear.

"Tonight," Louie had said. Some sort of gatherin', some sort of vote. MOONrats and Marcus. Three terraces in from the corner, next-door to where the canary used to live: the terrace I didn't get onto.

I turned to Schaeffer.

"I can take the rooftops. How can you get in?"

He said he wasn't sure yet. Said maybe he had a friend who could help.

Right then, my friends didn't amount to a couple.

I told Schaeffer to be ready for night.

"I'll be ready. What're you gonna do?"

I told him, "Sleep. Ya dummy."

SCHAEFFER

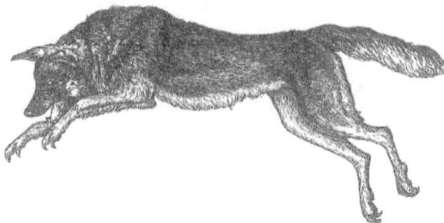

"Get some sleep." Get the cat — big comedian: acting cool, steam comin' off his ass, sidlin' away with a "Later," that meant, "I ain't expectin' ya."

Schaeffer looked at boats smelled the sea. Nix to sleep, too much to do. The next step, still not clear, Schaeffer looked down at his first problem — Louie — gazing up at him with wide eyes and an *I like you* smile.

He made Louie go through it again, straight-facing the incredible. The terrace tonight meant much more than just Frr's canary-murderer: it meant rats from the moon and lowlife Marcus planning to take over the city. And for 'take over' read 'k-i-l-l', and the BCPD had one — *one* — dog on the case. Louie was the sole witness and this didn't look as if it was going to trial.

Schaeffer thought about what to do with the rat now that he was out of the picture. A hit out on him back in the city. Zero chance of getting him onto the Witness Protection Programme. No use on the terrace tonight. Schaeffer looked at boats and thought about the disease that killed everything except stones and trees.

"Louie. Pick a ship. You're leaving."

Louie nodded and sniffed. He made this sad little squeak, "Say g'bye to Sax for me."

Then he played the prissy witness card. They spent half an hour sniffing for a boat with a cargo of cheese. Schaeffer watched Louie scramble up the mooring rope, then transfer to the anchor-chain and said a silent *goodbye, good luck,* when the tail tip disappeared inside the ship. Schaeffer shook, turned round and started pounding.

The breeze coming in off the sea ran at his back into the city, and on it, the scent of the only escape route. The further in

Schaeffer ran, the thinner the smell of the way out became: the city smell soon drowned it out. Now the only way Out was In.

Schaeffer ran, working scenes out. The terrace, the fifth floor. Rats always wait for dark, so figure midnight. Guards all over the rooftops, VERY security-conscious, no repeats of last time. How many rats not a problem. How the hell do I get up there? BIG problem.

Flash memory of Frr: he'd been up on the fifth floor inside the building.

Schaeffer wondered how to get in and decided he needed another partner.

CHAPTER 6

Convocation

A rattling tattoo of claws at the door brought Sai back to the present with a start, and the beautiful Florence he had constructed in his mind fell and smashed. The colours it had been dreamed in bled to grey and dispersed, ash blown across a marble floor. Sai blinked and shook his head, startled by the sudden noise and dismayed to find that while he had been reading, night had fallen.

"Lord Sai?"

Sai sighed and closed his book. Time had passed so agreeably while he had been hiding in his reading, but now the hour had come for Sai to face up to what he had been dreading for days. When he replied, his voice sounded weak, despondent and fatalistic.

"Come in."

The door opened, and Max stepped into the room.

"It is the appointed time, Lord Sai. Transport to the Convocation awaits."

The voice was once again toneless as if Max did not understand the words he spoke.

Sai came down the ladder to the floor and waddled towards Max, avoiding eye contact, afraid that his fear was on show in his eyes. Sai stepped past Max, through the door, into the corridor.

Max followed him. Sai felt his fur prickle, unsettled at having a killer at his back. The two guards closed the door behind them returned to stiff attention as Max strode past them, caught up with Sai easily and led on.

"This way."

They walked along the corridor until they came to another door, which two more guards pushed open for them. Ahead of them, rising from the carpet to a hole in the wall, was a ramp leading into a ventilation duct from which the grille had been removed, and where now waited a wheeled sled and a silent line of harnessed rats. Sai waddled up the boarding ramp and took his place on the sled. Max sat beside him and snapped to the guards, "Take the ramp away!" And to the sled-team, "Move!"

The rats strained and heaved until, with a lurch, the sled started rolling slowly. Sai collected his thoughts as the sled trundled. The walls rolled by, and the light from the corridor thinned and then went out. The sled suddenly turned sharply, then again, again, again, in rapid succession. Amid the weaving, Sai kept his balance but lost his bearings.

They rolled on for some time. Sai's pink eyes adjusted too slowly to the dark, though the confident cornering of the sled told him the rat-team saw perfectly. Sporadically, the sled would slow as they passed through the vent-shafts of occupied apartments, stations of light viewed through the meshes of vent-duct covers. Now a glimpse of a sleeping dog, now a skirting board, a cat basket, a flash of ankles, a crawling baby, smiling and gurgling.

Sai closed his eyes and collected his thoughts: Florence in the grip of the plague; other accounts and instances of the hideous might of *P. pestis;* the thirst for power and its insatiable parasite, the urge to follow... Caleb, Marcus.

The sled trundled on, grumbling softly through the tunnels. The rats' panting set a rhythm: the slow pounding beat of an uphill strain, the half-laughter of running downhill, in Sai's mind, a strange, insistent music — the mix of breathing, squeaking axles and the wheels' echoing rumble. And then the sled slowed, pulled up, and the music stopped.

Sai opened his eyes.

The appointed place.

The appointed time.

A ramp was hastily pulled up next to the sled.

Sai set his face like stone and walked down to the Convocation.

ERRR

I had about as much chance of sleepin' as I had of flyin': my head was boilin' over tryna understand what Louie had told us. An old, old rat story — hundreds, thousands of generations old. Once upon a time, nobody knows when, a disease appeared and killed everythin' it touched... humans, cats, dogs, rats. It was like this force was an enemy of warm blood. But it wasn't systematic: it didn't touch everything but there was nothing you could do about it if it did want you. It killed, it spared, and nobody could explain why one died an' another didn't. Everythin' the rats had ever believed in just fell apart... an' there's been war ever since. Louie said it was an old, old story, and lottsa rats didn't believe it... it wasn't a story you could prove, you just believed it, or you didn't. Louie'd believed, even before he knew.

"But the ones who don't believe it don't believe in nothin', they believe in anythin' — like rats from the moon. But the rats from the moon are real," said Louie.

An' four of them wanted to bring this death back.

Louie stopped makin' sense then started gettin' hysterical, an' I could see that he was still in the sewer, in a way. When I asked him the big question, he just shrieked, "Security! Security!" an' jumped between Schaeffer's paws, head down and shakin'.

I left things to do. No, I couldn't sleep. I slinked through the alleys, avoided by cats like I had a disease, thinkin', *I can't even put out the news on The Miaouw: a rat myth from a thousand thousand lifetimes back...*

I went to Sam. I told him why the rats were out on the streets, why the canary was dead. I asked him, "Help me, please, Sam: I think the whole city's in a pillowcase an' headin' for the river."

He just said, "Let's go."

Headin' through the streets, gettin' hissed at an' dissed from the walls an' trashcans, we looked back straight into every fiery eye scopin' us from the shadows, sayin' nothin', starin' back til the light went out. Lookin' up at the moon, I thought about what was comin'. I thought about Schaeffer, no use to me because he couldn't get onto the roof. I needed cats, but when you need them most, they ain't there: only your friends. I thought about The Big Miaouw closed off to me. Three days past the full moon. Louie said he'd been on the wall and heard them at the full moon. "Three days," Louie said.

The moon was waning but still givin' out strong.

So: tonight — the canary, Marcus, the guys who want the city... answers to all my questions.

Pity Schaeffer wouldn't be there, I couldda used an extra pair of jaws.

Sam an' me, an' how many rats?

An alley-war five floors up — blood: so much of it it'd splash the stars.

Us versus them. Our blood or theirs.

Sam an' I slipped through an open door in the opposite corner to the terrace where it was all gonna go down. We waited at the foot of the stairs, talked angles of approach and wind direction, team hunt-and-destroy strategies, signals, tactics... an' we reminded each other: "Never hesitate," an' "Ya ain't permitted t' run."

SCHAEFFER

Schaeffer crouched behind a car, hidden by the night.

Night was good: two-legs couldn't see, and you could smell them a mile off. Ears up, eyes wide, panting quiet, Schaeffer was alert. He was way, way off Fatso's usual beat, but he was still wary of uniforms and figured an APB on him by now: Detain. The station, questioning, the Chief in no hurry to get the lowdown on a police dog's night-owling. A night of the sweats pacing round a pound-outhouse, waiting for the Interview, listening to the cons howl and wondering if the Chief saw a canary-snuff as ok grounds for two days AWOL...

Schaeffer, still rogue, on stake-out.

Two-legs were always deadweight on stakeouts: always making 'I'm bored' moaning noises, smoking, farting, peeing into cups and throwing it out of the car window. Schaeffer sniffed, looked, listened, double-checked. The coast was clear. He got up, trotted over to the cop car he'd had under surveillance for an hour, and peed over the left rear wheel, then the right. He looked around, trotted back to his spot, all his senses working too hard. He lay down edgy, thinking, *Relax*.

He licked his balls. Lap, lap lap. *Ahhhh.*

Schaeffer's mind cleared wonderfully. He heard the station-issue boots round the corner, grinding grit half a street away. He crouched low, a sluggish city street breeze taking his scent away from the cop unit. Two cars downwind, snout down between the street and the chassis, Schaeffer scoped. The boots got louder, and, as they came nearer, the clatter of claws ticked into hearing, getting louder. Figure HUGE dog. The cop appeared round the corner, then Sergeant Rott crunched into view. Bulls-eye for Schaeffer's guesswork.

They strode to the car, the two-legs tinkling keys, while Rott — nicknamed 'Bone' but Schaeffer didn't know why — sniffed the wheels and pricked up stumpy little ears.

From across the street, Schaeffer watched Rott's two brain cells collide. *Bark, bark.* Way t' go, Rott.

"Derrr, Schaeffer. Duh... I can smell ya, ya know. Duh... I think I'm supposed to take you in, Schaeffer... duh... I think."

His two-legs rubbernecked to see what the action was, looked out across the street to where Rott was barking. Schaeffer barked back, "Rott! I ain't comin' in. You gotta come out!"

And stayed low, not optimistic.

Rott was typical of the 'weilers that'd been joining the force in recent years: dumb. The Station's alsatians ribbed the bonecrusher rotts full-time. Off-the-record they admitted the Crunch Bunch were great on crowd control, but they scored zero, possibly less, for detective work. So no shocks from Bone, then, when he barked the Standard Response.

"Doooooooooo... No. YOU gotta come in."

Schaeffer stayed down, wondered how to manipulate the thinking of an animal that didn't have any thoughts, and clicked on it: orders.

"Rott, I'm on a case, deep cover, on Captain Dobie's orders!"

Rott sat straight back flat on his ass.

"*Hrowwooo?*"

His ears flopped: too many thoughts in his head to remember to keep them up. Schaeffer made the complex rottweiler-simple.

"I need your help! This is big."

Rott whined.

"Dermmmm... ... ... Captain Dobie's orders?"

"Yeah, but it's all secret undercover stuff, Rott. Ya gotta believe me. Ya gotta help."

Come on, come on, ya dumb son of a bi...

"Der... ok."

Schaeffer heard it all go quiet, heard two-leg *What?* noises.

Rott barked again.

"Now, what do I do?"

Schaeffer double-took. Damn! He'd forgotten there'd be a leash.

"Bark like hell. Pull your guy over, get him to let you go..."

"Der... ok."

"Rott!"

"Der... yeah?"

"Don't bite 'im."

"Duh... no."

Two-legs said something to Rott. Rott jumped. A socket-popping yank stretched his partner's arm. Schaeffer heard, "*Yerk!*" and saw the two-legs lurch forward, his cap falling off.

He let go of Rott's lead to keep his balance.

Schaeffer leapt out from behind the car and barked, "This way, Rott!" and the two dogs tore away down the street.

GRRR

Me and Sam moved quick an' quiet on opposite edges of the roof: me on the plaza side, him on the far side, keepin' away from the edges. Slinkin' low an' silent with the breeze in our faces, eyes half shut so the fire didn't give us away — you can see it for miles if you've got good eyes an' rats do.

We approached the terrace from the furthest point, expectin' guards, silent but in touch. Signals: paw turned up — *What?* Tail flicks — *Go!* Ears up — *Wait!* Ears down — *Ready!* Ears back + tailflick — *Do it* !

Low concrete walls separated the roofs from each other. We jumped them at the same time, landed ready to fight, crossed the roof, did it again. When the roof did a dogleg around the corner of the plaza, we slipped over quiet, hugged the low walls, an' waited.

Sam an' me smelled them: rats on the roof up ahead.

I looked over at Sam, paw up. *What*?

Tailflick + shrug: *Go?*

Ears back.

Ears back.

Ears back + tailflick, an' we jumped, scoped the roof in mid-air, saw two rats, one lookin' the wrong way, the other's mouth droppin' to scream danger, an' we hit the ground runnin'. Sam went right, pounced, was on his guy before he could squeak. Sam did him without a sound as the other rat was turnin' round. I was on him, stepped on his back an' bit through his neck, fired up.

We waited at the next wall, counted one, two, three, jumped, landed, surprised more rat guards: same routine, different blood.

The plaza — six blocks by nine. Eighteen rats. Minimum.

Then, the terrace.

Sam flashed three claws, flicked his tail.

One two three.

We jumped.

SCHAEFFER

Making for the plaza, tongue flapping, head nodding in steady rhythm, energy burning off running, head CLEAR.

Maybes: the plaza under surveillance. On stakeout — two-legs: Fatso, Dog-pound crew and van. APB out on the city air, cops trawling through known haunts of Schaeffer, PD 647, alsatian. Fur: brown and black/grey, last seen app. 06:00 in the plaza, barking down drains... Two-legs whistling *"Here, boy!"* with a fake smile and a net ready if Schaeffer lay doggo.

Schaeffer sprinted.

A few paces behind him, Rott loped back-up.

The dog was a ground-shaker, rumbling like a truck. Round the edges of his mouth, white froth gleamed. Who needed a siren? Two-legs jumped out of their way, cars hauled up screeching when they dived across busy roads, pigeons launched, panicked at their approach, cats ducked under parked cars.

Schaeffer tore on, heading for the plaza, his new temporary partner coping with following — so far. Running, Schaeffer looked up at the moon thought, *Now, now, now, it's NOW!* He'd been planning his next moves since he'd picked up Rott. The quickest route to the plaza was coming in not from the entrance that gave onto the big open street but through the alleys: poor light, stink-rich — enough to go by.

Schaeffer skittered into a turn as the sidewalk veered off before a line of champing cars fuming at the lights and switched gear, changing down. Bone, behind him, crashed straight into a car, denting a panel. *Figure the rottweiler was nicknamed after the contents of his skull.* The driver took one look and stayed put. Rott shook, pointed his nose in Schaeffer's direction, and followed it.

Schaeffer slowed for Rott, watched him lumbering towards him, then ducked into an alley leading off. Straight away, he caught the smell of the plaza. *That* smell unique: hundreds of people, booze, cigarettes, perfume, dogs, birds, bins, cats, rats, piss, shit, trash. Schaeffer sniffed and went with it, nose down, watching the ground.

Alley walls closed in; the buildings seemed to grow higher. The light down on the street was spread thin. Schaeffer slowed. On the floor were dog turds — lots: cones, tubes, curls, twists, a rainbow of browns, some intact, others squelched into footprints. Glass-slivers glinted, Schaeffer trod careful. Dark turf-marker piss-stains bled down walls. Rott followed orders and didn't stop to sniff.

On the air, the plaza smelled less like a single thing now. They came snuffling through the alley, getting nearer, and then the smell started breaking down into its parts, information exploding outwards. The smell in the alley was a tiny yelp against the gigantic howl from the plaza. The smell of the plaza was a din, and it was its own language, one that Schaeffer understood. He came round the corner and saw the plaza ahead through the archway.

He stopped dead, hackles up.

Security was tight. The number of sentries and bodyguards had doubled or trebled since the Preliminary Convocation. Max had ordered rooftop sentries to be posted, and on the terrace, where the Convocation and final vote would take place, a pack of guard rats lined the walls, black eyes darting, noses twitching, alert for the slightest sign of danger. Sai walked to the centre, where the others had gathered, wondering if there was anything in the order of arrival that should worry him.

The Convocation was gathered, and the usual ritual was observed: each MOONrat had his or her rump turned to the centre so that none might speak before the whole was gathered. The overlapping tails still said, *We are One*, but when Sai manoeuvred into place in the centre and laid his tail on the pile, all the tails were whipped back as if in revulsion. Sai smiled inwardly and took a little hope: great division within the group. The stresses were palpable. As the rats faced each other, Sai scanned faces.

Caleb's was unreadable, Libo's was screwed into a scowl, Luxor's was vapid, and Athena's was a study in composed fury. Alvix's was dour, death in his eyes as ever. Mir's was impassive, his eyes half-closed, while Kaver was looking at Caleb. Marcus's face was a leering, wet-mouthed grin, awaiting coronation as King of the City.

Caleb cleared his throat. Heads turned to him, the Convocation's convener. Sai waited to see if he had correctly guessed the worst.

"Greetings, friends. We are all conversant with the protocols that govern our gatherings. You are aware that the matter in hand must be resolved tonight, one way or the other. There can be no equivocation. The matter is black and white: are we to be masters of this world, or remain as we are — marginalised, reviled, pariahs?"

Sai listened to the grating voice felt the stresses within MOON and the opposing tugs which threatened to tear them apart. What should MOON be? Masters of the world, or simply another animal — giving, taking, part of the whole...? The first impulse fed on pride and was almost irresistible, the second on humility.

"In turn, then, each to speak."

To Caleb's left, Kaver took a few lumbering steps forward.

"I've always argued that rat-kind is equal in strength to mankind and that MOON is its equal in intelligence. Yet we, rats, have always settled for the meanest existence wherever we go: in the cities or the wild, we are less than we can be. Wherever we go, we live the same lives: sewers, tunnels, rubbish-tips, charnel yards. I would have change. Why can we not walk about freely in the sunlight? Change comes about gradually, yes, but it can also come about cataclysmically. To all species. Nature's rules. And I believe it is time for that change."

He paused, then struck his sole note of doubt.

"I would like to know more exactly how Caleb would... effect this change. Caleb? Explain."

Yes, thought Sai. *Explain. Let's see exactly what you have created with your randomly bestowed, fabulous human intelligence. I think you must have received more of the formula than I. Because I don't understand how you can set yourself apart from the planet, wipe out its warm life and call it 'evolution'.*

Caleb spoke. Neutral, rational, cold.

"As you know, in my laboratory in the city, I have created cultures of the bacillus *Pasteurella pestis*. The bacillus is, like ourselves, highly adaptive. You will know that it takes different forms. I have moulded this adaptability, and created a mutation in a process called 'gain of function' to create a hybrid that embodies the bubonic, the primary pneumonic, pulmonary and the septicaemic plagues. I have infected some thousands of *Xenopsylla cheopsis* fleas and propose to release them in the city. The city's domestic pets will be the vector, and..."

"And what of the rats?"

Caleb flinched turned his head to meet the seething contempt gleaming in Athena's eyes.

"Athena?"

"What of the rats that will die too?"

Caleb rallied, affected a righteous calm.

"There will be... losses. But the survivors will quickly reproduce. And as masters of the city, there will be no predation upon us and no check to our growth."

"That," hissed Athena, "is precisely the problem."

"Athena..." began Caleb silkily, "I propose that we take control not only of this city but of all of them... the whole world. Rats will die, yes. But rats would die anyway. I am thinking of the future. The prize is worth the price. Luxor?"

Luxor, thought Sai, *the weakest of us.*

She half-looked at the floor. Her voice trembled a little, and she gave the answer Sai expected. She was in love with Caleb — loving without the slightest hope of any coming back to her. Caleb, Sai now realised, had no love to give.

"I agree with Caleb," said Luxor, with a kind of enthusiasm but still avoiding all eye-contact.

"Libo?"

Her answer was flat, her voice even.

"No."

"Your reasoning?" Caleb enquired.

"Rat and man is not a symbiotic relationship: we don't give, we take. If we kill them, we can't feed off them."

"The planet is vast…"

"… but finite. Eventually, our numbers will become too great. We will consume every last living thing, the planet will become a desert, and we will eat each other. Perhaps I should remind you of our origins, Caleb: we came *out* of the deserts. You seem to want to return to them. No."

Caleb turned for support, but Libo was not finished.

"Another thing, Caleb."

"Yes, Libo?"

"You're insane."

Caleb's face was momentarily a mask of surprise. He regained his composure quickly, and there was no room for doubt in his voice.

"Not at all, Libo. I am acting very much according to my rat and human nature. I am putting MOON — all of us — first. That's all. And if the planet must become a desert, as you insist, Libo, I would rather it was because of rat than because of man. Alvix?"

Sai knew before Alvix spoke what he would say. Of all the MOONrats, he had suffered most in the laboratories and still could not speak of it. He hated and resented what had been done to him. His life had been cursed since the first injection: an ordinary rat become a freakish miracle and a danger to his creators. His love, Nestor, had been killed by men. Perhaps he was remembering this when he croaked, "Kill them all. Give me peace."

He closed his eyes as if in pain.

"Mir?"

Sai knew already.

"Never, Caleb. The bacillus is too powerful. It cannot be controlled: it must not be loosed again. That's all."

"Don't you think I...?" began Caleb.

"Never again!"

Mir looked hard at Sai.

"Sai?"

Sai stood up, the speech he had rehearsed now jumbled and useless, all his reading an irrelevance, important only to himself. The others knew their own minds. For Sai, the choice was between the slaughter of a species he admired as much as despaired of or not.

"No," he said.

"Very well," announced Caleb. "A formal and final vote. Raise a claw: 'Yes' to the proposition," his own claw rising as he spoke.

Kaver, Alvix and Luxor joined him.

"'No' to the proposition."

Sai, Athena, Libo and Mir.

"Equivocation, then."

Caleb showed no surprise and turned to the last member of the Convocation — the holder of the host's vote.

"Marcus?"

All eyes turned to the rat king.

SCHAEFFER

     The cop car was doing a slow once-over of the plaza, and Schaeffer knew from the splashes up its side it was his partner's unit. He recognised the three-day-old filth acquired splashing around a trailer park on the Narco sniff-out, and Fatso, natch, hadn't washed the car. Or himself, probably.

The car crawled Schaeffer's way, coughing fumes.

Get lost, asshole! Schaeffer told it in his head.

He ducked back when the car turned the top corner. His two-legs partner now faced him side-on, rolling slow, arm out the window.

Schaeffer hugged the wall. Rott grunted, "Der... shall I bite his tyres?"

The least intelligent suggestion Schaeffer'd ever heard. He nixed it politely.

The cop car rolled. Schaeffer figured the angles out: *next turn, Fatso is parallel, right outside where we want to be, moving away... moving towards us... meet in the middle. Then he's blind...*

"Rott!"

"Duh?"

"Ready..."

"Duh."

"... to run... NOW!"

Schaeffer tore off, keeping low, low, belly fur to the deck, inside the arches behind lines of tables full of people, the view of the prowling cop car and its view of him all jungled up with legs and furniture.

Rott shook.

"Duh. Yeah."

And ran after Schaeffer, lolloping unquestioningly onwards in a straight line. He saw Schaeffer ahead stop at the corner and figured he should too.

He skidded up and sat down, breathing heavily.

"Rott!"

"Duh?"

"Ready?"

"..."

"ROTT!"

"Duh! Run?"

"NOW!"

Rott fixed his gaze on the bushy tail ahead and ran.

Schaeffer sprinted, saw the door ahead, rushed past the spot where the canary had been dumped and hauled up at the door. Rott bounded up.

They looked at the door.

"Duh... it's..."

"Not open. Thanks."

Schaeffer looked up at the bank of buttons by the door, knowing what happened when you pushed them.

"Push against the door, Rott."

Rott complied. The door creaked.

Schaeffer jumped up the wall and pushed buttons, came back down. He braced his back legs and stretched up again, got his balance better this time: paws pressing more buttons, the slitty mouth in the metal squawking angry noises... then, *Buuzzzzzzzzzzzzzzzzzzzzzzzzzzzz* and Rott crashed forward as the door flew inwards.

Schaeffer leapt and darted into the building, heading for the stairs. He took the first flight in two jumps and powered upwards, claws ticking in the stairwell. Behind him, Rott pumped uphill, crashing into the wall on every corner. Schaeffer, all senses alert... There! Smell it! Thin, but there in the still stairwell air: rat stink sinking down the steps.

Schaeffer tore upstairs, his only thought to get to the terrace and STOP them.

The smell got stronger with every step. Schaeffer tried to calculate how many rats made a smell like that. He arrived at the top in a breathless clatter and stopped dead in front of a large, locked door. Finally, Rott thundered up the last flight of stairs, stopping running only when his head hit the wall with a building-jarring thud. He made surprised noises and shook his head, but slow, like there wasn't too much to shake awake. When his head stopped moving, he noticed Schaeffer, helpless in front of the door, growling.

Down on the ground you got a feel for the size of the plaza. Real big, real busy. Up on the roofs, it was nothin', too small to even think about. Me an' Sam were makin' our way to the terrace, killin' as we went, not needin' to think much about it.

My nerves were stretched tight: movin' in silence was easy, but it was slow, slooow, an' the terrace had a pull on me, somethin' irresistible, nothin' would stop me. The guards in the way were just in the wrong place at the right time — nothin personal.

Personal I was savin' for the terrace. The tiny part of me that was thinkin' was thinkin' about a canary, but everythin' else was pointed at the moment: at Sam, at signals, at the next low wall that separated the blocks. One two three leap, checkin' the next patch of roof mid-air, always, always with the drop on the rats, either not lookin' the right way or else freezin' up when it mattered. Doing them so quick we hadn't had to fight yet, then dump the dyin' rodent, drop low, slink to the next wall, listen to the twitches weaken behind, sniff, signal. And then there'd be another jump, blind. I took the left, Sam the right. Gettin' the throat's the surest way of stoppin' any warnin' cries.

Stealth, frenzy, stealth, frenzy; everything stored up, then exploded.

My chops were wet, and I could see the black splashes on my whiskers.

The taste of rat blood filled my mouth. I'd swallowed lots, could feel the taste tricklin' down into my stomach. I looked at Sam, his face wet-darkened with blood, his eyes and teeth gleamin' bright and white.

He signalled, Wait.

Paw turned up: What?

Paw pointed back flashed: four claws, then three. Pointed forward, paw up: How many more roofs?

Flash two claws.

Old hands at roof warfare now, one, two, three go!

Three rats this time, one in the middle of the roof actually actin' like a sentry and two more in the corner. I rushed the alert one, pounced, pinned him and bit through his neck, making sure with a tearin' headshake. I looked up for Sam saw one rat gaspin', trailing black claws to his throat. Beyond him, Sam had the third pinned, head and back: couldn't get at its throat, couldn't let go its head in case it squealed. I bent down, Sam took his paw off the rat's head. He made to squeal, and I bit — *crelch!* — through his skull.

Sam crept up to the next wall looked at me. His eyes said it: How many rats?

We waited, listening. I could only hear my heart.

Sam looked over. I flicked my tail.

Mid-jump, I scoped just one rat, peeping over the edge of the roof at I couldn't see what. We landed silently. Sam signalled Wait. He crept low, closer and closer until he was behind the rat, then reached round and clamped his right paw over the rat's face, pulled him back and hugged him into his belly fur. He reached down his left, ripped across, kept his right tight over the rat's mouth while the twitches subsided, then quietly dragged the body away from the wall. Then we lay down and listened.

Marcus rose on his back legs and sniffed disdainfully. Civility disappeared.

"Thanks. Ya know, I wondered when I was gonna have my say in my own city. Reckon you MOON guys prob'ly got nothin' to do all day 'cept talk. Me, I run a city an' I live unnerground an' I don't like bein' out in the open, for reasons which should be obvious cos you got brains."

171

Then his face changed, and his tone: a part-snarl that carried part-threat.

Sai glanced at Caleb saw him wan and jittery.

"Least you better have, cos, ya know, I got a few problems with this whole plague thing."

MOON stared at Marcus: at his violent tics, his neck-writhes, his snorting and the furious circle he paced in front of them, every one of them, in turn, addressed: MOON, Max, the guards clustered along the walls.

"I got no problem with the bodies an' the smell an' that... an' the pay-off's good — aw hell, it's great — but I got questions. I got... concerns. Nothin' big. I jus' wanna bit of reassurance."

Marcus paused and paced, scowling, then finally span round and snapped, "Caleb!"

And Caleb juddered.

"You're the rat says where it's at. You say, we can do 'em all in one go, ba-boom, an' take over the city. But I figure they gotta be like us, no? Like, they get ill — ow ow ow, that hurts — but then they get better again. An' then what?"

He stepped closer to Caleb.

"I say if we do one, we gotta do 'em all. Cuz if you don't get 'em all an' some of 'em figure out where the whammy came from, they'll be real mad at us. They're gonna wanna get even. They'll come for us."

He stood in front of Caleb, taller, bigger, twice his strength.

"An' I don't fight what I can't beat."

Caleb gulped and nodded. Marcus scratched his head.

"For rats now... things are good. This modern life we got? It could be worse. We got the humans throwin' out food an' creatin' all that trash we live off of. But me, I say... it'd be even better wit' humans outta the way. Now, on *that,* we agree. But humans? Believe me: they know how to kill. They got dogs, poison, fire, gas... What've you got that's better'n that? I wanna know. The bug's been around before, an' they're still here. So what is it, smart guy? What've you got that's gonna help me take them all out?"

Caleb did not seem so assured now. The words were confident, the voice not.

"Well. The strain I have genetically-hybridised embodies all the known properties of the plague but is an improvement. Some strains of *P. pestis* transmit themselves with greater efficiency but are not always... fatal. Others transmit less successfully but, once established, are more certain to kill. My hybrid has both the superior contagiousness of the less lethal, combined with the more lethal virulence of the less contagious."

Marcus scowled.

"I hate big words. Max?"

His head of security appeared and stepped into the circle, an appalling breach of MOON etiquette, but one which Sai recorded as quite unsurprising, wholly apt to the disgusting company MOON had sought out.

"Boss?"

"Didja get that?"

"No."

"Me neither."

Marcus scowled deeper.

"Eh. Hey, Caleb. You made this stuff, right? How d'you know ya got it right? Like, what if ya got the bottles o' germs mixed up an' bred a wuss type instead?"

"I assure you my methodology was rigorous. Genetics was the first science I mastered after…"

Marcus curled his lip.

"Too many long words, pal."

"Very well, then: in shorter words. If we release the plague in this city, the humans will fall in their millions, and the city will fall to *us*. The humans do not have enough antibiotics to deal with an epidemic of any kind, and they certainly do not have any antibiotics which cure *my* strain of the plague."

"And what about the other cities? Like, they won't come an' help?"

"They will be fighting their own outbreaks."

"How do you know?"

"Because that is how I designed it. More certain to spread. More certain to kill. But with a period of incubation. While the bacterium takes hold in its host and before it takes its first victim, a million humans will have travelled into and out of this city, and some will become infected. Some of them will fly to every major city on the planet from this city's airport and be halfway across the world when the incubation period ends, and the bacterium turns aggressive. Once we have infected them, the humans will infect each other, all over the world. I promise you. You will have this city. And we will have the world."

Marcus turned, half snarling. MOON waited while he paced and thought.

"OK. So. Problem two. This has gotta go the black rats' way, I mean the bug, *an'* the blame. If rats find out, I did this... I'm food. Nah, we gotta pin it on the black rats."

"And what about the unfortunate security breach at the last Convocation? Have you taken care of the problem?" asked Caleb.

"I got guys on it."

"Black rats stay hidden in high places, if I recall. Very hard to reach, even if you know where to look, which I gather you don't."

Marcus shrugged it off.

"Nah, not so hard. That black rat? He didn't get far. He's up aroun' here somewhere. I got guys out all over the city lookin' for him. We'll find him, find out where they all are, round 'em up and send 'em in with the bug."

Sai surprised himself and spoke.

"Your own rats will die. There will be nowhere you can hide from the disease. And don't expect the black rat to tell you where his community is."

Marcus tossed his head.

"He'll tell me."

"What makes you so sure?" persisted Sai, not really knowing why but simply unable not to challenge the repulsive specimen.

"Because there's this thing we do."

"What thing?"

Marcus explained as if to an imbecile.

"We get the guy, we pin him down, pull his legs open, tell 'im, 'Where are they all? Now! Or I'm gonna eat your balls.' Then he spills, believe me."

Five MOONrats flinched, two groaning softly.

"Then..."

Guard rats tittered. Marcus grinned.

"Ya eat 'em anyway — make sure ya got the truth."

Athena stole his ugly laugh away, speaking up, softly mocking.

"And have you found this rat yet?"

Marcus snorted.

"Yeah, good question. Max?"

He turned on him.

"I like you, Max. Ya, don't use long words. But soon I wanna hear ya say 'I found 'im.' Very soon. Sooner than that'd be better yet. Then ya gonna bring the guy to me, alive, an' maybe I'll do the thing myself, but whatever. All of this is gonna happen soon... no?"

"Boss."

"Good."

He turned back to Caleb.

"I gotta know if this black rat knows about the bug. An' if he told anyone else. When we get the rat an' make him talk, you can do your thing. But your thing better work. So... do I vote now or what? See this paw? I'm in."

Caleb beamed. Kaver smiled, too. Luxor looked to Caleb for some sign that his happiness somehow had room for her and Alvix looked sick. Athena, Libo and Mir were gaping at Caleb, and none of them were looking at Sai — eyes wide, utterly still — or at where Sai's eyes had chanced to glance, where they were now fixed: Up, looking at two points of fiery light.

Marcus was smiling broadly, pacing around, talking to his guards.

"Hey. We're goin' to the top! I'm takin' you guys wi' me. We get outta the city while it's happenin', come back when it's done... Whaddyasay, Max?"

"I say, don't get found out, Boss."

"Heh, heh, like it, Max. I employ a worrier, an' already I feel safer. Hey, lighten up. Think o' dead dogs and lottsa lottsa dead cats... Heh heh. Paybaaaaaaack! So rats're gonna go too? They'd go anyway. An' hey, think of the fun we're all gonna have gettin' back up to strength again, knowwhaddimean? C'mon now, let's get off this roof. Everybody. Let's go. Ya can enjoy the view some other time. Yo, Max, hurry up and find that rat guy, huh? I'm starvin', heh heh. Hey, anybody else hungry?"

A voice came from the darkness above them. All eyes darted upwards. Two points of fire appeared above the edge of the roof and a voice came from them.

"Yeah. I am."

GRR

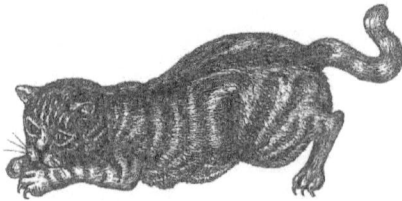

I stood on the edge of the roof and watched the panicked scamperin' on the terrace. Muscle rats came unglued from the wall an' formed a thick cordon around Marcus an' the others. I sized them up, figured a hand-picked élite tougher than the average rat, the way the average rat was tougher than a duckling. From above, I could see the shiverin' MOONrats' terrified faces, and Marcus, lookin' up at me with *I'm gonna eat you* eyes. One of the rats, the toughest-lookin' — 'Max', I figured — was hissin' orders an' the body of guards started shufflin', makin' for the bottom corner and the foot of the wall where I could see a dark square which I figured for an escape tunnel. They were tryna make a break for it.

The mass of rats moved slowly. The bodyguards were upright, facin' outwards, ringed around the MOONrats. The MOONrats themselves were so clumsy and near-immobile they had to be pushed from behind.

A voice came up from out of the knot.

"Hey, kitty. Whyncha come on down an' play?"

Marcus. His goadin', sizzlin' with menace, cut through the shufflin' and squeakin'.

"Ya got past the roof guards huh? Listened in on the thing? Didja geddit all, kitty? We're takin' over the city, hairball."

I couldn't help the low growl that came out.

Marcus squared off, safe in the near middle of the throng, a guard five bodies deep surroundin' him.

"Ooo, toughguy... comin' down?"

He stared into my eyes, beckoned.

"Yeah yeah, come on down kitty, do it do it do it... Eh, ya pussy."

A few of the guards were grinnin'. Max was scowlin'. Marcus was enjoyin' himself.

"Hey. Cat," he hissed, "better go home kiss everyone goodbye... all yer kin 'n' kittens. Take a good look, pal, cos the next time ya see 'em, well, they'll be kind of... pus-y. Yo, it's plague-time, folks! Heh heh."

The body of rats edged slowly nearer to the hole.

"Ya think there's anythin' ya can do about it? Miaouw all ya want. Me an' my fat friends here are down the hole an' gone an' you never see us again."

A minute — a minute or so before they reached the hole.

I looked behind me, down at Sam, saw his blazin' eyes an' flattened ears, claws tensin' in, out, in, out, barely holdin' it back, his whippin' tail sayin' WHAT THE HELL ARE WE WAITIN' FOR???

I looked back at the terrace, heard Marcus.

"So howja figure the odds against, cat? Like a hundred to one, no?"

I signalled Sam. He jumped up onto the overhang above the hole, a low snarl rumblin' inside him.

"Less," I told Marcus, thinkin' the odds were still too high

Max was shoutin', "Keep tight! Keep moving!"

But a tremor ran through the rats, an' the rat-heap stopped movin'. As their strength halved, alertness an' readiness doubled. The guard rats pushed the huddle in tighter, stiffenin' for a fight.

I looked over at Sam and signalled Go!

One two three.

We jumped.

Sai saw the outline of a springing cat silhouetted against the moon, perfectly balanced, perfectly dark, growing from cat to puma in the time it took to fall off a wall. Two shadows fell heavily on the MOONrats. Front paws landed on Sai, smashing the breath out of him. He felt cat's claws pinch in, and crush him once more before tearing out and powering the cat away into a long jump.

Sai felt the press of the rat-wall give. Sai turned his head, saw rats leaping into action, abandoning the MOONrats and rushing at the two cats. The protection around MOON was six rats deep.

The first layer peeled away and attacked.

SCHAEFFER

Schaeffer whined: he could smell rat through the gap at the bottom of the door. He paced the landing, knowing that inside the apartment the city's Most Wanted rat was negotiating terms with rats from the moon for the murder and takeover of the city. Next to him, slumped squat on his ass, Rott watched his furious pacing. Schaeffer looked at Rott's ears: floppy — zero thoughts. He reared up and put his paws up against the door. It didn't give by so much as a whisker. Schaeffer's impatience, desperation and urgency spilled over into a low growl.

"Duh... Schaeffer... ?"

Schaeffer checked the door handle. A round knob: solid metal — no working it with his jaws.

"Schaeffer?"

Schaeffer whimpered, the crime of the century going down behind this door he could not get through.

"Schaeffer?"

Inside was Frr's canary-killer, and what about Frr himself?

Schaeffer started thinking about how he'd buried his career, his pension, his reputation and years of loyal service only to be stopped from making the case of his life by nothing more than a door...

181

"SCHAEFFER!"

Rott's explosive bark boomed in the stairwell, rattling windows and doors, and Schaeffer nearly jumped out of his skin. Shaking, he turned to the massive heap of police dog and noticed that one ear was shyly poking up.

"Dummm... would you like me to... ummmm..."

The ear half-dropped, then rallied.

"Bite the door off?"

Schaeffer's jaw dropped. He nodded dumbly.

Rott heaved himself up and plodded to the door. His mouth gaped huge and he fastened his jaws around the door knob. Schaeffer watched as Rott's neck and eyes start to bulge. Rott altered his grip and tightened, snorting. Schaeffer watched in awed silence, fears and hopes dangling.

The rottweiler was straining into the pull — hind legs bent, front legs pushing back, frozen like a statue but for the drool gathering at his jowl-ends. His tail stump twitched like a tic as he snarled and bit. Schaeffer heard tiny tinny creaks. He looked at Rott. His eyes had rolled up into the dark, empty spaces of his head, tearing at the handle, violent tugs and jolting shakes sending slobber flying. Schaeffer watched with jaws agape as the door handle creaked, and the screws started to ease out. Rott's growl rose in pitch as the wood surrounding the doorknob started to squeal. Schaeffer heard high pings of splintering wood, screws bending, metal screeching, wood creaking and moaning. Rott kept the pressure on, rumbling and snarling, until, with a wrenching tug, he tore the door handle out and dropped it with a clang. Schaeffer stared as Rott backed up to the wall, rear-first. When his tail-stump bumped, he stopped, snarled, waddled his ass and charged. Schaeffer, sitting, gaped, astounded, as Rott hurtled past and crashed head-first into the quivering door with a crunch that made the alsatian whimper.

Rott backed up and did it again. And again. And again. And again. The door bowed with each blow, staggering back under the onslaught of what Schaeffer was now convinced was solid bone. Rott didn't even blink. If anything, he looked happy.

Schaeffer stared, staggered: there was actually *a brain* inside that head, issuing instructions to the mound of bone and muscle hurling itself repeatedly at the increasingly less solid-looking door. Order Rott to stop an oncoming truck with his head, and he'd obey — and quite possibly succeed. The door looked very wobbly indeed now. Schaeffer still was shaking his head in disbelief when the door finally collapsed inwards.

Rott went absolutely blank.

Schaeffer sat still, stunned.

Two rats suddenly darted out from the corridor now on show, and scampered past, down the stairs, jumping three at a time.

Schaeffer shook, came out if it.

He looked at Rott and got a blank expression. *Give me orders, please.*

"Rott. Good work, Rott. The Chief will hear about this. Now. Erm... now, try very hard to remember this, Rott, okay?"

"Duh..."

One ear twitched — signs of life. Schaeffer took advantage.

"Good dog. Now, two things. Bite all the rats you can. Don't bite any cats."

Two things to remember. Schaeffer scanned Rott's face: both ears perky — message received and understood. Schaeffer barked, "Let's go!" and bounded along the corridor. Ahead... a wide window at head height. Beyond the window... a balcony, night sky and moonlight.

Schaeffer built up speed and jumped for the sky.

RRR

More rats than I had ever seen at one time, let alone gone up against: this was a ten-cat job, not a two. An' whatever edge surprise might have given us, I'd blown because I'd let them know I was there. I'd wanted to know if it was all true, an' had to take a look. I let curiosity get the better of Never Hesitate, even though I knew all about what curiosity does.

We went for the soft landin', jumped in the centre of the pile, onto the MOONrats, then jumped straight off an' ran up to the top of the terrace, by the balcony wall, drawing them. Better that they come at us.... The first guys came at me an' Sam, squealin'. Sam dived straight in.

I saw him slicin' one guy open before I had my own to do — a rat jumpin' at my face, teeth first. I ducked, he went over my back, an' I went for the guy comin' up behind him, slashed him across his spine, leavin' him useless, turned back to the first, punched a claw into his belly an' ripped upwards.

I felt rats jump on my back an' I span, slashed one, had to roll to shake another off my back. I rolled an' crushed him, came up, pinned the rat, bit his head.

Rats kept comin'. I felt teeth bitin' into me, useless along my body because the fur was thick, but occasionally, I'd feel real pain from a bite to the back of my legs. I knew the rats were countin' on numbers, lookin' to weaken us gradually, takin' a little piece at a time, notchin' up bites, knowin' that it all added up. There were bodies all over. Blood ran in the gulleys between the tiles, an' the terrace floor was black and shiny. Some wheezin', bleedin', dyin' rats scratched at the tiles tryin' to crawl away, but always, more came, snappin' at our eyes, bitin' at our ankles an' throats, leapin' on us, weighin' us down. Stabbin', tearin', pinnin', slashin', bitin', rippin', jumpin', dodgin', flippin' an' rollin'; swipin' rats from each other's backs, Sam an' I fought, tryna get to Marcus an' the MOONrats huddled by the hole in the wall. Max was tryna get things movin' — pointin', pushin' an' slappin', shoutin', "Go!" an' "Get in the hole!" to Marcus an' the MOONrats. Marcus was laughin'.

"An' miss *this*? Get outta here!"

An' still rats came at us, leavin' the protective wall an' runnin' at us, keepin' us away from the hole. I slashed an' pounced, swiped at the rats comin' at us unceasingly. I had blood in my eyes, in my mouth, all over my fur. I heard Marcus sneer.

"Dah. These two chumps are dead. Let's go."

I watched him clamber over the rat-pile to stand in plain view, his soldiers between him an' us, a single claw silently raised in our directions.

Sai gaped at the pitched battle at the top of the terrace, barely registering Max's slaps and shouts. Sai heard Max order another wave of rats forward, saw them break away and sprint towards the two cats, looking, this time, as if they would be enough to swamp them. As the rats neared they jumped, landing on back and flank, some grabbing at legs, hanging on to immobilise the terrible claws on the end. The cats shook, thrashed, but the rats held on with tooth and claw, weighing the cats down. Sai saw the grey, flat-faced cat staggering under a covering of rats, saw him lurching and, finally, falling over.

He heard Marcus, still viewing the battle, saying admiringly, "Wait a minute... Maaaax, I'm gonna make you a General."

Then there was an explosion, a roaring **RRRR-UUUUFFFF!** and a window sprayed onto the terrace, shattered glass spinning and glinting, showering MOON, tinkling on the ground, crystal musical notes. A huge, shaggy, snarling dog hurtled through the blizzard of glass and landed on the terrace, then rushed at the rats, tearing at the prone cat. Then Sai felt the building shake as a second dog, a monster of muscle, landed ahead of him and tore into scampering rats with hideous, terrier-like skill, heading them off when they ran for the hole in the wall.

The guards ran in any and all directions, looking for an escape that Sai knew did not exist. Max didn't move — he watched the battle turn against him with stoic calm. Marcus's eyes darted this way and that, seeking a bolthole. Sai looked at the wolf-like dog: stooping, biting, tossing dead rats aside, peeling away the outer layer to the body beneath, the ginger cat thrashing to get out from under, shouting, "Sam! Sam!"

SCHAEFFER

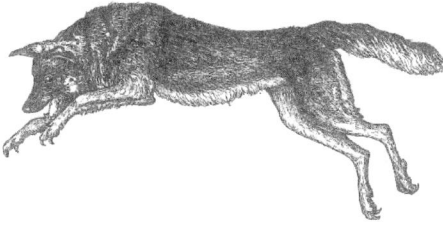

Schaeffer landed and sprinted to where he could see a ginger tail poking out of a coat of rats. Behind him, he heard Rott landing, the first crunch and the wet noise of a rat bursting. He tore up to the edge of the terrace and bit into the rats gnawing at Frr, plucked them off dead, threw them aside, carried on 'til he heard Frr gasp, "Sam! Sam!"

Schaeffer barked, "Rott!"

He ran to cover the escape hole as the big cop lumbered over to the mound of rats. Schaeffer saw Frr laying into the rats swarming over... who? Saw him stand aside for Rott. Rott's bite was a one-shot stop every time: rats splattered when he bit, flew when he tossed them aside, landed dead, ripped and saggy. Rott chomped and snapped, tearing off rats until a blood-stained grey cat emerged from beneath the covering of brown fur. The cat twitched, staggered upright and started lashing out blind at rats that weren't there, then fell.

Rats fled in blind, squealing panic. They ran into Rott, or Schaeffer, or Frr and died against walls, pinned to the floor, or bitten near in half.

Schaeffer barked, "POLICE! Give yourselves up NOW!"

And they did it.

"In the centre! In the light!" ordered Schaeffer.

They headed for the circle of rats. Schaeffer scanned and sniffed the MOONrats and Marcus.

Schaeffer looked at Frr, streaked with blood, eyes glazed, mouth agape. Frr was trying to speak, shaking his head, trying to come out of the daze. Schaeffer heard a gasp, leaned in closer.

Frr said, "Four of them... said 'no.'"

Schaeffer turned and looked at the eight very scared rats cowering in the corner.

FRR

     For a while it felt like I couldn't've killed another rat to save the world. I was giddy, sick with killing, gorged on blood an' I wanted to throw up. My head was spinnin' an' my eyes kept playin' tricks on me: I saw dead rats risin' up an' comin' back for more.

Sam was in bad shape. Bites all over his body, his ears nibbled away, one of his eyelids punctured an' bleedin', swellin' up an' half-blindin' him. He lay in a corner, too fragged even to lick his wounds. Schaeffer's big friend, square an' heavy like an apartment block, stood guard over the fat rats, Marcus, Max, an' whatever guards had managed to give themselves up. I looked around: dead rats everywhere. The floor was slick stank. I watched Schaeffer interrogatin' Marcus, his big-bark bad-cop routine gettin' nowhere because Marcus knew Schaeffer wouldn't bite if he didn't get answers.

Questions: Who voted yes? Who killed the canary?

Marcus, straight-faced, said he didn't know. Schaeffer couldn't, or wouldn't, force it, just kept repeatin' the questions 'til all I heard in my head was, "WHO KILLED THE CANARY?"

My head was spinnin'. I felt sick. More head tricks. I heard canary song an' the rage I'd thought I'd burned off sparked up...

I walked over to Schaeffer, burned-out calm.

"Excuse me, officer..."

I nudged past him, rammed a paw under Marcus, flipped him onto his back an' pinned him down.

"Those who voted yes. Who killed the canary. NOW!" I leaned in close, whispered, "Or I'm gonna eat your balls."

And Marcus spilled, pointin' and squealin'... Marcus ratted everybody out.

"Him! Him! Him! And her! And Max killed the canary! Max did! Max did!"

"Thank you," I told him.

I looked over at Max.

"That true?"

"Yes."

His voice was totally flat.

"Why?"

"Orders."

"Whose?"

No squeal. Max shrugged. I understood, *Whose do you think?*

I looked down at Marcus, squirmin' an' grinnin' uneasily. I smiled at him. He smiled back, very twitchy.

"Is that true?"

"Erm..."

"I see," I said, an' bit his balls off.

The terrace flinched, then groaned when I spat them out. All there was from Marcus was a thin gasp. His eyes were in the top of his head. He was totally frozen, doubled-over, claws clutched over his wound. I took him by the scruff in my jaws, not gently. I lifted him up an' heard him cry weakly. I carried him to the edge of the balcony, listenin' to his agonised whimpers. Another weak cry of pain came when I jumped up onto the ledge, bangin' him against the bricks. Marcus' mouth was open to scream, but his dyin' was almost soundless... just the hiss of the air goin' out of him, slow.

Thinkin' of the canary, I held him over the drop, then let him fall. I think he was maybe too far gone by then to know. Maybe.

I stood on the edge of the balcony, dizzy, one thing left to do.

I filled my lungs an' put it out on The Big Miaouw.

"DEAD RAT IN THE PLAZA!"

And then I turned back for Sam.

Sai

The sled rumbled through the darkness, making its strange music in the echoing duct. Its passengers, Mir, Max and Sai, were silent.

Sai tried to make sense of what he had lived through and witnessed over the past three days, but his mind was still reeling. The three days shrank to two terrible minutes where he had watched death rage in front of him, then stop before it touched him: a death that had averted the end of... warm life.

In shock, details flashed through his mind, impressions not wholly understood.

Dog justice — police dog justice — a blind eye turned to summary execution.

Cat justice — blood-spattered floor and walls — perhaps ninety bodies.

Dog justice — "Not *everybody*, Frr. Only the guilty."

Cat justice — Marcus's life for the canary's. Kaver's, Alvix's and Caleb's for Sam.

MOON — shivering witnesses.

Cat justice — Max, spared.

The bodyguards who gave themselves up — spared.

Sai, Mir, Athena and Libo — spared.

Luxor — spared.

"Mir, Max," Sai suddenly asked, "how is it that we're still alive?"

But the question fell away behind them in the tunnel: neither answered.

How long did I watch my death for? wondered Sai. *Why did it stop and not touch me? What held the cat back? Luxor's acquittal — an act of mercy amid merciless retribution.*

An image of the cat flashed in Sai's mind: drying blood, stiffening his fur, standing on the balcony, screeching into the plaza. The look of completion and contentment turning to horror when the cat jumped back down onto the terrace and tried to rouse his companion... closing

his eyes to block out the awful truth of the other's death. Opening them again and facing MOON...

Unspoken — the cat's price.

Caleb: pleading — silenced.

Alvix: dour dignity — no pleading, no begging. No complaint as the cat bit through his head.

Less calm, Kaver — not too young to die, evidently.

The sled rolled on, the rat-team pacing themselves for the long haul. Max had ordered them to make for the port. Sai stood next to Mir, all of his thinking fixed on how he could salvage the operation in play with Carlo.

Epilogue

Louie

Louie reckoned he was finally going to fill out. He was eating well, sleeping deep and getting strong climbing. There was even a chance he could get fat if he worked at it.

The ship was full of cheese. It was always night-time in the cargo holds, and there was no ship's cat. Engines hummed to you all day and all night, and the floor rolled with the ocean, rocking you to sleep when your stomach was full. There were other rats — blacks and browns of every shade and size — but nobody cared what colour you were because there were holds full of food. If it ever started to run short, reckoned Louie, things might be different: rats might not be so nice to each other. But there wasn't much danger of that.

"Biggest hill of cheese this side of the moon," laughed the old-timers and raised crumbs in each other's direction, toasting the good times. Ship-jumpers all, each had a tale of dry-land woe and of starving in holds full of coal or steel before finding their floating rat heaven. Sea-farers' tales was what you got instead of music. Sometimes someone shooting the breeze would mention MOONrats. Louie'd shiver, keep his mouth shut.

He'd go up on deck, whenever the dark of the holds became the dark of the sewer, to breathe in the sea air and feel the sun's warmth. He'd peer up, squinting at the wheeling gulls, looking for a pigeon. He missed Sax bad. Nights on deck he'd look up at the stars in the sky and hope to see the same configurations that hung out over the big city rooftops where he and Sax used to sing and dance. But the sky was different, like everything else... And maybe the big city didn't exist anymore, anyway.

Gazing across the vast sea-night, Louie'd get an ache worse than any he'd felt, even the one in his claws when he crossed the tunnel-arch climbing out of the sewer, death sucking hard from beneath. Fear would say: "Think Nice Thoughts!" and Louie couldn't find any. You can take the guy outta the sewer, but...

It still got bad, remembering, sometimes. That was when the Voice would come, rare these days now that there was so little to fear: *Maybe nothing happened, Louie. That cop dog... he was smart...* And behind the Voice was a gust of hot dog breath, and it would warm Louie to his heart. In his head, he'd hear music, see the emerald greens shimmering over the golden tonsils of the world's best friend and singer: Shibbendaddy shibbendaddy skiddley-bop doo-wop !

A fur-raising shiver would slide down his spine like a long, warm wave.

Louie'd dance on the deck with tears in his eyes.

SCHAEFFER

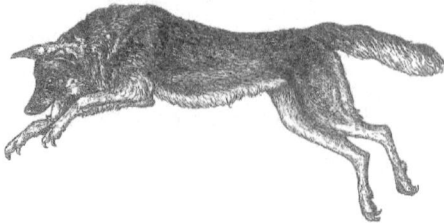

Procedure: turn yourself in — police dog thinking.

Instinct: save your ass — street cat thinking.

Going down.

The awful scene behind him, Schaeffer walked slowly down the stairs. Rott lumped unsteadily at his side at the same pace. His ears were droopy. No-one spoke. Frr moved in silence, but Schaeffer could smell him beneath the sharp stink of rat blood. Plenty of that in his own fur, too.

Going down.

Outside — the plaza. Schaeffer'd been away for two days, figured the square buried under dogshit by now.

I used to be a poop-policer, he thought. *Now I'm a cop. Correction: ex-cop. Any way the stick lands — shit — splat!*

Think!

Options: two — both ugly. Report to Captain Dobie and have your ass chewed off, or live in the street. Full Report too incredible to believe: routine murder follow-up, leading to... AWOL, association/partnership with known felon, intimidation, abuse of rank, exhorting fellow officer to dereliction of duty, B&E... More, line-of-duty killing for the first time — rat blood — real police work — nasty taste in mouth.

Averted: what? "Attempted Metrocide"?

UNBELIEVABLE.

Sole corroboration: Bone.

UNBELIEVABLE.

Scrap to toss to Cpt Dobie: Marcus dead, but figure replaced.

"Well done, Schaeffer."

UNBELIEVABLE.

Dog-house.

Believable.

Foot of the stairs.

Think!

Blood-stained... Rott my partner... tell him anything. Fatso in the plaza... street cat thinking... YES!

They came to the last flight, claws ticking, no-one speaking. When they reached the foyer, the door opened from outside: a two-legs, drunk, staggering and staring.

The cops and the cat filed past. The guy got out of the way, pronto.

Schaeffer stepped outside, breathed deep, sat down, looked over the plaza at the teeming crowd drinking in the summer late, late into the night. Dogs, action, night-pigeons, a prowling cat, a prowling police unit...

Schaeffer bent down low to lick, and felt his head clearing with the soothing strokes of his warm, wet tongue.

Here comes Fatso.

"Rott!"

"Duh. Yeah?"

"Two things. One: you found me in an alley."

One ear twitched, wobbled, and poked up.

"Two... that's all."

Boing! Went the other.

Cop car crawling closer...

Schaeffer looked round: Frr was gone. Schaeffer got up, started limping towards the car, a three-legged fakeass hobble with matching whine. The unit turned the corner. Schaeffer got in its path, dip-beams either side of him. The unit stopped. The door popped. Fatso clambered out, soppy smile on his sweaty face. Schaeffer whimpered and limped. Fatso crouched, threw his arms around Schaeffer's neck, big hug... smelly like take-out cartons and ashtrays. Happy noises, rough-friendly fur tousles... This worried expression as he noticed the blood and made a *what-the-hell-would-he-know-anyway* once-over of Schaeffer's fake leg trouble. *What?! You're a vet now, asshole?* Fatso nose-to-nose with Schaeffer: Fatso's breath soooo bad, *please don't lick me!* Pat pat pat — dog tag tinkles — stroke stroke stroke... get that ugly face... yeuch!

But get the smile on Fatso's chops.

YES!! *Faked it.*

Schaeffer could have howled.

Partner, sucker, let *him* square things with the department.

Schaeffer, tasting rat blood and his own asshole in his mouth, dishing happy-dog face-licks to Fatso: right on the mouth.

ERR

Sam's death was out on The Miaouw by sun-up. I don't know who found him, but by midday the word on the street was that Sam had taken nearly a hundred rats with him. I hadn't realised just how popular Sam had been or just how big his family was 'til I heard the singin' from the terrace: a city of cats wailin' mournful and choked and screechy-sad: a street-cat requiem.

Tears runnin' down my face. Sobbin'.

All *my* fault.

My obsession, *me* gettin' caught up in the flow of mad events and draggin' Sam into it: *my* curiosity.

I went down to the port, to where Sam and I had napped and fished only a few days before. I looked beyond the harbour to the wide ocean and the horizon, wishin' I was a fish, or a bird, so I could just... go. Go. Leave it behind.

Saving the city: just a dream. Nobody would believe it.

Schaeffer — back in the plaza now. I go there sometimes just to look at him. I don't speak, I just look. To know that he's real, to know IT was real... if I didn't I'd go mad: ghosts comin' at me in the alley, rat bites all over them....

Can't take the alleys no more. No friends left there.

There's no music now: Sax flew the coop. The Combo ain't no more. Ya, hear me? *There ain't no music.*

I got it bad. I prowl jumpy, keep to the roofs. I dream of rats, wash more than I need to.

I hear birdsong an' I wanna cry.

I'm afraid of what I'll hear on The Big Miaouw.

PART 3

THE YEAR OF THE WHITE CROW

WHITE CROW

In the beginning, as none but I remember, there was not one sun but ten.

Who shall carry the suns? asked the gods.

Only the most beautiful of birds, said the angels.

My brothers and sisters and I, with our rainbow feathers: we were chosen to raise the suns.

What shall be our reward? my brothers and sisters and I asked the gods.

To dream the dreams of all things, replied they.

And we carried the suns.

And their fires burned us black.

And to all creatures, we became hated and feared because as we gave the day, we also brought the night.

Til one day, we rose together, my brothers and sisters and I.

All the suns rose at once.

The earth scorched.

The rivers dried.

The fields burned.

The creatures died.

All starved.

But We fed.

Then came Houyi the archer and killed my brothers and sisters.

He pointed his arrow at me, and loosed it.

And I ceased to be.

And now only one sun rises.

But now I live again.

Not hatched but become again.

Re-born. In the nest of a hawk away hunting.

Two chicks squawled for her, until, eaten, they were silent.

Their souls nourished me.

I am so strong.

Again.

I have lived before, many times.

I have perished but never died.

I have been dead for centuries.

Now I am reborn.

I know why: I feel it.

The pain and fear of the world cast a longer shadow than the light of peace and joy can dispel.

I am come to destroy.

To feast on the pain and the fear.

I would see the ten rise again.

And after the world's burning… the feast.

I am. Again.

It is my turn to kill.

I will kill Hope first.

But slowly.

Slowly.

Yes.

My brothers and sisters will take me to the heartstone, and I will find my instrument, my weapon, my Ghoul.

CHAPTER 4

The Mission

CARLO

"So... it's a snake goin' between two round rocks, right?" said Mauro. "An' then another snake bumpin' into another snake... that it? That's what he said?"

Mauro hovered a little in front of Carlo, who nodded. Mauro darted away again.

"And then it's a snake tryin' to eat its own tail?" asked Emilio.

Carlo nodded again.

"Snakes don't do that," Emilio said.

"He's right, boss," offered Mauro. "Even really dumb snakes don't do that."

Mauro darted forward again and was back a few inches in the air from Carlo's face.

"… an' then there's another snake going around a tree trunk, right? Why? I don't get it. Is any of that supposed to be funny?"

"It's what the white rat said," said Carlo, but he did not say what he was really thinking: no... it isn't funny.

"And only you can deliver this message?" asked Emilio.

"Yes."

Mauro was buzzing, agitated, irritated, and partly angry about being out of the loop, not let in on Carlo's thinking.

"An' it's life or death. You gotta risk your life for this guy... why?"

"Because I'm the Don and nobody else can do it."

"It's a long way to the edge of the forest, Carlo..." said Mauro. "For you, anyways...."

Emilio asked no questions: he had plenty, but he could see when Carlo was thinking. Part of him, though, as Carlo's adviser, *consigliere* and bodyguard, could not let go of the suspicion that the whole thing could just as easily be a set-up for a hit.

One reach at a time, slowly dragging himself forward, Carlo saw the ground now for what it was and wished he had never left his tree. It was such hard work walking, and he missed hanging on a branch, feeling the lulling sway of the breeze, seeing everything from upside down and having time to think... when all he had to do was run the forest before the white rat came, the one who had come to find him, and had survived doing so, impossibly. The one who said he could *talk* to humans and make them understand, the one called Sai, his name a soft exhale, and so like *ai*, his kind's name, that Carlo felt... kinship. And when the white rat told him that the forest was not alone, that there were others, just as rich, just as endangered... and that the destruction could be stopped, he listened to the white rat who said he knew how humans communicated, using tiny scratch marks that told stories.

"Give them this message: a snake going between two round rocks...."

And then Sai showed Carlo alone what the message meant and told him where he should take it: to the end of the forest, to the very line of devastation where the death of the forest was marked out and....

"You'll be in the greatest danger imaginable," the rat had said. "But my organisation can keep you safe. We are very powerful."

In the darkness sounds were amplified, not just because of the echo in the tunnel. It was Sai's senses heightening: when he could not see his hearing became more acute, his sense of smell became more acute, and so did his sense of danger. And he had never come through so much danger before in his life. Compared to this, the jungle was safe.

Sai and Mir stayed silent and held on as the sled swayed around corners, speeding up on the downhills and slowing down for the uphills, listening to the regular-as-clockwork squeak of the front-right wheel on its ungreased axle and the rhythmic and laboured gasping and panting of the sled-crew.

In his mind, however, he could hear something else: the groans and the screams of the dying and the wounded on the terrace. He could still smell the blood, could still see the blood, the floor of the terrace spattered and splashed with red, red pooling, red flowing along the gaps between the tiles. There had been no time yet to mourn the deaths of old, old friends, and Sai was just thinking that the only option for MOON now was flight, escape, dispersal and the end of all hope of any chance of Carlo's mission succeeding, when Max shouted "STOP!" clearly enough to make himself heard above the echoing din of the sled and its crew. The rat-sled came slowly to a halt.

"We're going back", said Max. "You...",

Sai knew Max meant himself and Mir, even though he could barely make out Max's outline in the darkness.

"… you ain't leaving yet. Get off the sled."

Max spoke to the sled-crew.

"You're done here, guys. Take the night off."

The crew-rats shrugged off their harnesses and moved off laughing.

Max pointed back down the tunnel.

"We're goin' back to where we came from. You made a mess. You're gonna clean it up."

ATHENA

In the apartment where she had stayed for the duration of the convocation, Athena waited, alone. She was singing very quietly to herself as she does when nobody is around to hear it. She sang beautifully. For rats, to hear her sing was to hear The Goddess. Except Athena knew that she wasn't The Goddess, or even a goddess; she had never been one, would never be one, wasn't one and didn't want to be one either. She was sure, only of this one thing: she *knew* that she was *definitely not* the reincarnation of an ancient Moon goddess from Sumeria or a goddess of Wisdom and War in Greece, or any other goddess.

If I were, she thought, *I think I'd know it.*

But everywhere she went, everybody else believed it. In cities where she had hidden before, when she appeared as a goddess to rats, wars had broken out. Rival interpretations of what she was what she meant had divided rats in cities the world over. And it was always all about war and power. Rival rat kings had pitted everything to have her as queen. For status. She had accepted none of them, and outlived them all many times over. Whenever she was seen as a goddess, there were consequences, thousands of lives changed on each one's whim of what she was, or what they thought she was. Not what *she* thought she was. Rats fought, killed, died in her name. It was unbearable. The lying was choking her. She did not want to be The Goddess. Nothing *good* ever came of it.

But as much as she hated it, she *was* the goddess to millions of ordinary rats worldwide. She gave them hope and something to believe in. If she stood before them – and she had, many times - and commanded them, they offered her everything they had did anything she asked. And these rats, all over the world, had kept MOON, all of them, safe now for many, many years, so we – I- owe them, Athena told herself, for the thousandth time. So, if she had to be a goddess… she would be a goddess even if she was not a goddess. Right now, though, she told herself, I had better be the goddess. Because if I'm not, I think these rats will kill us. It's not the first time I've been in this situation. But I wish I could be sure it would be the last because someday soon… I'm going to give this goddess crap up.

She sipped water from a dish and then stood when Max, Sai and Mir emerged from the tunnels through a ventilation shaft with the grate removed.

Mir and Sai came immediately to her side and laid their tails over hers.

"Are you all right?" asked Sai. And looking at Max, he asked:

"Has he harmed you?"

Max stood some way off and did not approach her.

"Here. I got 'em back for you," he said to Athena.

"Thank you, Max," said Athena. "Can you let us talk alone?"

"Yeah, but remember what we talked about."

"I will."

"I'll be outside."

"Thank you, Max."

She was calm and serene and Max obeyed her too, noted Mir.

She waited until Max's tail disappeared into the skirting-board and said,

"Libor and Luxor have gone."

"*Gone*? Where have they gone?" Mir was shocked, looking at Sai. Sai took the news in with another deep sinking in his spirit like hope being snuffed out slowly...

"They left. They're gone. They want nothing more to do with MOON," said Athena flatly. "It's just the three of us now."

"We can't protect them if we don't know where they are," said Sai.

"They don't want protection, Sai. Libor told me that after tonight, she thinks we should all be dead."

"Dead? Why?" demanded Mir.

Athena's composure broke:

"'*Why*'? Because we nearly started a war with biological weapons and killed billions of people! That's why!"

She turned to Sai:

"Sai, how the hell did Caleb... *happen*? Why didn't we know what he was *doing*?"

"Because we were all involved in Sai's plan," said Mir.

Athena sighed. Sai's plan to save billions of lives. His visit to Carlo.

"Is that all still in progress?" she asked.

"Yes. It has started. It's happening. Just very, very slowly," Sai replied.

Mir grinned. He was used to communication that happened in nanoseconds. Sai sent his message by sloth.

"And the asset? The network of birds? Is it still ours to use?"
"Yes."

"So everything you set up is still..."

"... an ongoing operation, yes."

Mir was not grinning now. Sai, the overweight, bookish, distracted-looking rat risked his life to travel into a rainforest to recruit an agent for his network, a sloth who talked to birds. And now MOON was part of this network, hearing and sharing information. The birds carried their messages now and brought them information. And in return for access to that communication network, MOON must do something to help them. That was what Carlo had asked for in return for agreeing to Sai's plan. And Sai's plan, thought Mir, definitely needs what I do.

Athena will command, of course, because she's a goddess.

But now there were only three.

Athena called out to Max.

He climbed into the room. There were no guards posted anymore.

"Why are we back here?" asked Mir.

"I brought you back because I want you in the city," Max told him.

"As hostages?" asked Sai.

"No. I want you to help me run it."

"You want to be king," said Sai and looked at Athena.

"No. I don't."

Athena was calm. She knew how Max had come to feel about her while has served as her bodyguard for the week of the Convocation.

"We tend to attract trouble, Max," she told him, "maybe it's best for you if we aren't here."

Max was under the spell of her beauty; Mir saw this. And Max had no idea at all, of who Athena really was.

"Why do you want us here?" asked Sai.

Max stood on his hind-legs and looked hard at Sai, a look that reminded Sai that Max was a killer.

"Okay. So every rat in the world has heard of you Moonrats, right?... an' your amazin' intelligence?... how you've all lived more than ten times your normal lifespan... how humans want to kill you? Well, get this: humans want to kill us too. You think this makes you special? You might be gods to some rats, but you ain't to me. I don't know what you are, but I can see how you live. You got every rat in the world serving you. But with what your friend Domus and his buddies had planned?… I'm wondering if that's a good thing. I'm wondering… are you even a good thing? I mean, what is the point of you?"

He spoke directly to Sai and Mir, now:

"You should know from the off that my orders from Marcus were to kill all of you guys right as soon as the disease started. Yeah. He knew you were stronger than him, an' he didn't like being challenged."

Max paused.

"And I'd have done it too."

"Max..." started Sai, but Max cut across him to address Athena.

"Do you know how rats live here? Mostly? In sewers. Hungry, angry. Never see the sunshine, or go up top an' breathe clean air... That's how I came up. I was the toughest rat down there an' it got me noticed by Marcus, okay? Now listen…. Marcus was king, which means he got a piece of everybody's food. One day in every five, every rat in the city has to bring the king something as tribute. Any other day, you keep what you find, which ain't much. But the tribute?… tribute has to be your best, has to show your respect for the king. But going hungry for a whole day, working like that for King Marcus?… rats hated him. I hated him. But he was too big to kill, even for me. You know how many rats Marcus ordered killed because they came up short on the tribute? Thousands. 'Cos he only accepted the best. The freshest scraps he'd eat 'em there an' then, but stuff that didn't rot, he stored … I'm talking rice, grain, seeds, nuts. He had whole crews stashing it away, an' I know where, because my job, before this job of taking care of security for you guys... was maintaining the tribute system, an' protecting the

213

stashes, which are all over the city. It's what rat-kings do… they store food against the day."

"Against what day?" said Mir.

"The day it goes bad. And we just had that day, didn't we?"

Now Max addressed Sai.

"No. I don't want to be king. But I do know where Marcus put all the food. And I want to give it back. An' I can't, because I'm not the king. You kill the king, you become the king. But I didn't kill 'im. An' we can't make that cat a king."

"But *we* can make you a king," says Athena.

"Yeah. If you tell the rats. They'll listen to you. You're the goddess, right?" said Mir.

"If we make you the king, will you end the tribute?" asked Sai.

"If you make me king, I'll end the war."

"What war?

"The war against the black rats."

"You could end the war?"

"Oh, yeah."

"How?"

"Easy. If there's food, there's peace."

THE GHOUL

... and when ze world asks me, "Juju, where does your genius come from?" I will say, "I ad a appy childhood." Ma famille was loving an' cultured an' riche. We ad ad ze mountains for our estate for generations. We ate well, meals were vairy important an' we ate as a family. We would go on walks and picnics by ze river, we shoo off les bears oo are trespassing on ze estate an' ze fish swim up the river and zey are 'appy to jump into our mouths and we laugh and we eat and are 'appy. Ma famille teach me to appreciate all sings for zair beauty. Ze trees and les fleurs, ze sky an ze stars. Ze birds and ze butterflies. Ze petit bears and ze bees' nests et jacques-lapin. Maman knows I am fond of jacques-lapin and she spoils me. Yes... it was a perfect child'ood.

And zen Papa one night after dinnair 'e sez:

"Your muzzair and I we 'ave been talking, Julien."

And Maman she cannot look at me!

"We love you. But eet eez time for you to leave 'ome."

Zat night I go to sleep vairy urt and vairy afraid, and I cry because I am vairy sad. Zey do not love me, maman et papa. Ze world is so big and scary. Zere is cold and unger. I do not want to leave maman et papa and my 'ome. But zat night I av a vairy strange dream. A white crow come to me an 'e sez to me, would I like to taste everything that is beautiful? and I say of course, I am an artiste, I live only for beauty. Life is brief, beauty eternelle. I must taste all the beauty that I can in this life, or I 'ave not lived artistically, and 'e says, vairy well... would you like to eat me?

And I sink about zis. He is purest white, whiter zan ze bones of ze petit bear I sample today, he is white as ze snow where I created ze lovely abstract fresco wiz le petit bear's blood, and I am thinking, wiz zeze fezzairs this would be a daring original medium for me to experiment wiz, but in ma dream 'e smell bad. Very bad, like dead sings, so I say non, merci. I will only eat ze dead sings when there is nothing else to sample. Non. It is beneath a de Goulot to do so, so zair.

An' 'e says Bon! Would you like to taste all ze beauty in ze world like an artiste, an' I say of course, an' 'e sez then you must travel, an' e iz right.

I must see ze ole world an' taste all of its beauty so I can turn zis into beautiful art an' he sez, you must sample ze most delicious thing in ze ole world. And what iz zat? I say, an' it is a slow thing an' it is… perfection! An' ze most delicieux thing in zis beautiful world.

Where is this thing? I ask an' 'e say:

"Sowsse."

Et voila! suddenly I know why I existe!

I must taste ze beauty of ze world.

An' turn it into art.

In ze morning I wake.

Maman 'as prepared jacques-lapin for ma journey.

I kiss Papa.

I kiss Maman.

She is crying.

I tell zem:

"I will be a famous artiste!"

An' I 'ead sowsse.

ATHENA

The rats waited below her in silence in the darkness of the sewer. If Athena could have seen them, she would have amazed at their number, but she could not. She was above them, on a balcony. She could not be seen, ever. Not as the goddess. She was the Goddess and none was worthy to look upon her. The rats had been summoned. They knew already that a cat had killed King Marcus. The King lay dead in the dirt of the plaza, unmourned. The rats had gathered in the sewers in their tens and hundreds of thousands and now wait to be told who was to be the new king.

Max, standing among them, rose on his hind legs and shouted:

"King Marcus is dead!"

And still there was silence until, out of sight, hidden, Athena sang to them:

"I am the Moon. You have waited for me. Waited for me to come and end war and hunger. I am here now."

She heard the gasp rise like a wave, and she waited. They were in awe of her, she knew, as rats were everywhere she went when she sang. The rats' silence had broken now, and the sound from below was a rising whisper of... hope. Did the Goddess say an end to war and hunger? Excited squeaks started to break out all over.

She sang again.

"This is your king. Hear and obey his first command."

Max raised his voice for everyone to hear.

"I am the king now! Hear my word! No more tribute! The tribute is ended!"

The first sound as Athena heard it was a collective gasp, then laughter broke out, then joy began to build to a roar. Then the new king silenced them again with a raised paw, and told his subjects where Marcus had stored the food. Athena could hear their joy as they ran in the direction of the feast and thought, *he will be a good king, this rat.*

Later, in the apartment, alone, King Max proposed to her, to her disappointment.

"Stay. Live in my city."

She could not stay, she knew.

"The others, yes. Not me."

"Be my queen."

"One day, perhaps. But for now, promise me three things… keep my friends safe…",

"Yes."

"And when the stores are empty… that's where you hide the flasks with the disease that Caleb created. Nobody must ever find them."

"Yes. What's the other thing?"

"You might have to receive the ambassadors of the birds."

"Huh?"

"You're a king now, Max," she told him. "Don't say 'huh?'.

ATHENA

It was decided. She was heading south. It was her part in Sai's plan. Mir and Sai would live in the city, in this building, but not out in the open, or in luxury, or in any way that would draw attention. Max was the king and he would see to it that they were protected. But they would not live like gods the way they had before. They would live like rats. They would be protected, but they would not be served. They would not have teams of rats to pull them to where they wanted to go. They would have to learn all the tunnels and ways of the building

for themselves now. They would have their meals with Max, and Max was determined about one thing: Sai would have to lose some weight if he was to even fit in some of the tunnels he was going to have to use. Mir and Sai would have to take care of themselves now. Max's rats would find the computers that Mir and Sai wanted, they would set watchers to map the comings and goings of the humans in the building, so they knew when apartments were empty and safe, but getting inside the rooms where they are kept would now be all on them.

Here we go again... she thought: differentjungles.com.

"India. Rajasthan." said Mir, "Karni Mata temple. Got it."

Sai nodded.

And with that, Mir was gone. Within a few hours, Sai knew Mir would have everything they needed done on differentjungles.com. He had talked to Athena at length about where she was going and what she must do when she got there. He had assured her that she would be safe, that she would not have to be a goddess, except perhaps on occasion. Above all he was concerned for her safety, but after that, her happiness.

"I don't want to be a goddess, Sai," she had told him many times, "except when it has a purpose."

"You could just be a queen if you wanted. I think Max is…. " he now said to her.

"No."

Sai knew she would say that and why. Athena had outlived any lover she ever had, and losing them hurt her too much.

She had to take this journey.

"So, you're going to Karni Mata," said Mir with a grin. "You'll love it."

It was Sai's idea. He had, he said, found a place where Athena would be safe, where she would not have to hide from rats or humans. The perfect hiding-place for the rat goddess who didn't want to be one. Now, it was down to Mir to do what he alone could do for MOON.

He unrolled a tiny keyboard, a mat, a masterpiece of miniaturisation with intricate filigree wiring and tiny keys. It had a loose string coming off it, rather like a tail. Mir took the bulbous end in his jaws, climbed onto the computer and pushed it into a slot in the side of the machine, called, he told them, 'a USB port'. Claws ticking, he started doing what he had to. Sai and Athena watched as he typed, screen light playing on his pale fur and sparking in his black eyes as his claws flew over the keyboard and the screen flowed with sparkling rivers of computer code. They watched, but they did not know what he was doing. He entered the code he had written and opened a terminal, creating his command line. The remote access tool that he had designed opened a backdoor into the system and allowed a manipulative programme to bind to its host. Remote Access Tool, a RAT. Now Mir had control.

"What are you doing now?" asked Sai.

"Moving some money."

"You always said that was dangerous," said Athena. "That humans watch money more carefully than anything else."

"True. They do," said Mir, "but this is from an account in a tax haven. I've got encryption running, I'm re-routing through different servers in thirteen countries, and… I'm out."

He grinned.

"Well, there's the money. Now let's arrange Athena's holiday."

He went back to his work. Sai and Athena watched without understanding how he was doing what he was doing.

"Ta-da!"

Mir hummed and clicked, releasing another RAT. Seconds later, his programme was manipulating flight cargo manifests on three different airlines to move Athena across the world; he had arranged transport door-to-door. The necessary forms and permits and medical regulatory paperwork were suddenly, miraculously, digitally real. His RAT ran silently and found its way in. Mir followed it, claws ticking softly and rhythmically on the face of the tiny keyboard.

The computer work was fiercely complicated, but the idea behind it was beautifully simple: www.'differentjungles.com'. 'Pet delivery anywhere in the world'. The website had only ever had one client, MOON, and Mir, who built it, still thought it was one of his best ideas. It was the secret of how they travelled. On the surface, it was entirely plausible: you had only to contact the site, arrange dates, collection, and destination, and then make payment, all digitally. Mir had just placed Athena on a flight to Rajasthan and arranged her collection from the airport, and delivery to her next destination. Tomorrow morning, she would climb into a cage outside this apartment and wait to be collected. Humans would do the rest. They would convey Athena to the Rat Temple. It would take less than twenty-four hours. Mir's final touch would be to fetch a sedative from Domus' laboratory in the city to make the journey pass less disagreeably.

"Finished?" asked Sai.

"Done."

He pulled the tail of the keyboard from the side of the machine and rolled his miraculous mat up. The screen went off, and the room went dark. Now, there was only moonlight to see by.

222

"Is it safe?" asked Sai.

"Not here. The occupier will be back soon. And he has a dog."

"I mean for Athena."

"Yes."

"When do I leave?" she asked.

"Tomorrow night. It's all arranged. You'll be there in under twenty-four hours. And you will be *very* well-treated."

"And there's no risk?"

"Sai, there's always risk, you know that."

"Athena?"

None of them liked risk, and exposure of this level – literally putting yourself in the hands of humans – was the greatest, but there was no choice. All three of them living in the same place in the same city was not safe; one of them needed to be in the animal world again, and Athena was the best choice: Sai went last time, and Mir was too important here.

She would take refuge in a place where she would not be noticed, yet a place where she would be at her most powerful. But Sai fretted for Athena, she knew. Because Mir had explained to them the dangers of what he was doing, what Sai and Athena had asked him to do. So now, even though they could not understand how he did what he did, they now knew what he knew: that this could get them all killed. This was how the humans could find them.

It is getting harder to evade surveillance, explained Mir. The humans are watching the human world, and they can see everything: there are surveullance satellites in orbit, there are face recognition algorithms looking through street cameras; optical recognition cameras in any place where traffic moved. They can see everything. So we hidefrom that world. But if we use this world... we cannot hide our digital paw-prints. And even if Mir mostly went under the surface of the net, hiding his actions with clever sunbterfuges, he could not operate without leaving some tiny elements of a trail that could be followed, even though he had hidden their tracks behind myriad layers of false identities, dead-ends and stayed as much as possible in the darknet. But if they were still looking for them, they could catch scent of us there, in the world of ones and zeroes. Because they were still looking. They just had to be.

It wasn't about the intelligence the injections gave us. They all knew.

The humans already *had* that.

It was the ten lifespans.

That was what the humans wanted.

And that was why they must never be caught.

The Ghoul

I am far from 'ome, from Maman et Papa. But I am not 'omesick. I am never zis 'appy. It is as if I am living ten lives at ze same time, zere is so much zat is new all around me. Ze world is beautiful. Ze sky, les mountains, zeze ills, ze desert I see ahead an' ze stars. Ze smells. Les fleurs! Ze perfume of ze trees. Ze birds sing. Ah. Beauty, all around. An all ze délices I sample. A paradise of flevveurs and aromes and so many things for me to taste.

And my art, my talent az never been so riche, nor I, ze artiste, so productif! Ze fruit of my talent I put on display to ze world.

What is zat? A moth?

Hmm. Intéressant. Crunchy, wiz a succulent fondant centre.

Zen I snuffle and zair! un squirrel! Ze nuts of ze squirrel are exquisite!

I follow my nose and voilà! I taste.

Ze squirrel first sings to me then is polite and quiet as I dine.

Délicieux.

Ze rest of im is quite good too.

Oh. It 'as started to rain.

I will sleep 'ere, under zis tree. Zen I 'ead sowsse.

White Crow

In this black night, thick with the hiss of rain, the cloud-blinded moon is powerless as I float up and land atop the Heartstone, the great hammering pulse of the world. I close my eyes and empty my mind to enter the dream of all things, the swirling, flowing, ever-changing murmuration of the dance of life.

My soldiers stand guard, a shadow-black legion of sharp beaks and honed cruelty, my army, my protection.

The walls of the universe melt, and I enter: into the minds and the lives of the waves and the winds, the mountains and the seas, the woods and fields, the rock, the soil and the flesh... and I find you, my Ghoul.

I hear you slavering, grunting, panting, your heart bursting with joy as you lope on and on, ever southwards, hunting for the slow thing, the forest king, who dreams of peace. You will find him, I know: you will devour him and end him.

Oh, but I have chosen well! My fool, my Ghoul, my weapon: dreaming your dreams of beauty and bliss, believing yourself the messenger of joy and all the while wounding and ripping and tearing; thoughtlessly, wantonly killing, besmirching and polluting, you - the stinking, savage embodiment of greed that would consume the whole world and still want more - you are joy to me, my child, my weapon, my Carcajou. Blood-spiller, grief-bringer, captain of carrion... go... onwards... follow your path and your dream... do my bidding: find the slow hope. Tear it to shreds.

ATHENA

Max's rats waited until the human left the cage outside the apartment door and then waited for him to leave before Athena was escorted into her travelling quarters. There were no goodbyes, not in this corridor, with its humans coming and going. Athena willingly stepped inside the cage. The guards shut the door and left quickly.

Athena sighed in relief. She needed to be away from here, this building and the plaza it overlooked and the awful horrors of that night. She needed to not be a goddess and needed Max to understand that she didn't want to be a queen, either. She remembered her first cage.

When 'Moon Goddess' meant M.O.O.N.

And that it took her years to find out what M.O.O.N. meant.

'Mil Ops: Origin Neuropsych.'

They were a medical experiment funded by the military.

She walked to the water bottle hanging from the bars in the corner of the cage. The water meant sleep, and this cage was not like the cage where she hid cowering away from the sharp stinging thing, the injections, in the corner, until the sharp stinging things came, anyway. And the human who did it to her was singing. She drank from the water bottle. Her last thought before sleep was of swifts.

Ah. Again, I dream of ze white crow. It is such an 'appy dream because ze white crow understands ze beauty of my purpose: to make ze life of ze ole world better with ma art. But what is life? What is art? What is 'appiness?

Ah, but siz is a beautiful landscape, an' ze night sky is starry an' I see some stars I know from 'ome which make me feel sad for 'ome an' some I do not know yet but I am 'eading south so I will meet more of you, I think.

Bonne nuit les stars!

C'est moi: Julien de Goulot. Artiste!

Now ze artiste must stop an' repose 'imself in contemplation as 'e produces iz art.

Oo. Aa.

Et ... voila!

The latest from Julien de Goulot.

Ah.... ze arome, snff, snff, parfait!

Oh.

     Each day is more perfect than ze last as my art becomes more refined, daring and powerful. Ze material I am working with... such variety! An' my tummy it iz producing so much zat is good.

Bon.

Eh? Oh!

Voila!

Encore!

Ah...oooh...

Oui.

Snff, snff.

On a smaller scale zan earlier works, but en miniature, a work of delight. I snuffle an' zair... in ze air... moving so swiftly, I wonder... 'ow can I eat you? You fly so very quickly an' never land, oui, I know oo you are, Martinet... Papa taught me. But if I did sample you, lots of you... would that speed up ze artistic process, I wonder?... indeed.... an' will ze slow thing zat ze white crow tell me to sample make ze the act of creation slower.... but 'ow much more satisfying…?

Hmmm.

I am vairy philosophical today, I find.

I am also ungry.

I 'ead sowsse.

ATHENA

The sun was blazing hot but she was standing in the shade and the smooth stone floor of the temple was cool beneath her paws. The air around was warm and still and sweet-scented with the perfume of sun-bright marigold and snow-white jasmine garlands which hung in thick tresses from walls and rafters.

Even breathing here is delicious, she thought.

She had never known such peace. Or freedom.

She had never felt safer, even though there were humans in every part of the temple, always. They would not, she knew, ever harm her. They were Jains and lived lives devoted to taking no life so that they will live better lives in their next lives. She was among humans who did not take life. That, she thought, was a safe as she could be. As for the other rats... well, they didn't have it so bad either. Sunlight glinted off the steel, copper, silver and gold dishes and bowls and sparkled on the water inside them. Food was laid out everywhere: grains, vegetables, lentils, nuts, fruits. Athena was comfortable and at peace, and she was not even remotely treated like a goddess, and the normality and the simplicity of this was a luxury she had never had before, and she relished it. For the first time in her life, Athena could hide in plain sight and be no-one but herself. I could stay here forever, she thought, as long as none of the rats find out that, in fact, actually, she really *was* The Goddess.

Then again, maybe not. Because there was still the whole goddess thing.

Let's see, she wondered… She didn't want to be a goddess, so she left the city where she was a goddess, and she travelled, like a goddess, to here, where she was, once again, in spite of everything she did to avoid being a goddess, still a goddess. She didn't even have to

say, hi, it's me, the goddess, for it to happen. *Because for someone who wanted to get away from the goddess thing*, she told herself, *for a goddess, you sure messed up.* There were twenty thousand rats here in the temple. And all the girls were The Goddess, Karni Mata. Here they go again:

"Hello. Have we met? I'm the Goddess. Lovely to meet you. *She* says *she's* the Goddess but she isn't actually, because I am."

"Actually, I don't think you can *actually* be the Goddess, because I am."

"Oh, are you actually the Goddess as well? How quaint. I thought there was only one and it can't be you because I am the Goddess."

"Oh, really, and what were you in your former lives?"

All rats were sacred in this temple. She had been here for three months now. She was recognised but ignored. She was, she thought, the only female rat here not claiming to be the Goddess. When she first got here, she tried to make herself invisible, determined to give not the slightest indication of who she was, talking to few, investigating the temple, looking for a place to leave her sign. She kept out of temple politics but listened in on the temple gossip and amused herself by following the shifting hierarchy of who, really, actually was the Goddess today. ("No, but really, I'm, like, really sure *I'm* the goddess, because I feel, like, kind of, y'know, really *goddessy?*").

Some of the goddesses were nice, thought Athena. Some were really nice, but some not so nice at all. Some of the goddesses were real cats, all claws and hisses. The younger ones? They needed to get better at it:

"Her? Being reborn with a rump fit for Ganesh does not make you a goddess."

They should learn from their elders:

"That is the golden goblet of a maharajah that she drinks from, yet she sups from that cup as if she dines in a Himalayan midden."

And everybody knew just what they were going to be in their next life, and it was usually a cow.

And the guys? Oh, they were all going to be tigers. Brahmin bulls! Buffalos! Elephants! Yeah - still hitting on all the girls, same as everywhere, except here they did it better.

They didn't grab you or even touch you; they stepped out of the way to let you pass, stepped aside at the water bowls to let you drink and offered to bring you food.

They didn't bring up 'mating', just like that, in conversation. No, they said things like:

"Oh, Goddess, would the flower of perfection permit one to convey to her, in the jaws of supplication, a morsel of delight?" Or, "Oh, Goddess, would the eye of beauty walk upon the paws of enchantment with one to the golden drinking bowl for some refreshment?" (No, the Goddess would not.). And they didn't ask again. They would usually go try the same act on another couple dozen goddesses, and when that didn't work they'd find a human to toy with: running across their feet, or lying on their feet because that would always get you a treat because here it was considered a blessing if a rat lay on your feet.

Athena sighed. For the first time in a long time, she felt happy because she felt free. Or free-er, because she had not forgotten why she was there. Once she had come to feel safe in the temple, after the first month, she had started her mission: she found a whitewashed wall made out of soft rock, a wall onto which moonlight fell, in the quieter, older part of the temple, and scratched her sign where birds could see it: The Owl's Identity, her sign, the sign of The Goddess.

$$e^{i\pi} + 1 = 0$$

And she waited to see who it would bring. Those who would come would be expecting her to be an owl. Instead, they would see a rat. In this place, that was understandable. But at all costs, Sai had reminded her, you must act as The Goddess. So she came to this spot, by night, every night, while other rats slept or went looking for food, to the place where there was never any food

232

left out, that rats never came to, to wait for whoever might come, and to look at the moon. Until one day there was another rat who came to look at the moon as well. Athena knew him from the temple. The first time she ever saw him she had been afraid of him. He was slow and grim and worn and thin, scarred and scabbed across his back and his face. He was missing a front paw, and his back legs were weak, and he walked with obvious pain. *He is mad*, said the others. *He raves. He screams in his sleep, and he is ugly. He is cursed. Look at him. One of his feet has been bitten off.* Normally, the crippled rat did not dare approach her or any of the other goddesses, who greeted his presence with shrill shrieks of disgust, and now the rat still did not speak to her or look at her. He merely stood and looked up at the moon in rapt silence. Then, from his throat began a low humming, and the sadness and pain seemed to leave his face.

Athena looked at him and listened to his soft song.

And then he spoke.

"One comes to you. Before tomorrow's moon."

She stared at him in fright. How did he know? She'd done everything to avoid being identified as the Goddess.

And he seemed to know what she was thinking because he dared to look her in the eye when he said:

"Your sign. 'Add only one to the chaos... and all will become nothing'. Three of those symbols were born in this land."

She did not reply. The rat looked at the floor.

"Goddess," he said, "the one who comes knows of the White Crow," then he turned back to look at the moon and started humming again.

CARLO

Carlo hung in the tree quite still and gazed at the moon from upside down. Emilio was coiled at the foot of the tree, and Mauro was hovering nearby, the hum of his wings still reassuring after all their years of friendship. This was luck, thought Carlo. This was life. To hang in a tree, safe and content and free to look up at the moon. Tomorrow, there would be the tree to come down, another mile to travel as they made their way towards the men, to reason with them. Carlo wasn't worried that they were getting there slowly. The humans were coming to them, and the line of destruction that came with them was moving a lot faster than they were. They'd meet soon enough. He yawned and fell asleep, and Emilio and Mauro watched over him.

ATHENA

Athena waited in the quiet part of the temple, at sunset, alone, and tried to ready herself for whoever was coming. She peered intently into the sky, watching for their arrival, whoever they were. Most likely, Sai had briefed her back in the city, it would not be the kings of the Eastern World, but the swift, the kingfisher, the crane, their emissaries. *At all costs convince them you are The Goddess*, Sai had implored her. *Sing if necessary. Just get the swifts on our side. With them we can connect further into the bird world, and help Carlo.*

Again, she felt like a pain in her chest, the heart-sickness of the lie, the myth, the absurd joke tearing her apart - 'You Are The Goddess' - when she wasn't, never had been, didn't want to be but had to be.

She looked out across the sky spread out before her again, then turned her back to the moon to look at the sign she had scratched into the wall, the owl's sign, the sign of the...

"Goddess!"

Her heart leapt, and she squealed. It sounded like a cat. She spun around and, for a moment, knew perfect terror. Standing on the wall was a large bird of prey. She hadn't heard it or seen it or sensed its arrival in any way, and its stealth terrified her.

"Goddess!"

Athena nearly shrieked with fear again and then remembered that this bird would never harm her. (For once, it was good to be a goddess). She breathed deeply, slowly, feeling her fear and her heartbeat slowing down as she regained her composure.

Then she looked at the bird and formed these impressions immediately: it was a female, and its head was bowed; she was young and malnourished; her feathers were dusty and without lustre even in this evening light. Athena formed one final impression: she's in pain. She bears no wound, but she's hurting. And she needs The Goddess.

And then the bird spoke, and just from the pain in her voice, Athena was overwhelmed with pity.

"I am damned, Goddess!" said the bird.

Athena pitched her voice to its sweetest song of gentleness, so that when she spoke, it sounded like the loving whisper of a mother comforting her young.

"Why?"

"I feed on filth! I am cursed! In this life and the next and all beyond.".

"No..."

"Yes, Goddess! A white crow fed on my children! The very life I created feeds evil! I am all pain and fear! I am calamity! I wish to die. Release me from this life!"

And then the bird began, softly, to weep and looked at Athena with eyes full of... what?, wondered Athena: hope? *Hoping to die?*

And what Athena did next surprised even her.

"Come down here, child," she said.

The bird dropped off the wall to land before her, and Athena walked to her and lay down across her cold, hard talons. The bird softly began to sob, the sobs shaking her frame, and she wept until she cried herself out and sighed:

"I will be so happy to die."

So Athena told her:

"No." The bird stared back at her. "Goddess?"

"Live again. Fear and pain hone weapons. Become one. The White Crow... purge it from your life."

"Yesssss...."

"What is your name?" "I am Chila. A name I am ashamed of."

236

Athena looked the bird directly in its eyes, without fear.

"Then become another," she said.

"Name me!"

Athena looked up into the sky, and whispered her name.

"*Dusk.*"

Without a sound, the bird turned and jumped into the air. And she was gone. Leaving Athena standing in the moonlight, wondering… what have I just done?

The Ghoul

Every night I look at ze beautiful moon, and sometimes it is so pretty I 'owl in sadness because only an artiste can appreciate such beauty – an artiste like Jules!

I am tasting ze beauty of zis perfect planete, oui.

I feel anuzzer masterpiece growing inside me.

It is made of many different animals an' eggs an' insects, oui, but ze butterfly wings when I ran through ze meadow an' all ze petits papillons fly away, except the sixty or so zat I sample, zey are all ze couleurs of ze world, zey are beautiful an' add ze most poignant emotion to ze work.

Il arrive!

Ze pain an' pleasure of creation!

Zis iz 'ow art is born!!

Et regardes!

Ma latest exhibition!

Oh.

But it is very nouveau an' complexe. We 'ave not seen zis before from le Julien. It iz ze evolution of ze artiste. Ow daring it is an' originale! Ze use of flies' wings an' ze butterflies is pure genius an' zis latest work sparkles with light, couleur and irridescence. It is entitled… 'Untitled.' An' it smells…

fantastique!

This movement… will start a mouvement!

Zen I snuffle an' zair! a snake.

Snak! Snak!

Un petit snack.

I 'ead sowsse.

ATHENA

Some weeks later, by day this time, the crippled rat found her in the temple. She saw him across the floor, by a column, looking to catch her eye. Hundreds of rats were scurrying about, feeding, and he could not approach her, so she moved towards him.

The glances he was drawing of the rats passing him by were of distaste and disgust, and the muttering that followed him was not even trying to be discreet:

"Him... again!...."

"... how dare he...?"

"... shameless..."

"... ukh! look at his foot..."

"...eek!..."

"Three ask for you by the moon," he muttered as she moved past him.

So she was waiting in the moonlight and it was cold.

Three ask for you.

The Three. Sai had said they would come. That was six months ago. The Three: the messengers and emissaries of the kings and queens of the eastern realm of birds. As Athena is to the rats, so are they to the birds. God-kings, goddesses. And even though she knows, she is *sure*, that she is not a goddess, she knows will have to be one now. The messengers will come, and she will know who they think she is when they call her by name. It might be Eingana, Inara, Sekhmet, Bastet, or Artio. It might be Hathor, Mehit or Hippeia or Manasa. Depending on what they call her, they will want the hunter, the protector, the mother, the birth goddess, or the death goddess. She was The Goddess. And they would expect her to act.

There. They landed quietly on the wall at the same time, The Three, in a whispering rustle of feathers.

Lie like your life depended on it, girl, Athena said to herself and assumed a facial expression of placid haughtiness.

A heron, all elegance and perfect angles, was bowing to her, in respect, its wings outspread.

A kingfisher, its blue deeper than any sky, its breast sunburst orange, aglow like a casket of jewels in the moonlight, spread its wings and bowed.

A swift. Who did not bow but looked directly at Athena. She had already paid the greatest obeisance of her life to the goddess: she had touched the ground.

Athena bowed back.

The swift trilled: "Goddess. Sekhmet. Lionness."

The heron croaked: "Goddess. Hippeia. Chariot."

The kingfisher piped: "Goddess. Aranyani. Forest."

"You honour me. Speak," said Athena.

"One hunts."

"The jungle is its prey."

"The Ghoul hunts the slow hope."

"I know," she lied.

She could not show that she did not know, that she could not understand what they were saying: the words, yes, but not the meaning. Or her fear that they would guess this.

"What little do you know?" she asked them. To save face, now, she knew, they would tell her everything.

And the heron and the kingfisher did, each talking one after the other as if reading each other's thoughts, but never once speaking over the other, while the swift stayed silent.

"The Ghoul is the weapon of the White Crow,"

"The White Crow sits atop the island Heartstone and has dreamed The Ghoul awake... not a myth but a truth,"

"The White Crow is not hatched but born, again and again,"

"Only crows shall feast,"

"… when there is more pain and fear,"

"...than joy and peace,"

"...comes the White Crow,"

"...it travels in the black cloud..."

"... its stench is that of death..."

"...burning and death follow..."

and then they spoke as one:

"It is Calamity."

And she didn't understand anything they said. All she could understand was a night from months ago when a bird of prey shrieked in pain: "A white crow ate my children!"

And she can remember what Sai told her.

Get the swifts on our side.

She pitched her voice just between song and speech and replied.

"I have sent my weapon against the White Crow. I will send another against The Ghoul."

As one, they gasped:

"Goddess. Thank you."

So she pushed the advantage:

"But you must serve in this, too."

Again, they rushed to oblige:

"Yes... how? Goddess..."

"Swift. You honour me by touching the ground you despise. You who do not rest... must be my messengers."

The swift seemed to grow larger than both of the others, her eyes bright with fierce pride.

"Find Sai. I will tell you how. Tell him: *Our forest friend is being hunted.*

I hunt the White Crow. You hunt The Ghoul.

The Ghoul

Oh, but I am so 'appy today, an ze sun is shining an ze birds are singing in ze trees and flying all around me an' 'ow I wish I wuzza bird like zem so I can fly up on 'igh an' sample zem, they look delicieux... zo I mus say I am eating vairy well down 'ere so it is not so bad an' oui! ma tummy tells me zat now I must create again.

It begins… oh… oui… ze splitting, ze stretching, ze pain, oui! but ze plaisir also. Ze fezairs tickle... ho ho... stop it!

Et voila!

I unveil ma latest création.

Oh.

I examine ze finished work.

Hmmm.

Intéressant.

Very dark, but ze composition is firm and strong, ze artiste absolument in control of iz materiels. Répugnant! But irresistible. Répellant! But brilliant. Look 'ow ze sun shines on ze wet surface! Ze white fezzairs lend depth and contraste to ze whole, in a dazzling exploration of a daring new media. Anuzzer masterpiece. An' now, I shall smell ze bouquet.

So powerful! Ah! So delicate, pungent an' profound. Such subtle perfumes in perfect 'armony. I shall call it, "White Dove," after ze dove I use. Ma art will bring joy and peace to ze world. Oui. Zat is ow I say thankyou to zis beautiful world an' all ze delicious sings in it. I am 'eartbroken to leave it 'ere unappreciated. I can only 'ope it lives on as art an' inspiration for 'uzzers, but in my 'eart I know only ze 'orrible flies will enjoy it. Zen I snuffle an' zair! something in front of me which I 'ave not sampled, a nouveau lizard.

But I have not long eaten, monsieur!

Bof. Il faut manger.

I 'ead sowsse.

One word was pounding in his skull like a headache and it wouldn't stop: *Ghoul.*

The first swift arrived two weeks ago, doing the bidding of her king and the Goddess, Athena. Max received her on the roof of the building as she refused to land or speak to anybody lower than a king.

"Carlo has been targeted. By The Ghoul, which is controlled by the White Crow."

Myths, or real? wondered Sai.

Out in the world, the birds had heard of the ghoul's passage, its southward journey, and they were looking for it. They were starting to pick up the line, a swathe of killings, and they were following it back to where they began to learn where this Ghoul thing was from and what it might be. Now that the swift king's emissary had made contact, swifts were coming daily to the rooftop to tell what they knew: they were all over the world, instructed to pick up information and bring it to Max. Athena had sent her own agent to find this White Crow, whatever it may be.

His job was the find The Ghoul.

And he couldn't even say what it was.

All he knew so far was the ferocity of its killing-spree. It came from the mountains of Canada. The victim list included bear-cubs, wolf-cubs, bears, bobcats, skunks, squirrels, snakes, moths, frogs, birds, butterflies, beavers and beetles.

It just kept killing.

Sai's footfalls were heavy as he wandered the tunnel to the place where he could find Mir. The sound they made on the metal cable tray he was passing along even seemed to be making the same sound as the word that was going through his mind: a dull clang:

Ghoul.

The word tolled in Sai's skull like a doom-laden bell, like a countdown.

Ghoul.

It's killing. It's coming. It's been summoned by the White Crow and it was going to kill Carlo. That was what the bird-kings told Athena.

Ghoul.

Sai's mind was fixed on the meanings of the word. 'A malevolent spirit of ancient times in far eastern mythology'. 'One with a fondness for the morbid or disgusting'.

Ghoul.

Why does it do this? Sai asked himself. Why does it kill anything, everything? Does it like the pain and fear of its victims?

Ghoul.

'A taste for morbid or disgusting things'.

Ghoul.

Then something rebounded in his mind, something in his memory stirred. Silently Sai repeated the word to himself over and over until it didn't mean anything anymore: ghoul ghoul ghoul pool fool cool rule gule tool spool. He had the letters g-h-o-u-l in his head and he

played with those too: ghoul pool fool cool gool rule gule tool... and then he had something: not 'ghoul' but 'gule'.

'Gule'. An archaic word. 'Greed. Gluttony.'

Greed, thought Sai. *This ghoul thing kills and kills and kills but it doesn't kill to just kill, not like a cat. It's eating them too. It's always hungry.*

And then his memory sprang open: Linnaeus, the great taxonomist, named a creature *gulo gulo*.

It's real, thought Sai, it's not a myth: *there's an animal out there called 'Gulo gulo'.*

Minutes later he was struggling through a hole in a skirting-board and once through he found Mir at his computer again.

"*Gulo gulo*," he said.

"Gulo gulo to you too."

"Latin, taxonomy, Linnaeus. I think that's our Ghoul. Can you find it on..."

A clatter of claws and...

"Yes, I can."

"That's it."

It was a wolverine.

They both stared at the screen. There were films of wolverines. There were articles about them, photographs of them. Sai spent an hour scanning everything that Mir could find and formed a picture of the ghoul. Grizzly bears ran from it when it came ravening in their territory. Pound for pound it was perhaps the most savage mammal alive, greed made flesh, carnage incarnate: no glut of dead red meat could sate its rapacious appetite. And it was coming, killing tirelessly as it loped south, fueled by blood and the hope of still more, loping through the mountains and deserts and forests, slaughtering. It didn't care whether you ran or

 stood your ground and fought – get in its way, and it would kill you and eat you. Claws would rip, and fangs would tear. Bones would snap when it shook you. *Carlo.*

"It eats everything it kills or pieces of them," said Sai.

"It's not just a killer," said Mir. "It's a *foodie.*"

The Ghoul has come to kill the hope, was Athena's message.

And it was targeting *Carlo.*

It seemed impossible.

Sai had been there, in the rainforest, where there were so many fierce, fierce creatures… could this thing really get to Carlo?

Assume the worst, thought Sai, and imagine what happens if Carlo doesn't succeed.

The Ghoul was the most dangerous mammal on the planet for its size.

Bar one.

A human.

And I'm human, thought Sai, *or, at least, a bit human.*

What would a human do?

Kill it.

How do I kill it?

I don't know.

And then he was heading back along the tunnel, and the echo of his footsteps on the metal walkway seemed to be whispering, "Kill kill kill" as he made his way through the building to talk to the only killer he knew.

THE GHOUL

I 'ave zis lovely soft bed to sleep on, under zis tree, an' ze night is warm… but ze artiste 'as 'ad a vairy strange day.

Hmm.

I wonder what I will dream of.

Of 'ome, I 'ope.

I am not 'appy.

Per'aps I am sad.

I do not know.

I do not understand.

I do not understand anything anymore.

I met ze vairy slow sing today.

But I could not eat it.

An' I am vairy confused.

Because ze white crow oo comes to me in my dreams an' tells me zat I am ze greatest artiste ze world 'as ever known....oo sez to me zat ze slow thing is delicieux an' only for ze artiste oo can make 'im into perfect art. 'An zat is moi, Julien de Goulot, non? Oui. Well, I did not enjoy zis, at all. 'Ow could I, when I could not sample ze slow sing?

Non.

I could not.

It is not because it was not slow. Because it was vairy slow. So slow, nothing could be slower.

Non.

An' it is not because I cannot 'unt a slow sing, because I am a vairy good 'unter.

An' it is not because I could not eat. I was 'ungry. I tried.

It was impossible.

No artiste can work under zeze conditions.

I 'ave not seen un animal like zis before. I am 'eading south an' zen I snuffle an' zair - I do not even 'ave to 'unt 'im - 'e iz right in front of me. 'E is round like a little rock an' 'ave a little 'ead an' little legs, but 'e is also vairy grumpy an' he is not 'appy when I invite him to dinnair with Julien - poop! - iz 'ead an' iz legs zey are gone an' zair is nothing to eat an' 'e will not come out.

Non.

'Ow rude.

It is lucky zat I 'ave found zis lovely place 'ere, under zis beautiful tree as ze sun is setting an' ze stars are coming out to say 'ello, an' I 'ave eaten well. Mah dinnair companion was another oo lived only for art: 'e woz un acteur. A great one, oui. It was an honneur to meet 'im. At first I thought 'e wuz dead, an' eating dead sings is beneath a de Goulot. An' zen' I remember something Papa tell me: *"Pah! Zey are called 'possums', an' zey are only acteurs. Zey pretend to be dead so you will not eat zem."*

Zis acteur?

A superb performance. 'E was born to play zis role.

He played dead. An' zen 'e woz. Bravo.

Hmmm.

Life imitating art, or art imitating life?

Now I sleep.

Zen I 'ead sowsse.

"Max, I need your help."

"Yeah? How?"

"Helping me understand something."

Max actually laughed.

"Me? Help *you* understand something? What, you can't find it in a book?"

Sai shook his head.

"Not this. How does it feel to kill?"

Max looked sharply at him.

The atmosphere between them went very frosty.

"Why do you want to know?"

The question was too intrusive, too personal. Max knew how it felt to kill. He'd done it in hunger and anger and terror in the sewers. He'd done it to rise through the ranks of King Marcus's court, and, once inside, he had done more: in coolly-planned assassinations, killing off Marcus's rivals, or rats Marcus just didn't like. He'd killed with his teeth, with his claws, even with poison. He'd had enough of the killing. Now Sai had just reminded him of all those murders, where being with Athena could make him forget them.

"Because I need your understanding. I have to kill an animal. I don't know how to."

"What is it?"

"A wolverine."

"Never heard of one of those. What did it do?"

Sai shrugged.

"Killed."

"Lots of things kill. What's so bad about this one?"

"It's targeted a friend of ours."

"So it's a hit? Who's the target?"

Sai told Max about Carlo the sloth.

"So that's the target. Vulnerable. But well-protected. Go on."

Then he told him about the prophecies of the bird kings of the east: The White Crow, The Ghoul, the threat 'to the slow hope' and to the forest. Athena was sure they meant Carlo.

But his job was to find the Ghoul. And stop it. And he had no idea how to go about this.

"How do I kill it, Max?"

"You find it first. Then you work out how to kill it. What have you got tracking it?"

"Birds."

"Where is it headed?"

"South, quickly, at thirty to fifty miles a day. It's been travelling for months now."

"What're the birds saying it's doing?"

"Killing and eating."

"Killing an' eating what?"

"Everything."

"Everything?"

"Butterflies, beetles, birds' eggs, birds, bear-cubs, beavers, bobcats...."

Max shook his head.

"Nah. Nothin' eats like that. Nothin's that hungry. You eat what you need..."

Sai shook his head back.

"Not this… it's… insane. It seems to exist only to kill."

"Nah, nothing's all bad. Probably got a mother somewhere."

Max stood, his tail swaying from side to side.

"What weapons has it got?"

Sai told him. About the claws, the teeth, the low-centre-of-gravity, squat, solid power it had and about the speed in it: about its strong muscles, thick fur: about its swimming, tree-climbing, its imperviousness to cold or heat, its tirelessness, its fifty-miles a day lopes for food, about its keen, keen sense of smell and hearing, about its scent-glands, its marking of territory, about its constant cycle of move-kill-eat-defecate-move-kill-eat-defecate, its violence and savagery and its never-ending appetite.

"You say it has scent-glands? That it marks its territory."

"Yes."

"And if it eats a lot then it's gonna crap a lot..."

"Yes."

"Well, that's one way to track it. Get guys on the ground to start following the scent."

"Yes!" said Sai.

"This thing? What its name again?"

"'Ghoul'."

"Does that mean anything? 'Ghoul?'"

"Well, either a ghoul is a blood-drinking evil spirit who digs up corpses and eats them. Or it's something obsessed with disgusting things. Or both. This ghoul's a kind of weasel."

Max burst out laughing:

"A weasel? You're worried about a weasel? Two good rats together could take a weasel. A dog, a cat could do it...."

"It's in the same family as the weasel, but it's much, much bigger."

"Where did it come from?"

"Mountains, in the north."

"Where's Carlo?"

"Thousands of miles south."

"What's in between?"

"Territory that I think this animal's capable of crossing. It doesn't seem to mind cold or heat. And I really don't think it has any predators."

"Headed for the jungle?"

"Yes."

"And you've been there, right? The jungle? What's it like?"

"Oh! So beautiful! Such variety of life! The flowers alone represent..."

"No. I mean as a kill-spot, as a hunting ground for this thing. For you. If this thing is there to do a hit, you need a hit set up an' waitin' for it when it gets there. If this thing has never been in the jungle before, it can't know what to expect, so it's got a blind spot... that's how you're going to kill it."

"Oh, yes... good thinking..."

Max looked hard into Sai's eyes.

"So tell me how you're going to kill it."

"I need to set a trap."

"Right. And to set a trap you need... what?"

"Bait."

"Whatever it likes to eat most," said Max, "that's its weakness."

"Okay. I'll try to find out what that's most likely to be."

Max said nothing until Sai was about to disappear down the hole:

"Before you go, Sai... You asked what it's like to kill?"

"Yes."

"Well, as you're about to find out, I thought you'd like to know: you're about to find out that you'll wish you hadn't."

"I have to kill this thing, Max."

"Yeah. I wasn't thinking about this Ghoul. I was thinking about the bait you're sending out there to die."

Sai was still thinking about those words hours later as the night fell and he waited on the roof overlooking the plaza when he told the swift the message for Athena:

Help me.

I need you to find me a hare.

CHAPTER 8

An Agent In The Field

HARE

Not far from the road a hare was lying still.

That'll bring a crow soon, that will, he was thinking to himself. He was young and hasn't mated yet. He was fast and wiry and wary, and like a lot of young things he believed he was world-weary, when in fact he was just bored. He lived afraid by day, and sometimes by night, he dreamed bad dreams of wheels crushing flesh, and of red red blood, and all the animals he'd seen dead. He didn't know why he was alive still or what for. His life was just one of running and grazing and drinking and sleeping and waking and then doing it all over again, a life of looking over his shoulder or up into the sky, always listening and looking for the things that would come looking to kill you, a life of always running or hiding when there was nowhere to run to or to hide behind because you just came up against more roads or else you just stayed where you were and lived the same day over and over again until you died. Wherever you ran to or hid, you just came up against how pointless you were and how you'd end up one day, he decided, squirrelnutjob, screaming from a tree. So he'd taken up danger for fun: find a road and run out in front of cars to test his speed or just die, he didn't care which. He'd seen the crushed hedgehogs, rabbits, foxes, badgers out there on the roads, but the noise and roaring motors and the danger made his blood jump with excitement, and it was the only thing that mades him *feel* anything, even though he could hear his instinct telling him that it would get him killed one day.

He'd done another road-dash just now, and his breathing was even and he was calm, not moving, in the field next to the road. And the rider he had just run out in front of who had

swerved to avoid him, who had gone off the road and hit a tree, was dead. Hare could smell blood. He could sense the heat leaving the body. He felt more alive than he had ever felt. It was dusk, and the sky was red. It was the greatest sense of peace he had ever experienced. There was silence. No bird-song, no breeze, no cars.

And then, only a few heartbeats later, came agony he had never imagined possible.

Sudden pain, so pure and so complete he couldn't even cry out. It was death, he knew. He was pinned and crushed, and strong, sharp, cold teeth were gripping him along his spine. Different pains - all new - all at once. He couldn't move. He couldn't see. His breathing was cut off. He was passing out, and he accepted that he was dead.

A voice cut through the darkness, filling his eyes and his mind.

"Shabash!"

It was a soft mewing sound, as quiet and as cold as the winter wind which killed hares.

"You are in the talons of a she-kite."

She squeezed again.

This time he screamed. In pain. In fear. In fear of death and in fear of pain. All one.

"It is your day to die."

The voice was soft and close to his ear; it would almost be gentle but for the agony she was causing.

"You wished to die. You killed. I came. The wheel."

She loosened the grip of her talons, a little. The relief was instant. Breathing and vision returned.

"Ah. You feel that - some relief from the pain? And now you are thinking, perhaps this is a chance for escape, yes? But no, it isn't. Give me reason to cause you pain and I will do so. I am *very* hungry."

And then she simply let him go and stepped off him. The relief was bliss, and the ending of the pain and the fear of dying was like being reborn.

And then she stepped in front of him, and for the first time, he saw her face, and he was more afraid of looking at her than he was of pain or of death. Her eyes pierced his as if she saw all the way through him, into him, and beyond him.

The soft voice again.

"Do you accept that I can kill you?" she asked.

"Yes."

"That your life is mine. To spare, or not?"

"Yes."

"Good. Now listen. The path you chose today put you here, just now, in my talons. I could have killed you and eaten what I wished of you until some bothersome crow invited himself to my feast. Like that one up there. Do you see him? The crow watching us? He senses the kill. He wants to eat too. Of course, he does. Never mind. Don't speak. And do not move."

Hare lay absolutely still.

"I offer you another path. It begins here, in pain, and ends in death. Such is so. But it will not be all and only pain and death - just some of the way. The rest will all be life. So… choose now, please. Do you wish to live or to die? Please, I am rather busy: choose."

"Live..." he managed to croak.

"Good. Most wise. So... I don't kill you, I prepare you. Mostly to be eaten. Yes? Actually, better is 'definitely'. Ha ha. Still. 'Yes?' Good. Fail me, and I will kill you. Yes?"

"Y..."

"Good. Thankyou. You are now a soldier in a war. And I am going to tear your flesh with my talons to make you scream."

And she did as she said, and he screamed, as she said he would. As never before. Ever. When she had her talons dug in along his spine, it was cold agony, but this was worse, this new hot tearing pain like nothing he'd ever known. But he bit back on the scream and let the pain happen.

"Now. Let us look at you. You are the colour of dirt. You have large ears and can hear a threat from far away. And you can run very quickly. Very good. Camouflage and speed of flight. Such skills: you have all the makings of the perfect coward. But death and pain, and fear are always on the path, and you are on it too. Running and hiding will not always be options. You will be tested on this path. Many times, I hope. Your problem is... that you are very… fearful, and very, very unknowing because young. All one. Such is so. But now I use you as bait because you are not at all useful to me in any other capacity."

She leaned in close and whispered:

"And I want you to learn how I hunt. You are not the reason I am here. Please stay perfectly still, as if dead, until I return."

And she was gone.

Hare played dead. It was easy. Because he almost wished he was and couldn't believe that he wasn't. And he wondered why he wasn't *sure* that he wasn't dead. Or that he wouldn't be soon. His body told him this because *it* couldn't move. He was hollowed-out, exhausted, still half-paralysed, and in shock. He could feel the gashes in his flesh, the shape of her talons. Pain had emptied him out. His wounds screamed at him, but now he'd seen her beak. Her face. He dared not look at her face ever again. Her eyes alone scared him more than the thought of being crushed by a car.

DUSK

She flew swiftly and silently away from the crow, leaving her kill to the dark scavenger. Had she stayed, it would have called to others, and they would have come and mobbed her and harried her and tried to chase her away from her meal. And she would have killed all of them, one by one.

It is, she thought, an auspicious day: no sooner does word reach her from the Goddess's messenger swiftly that a hare is needed for bait, and here is one, careless enough of its own life to be worthy of sacrifice.

She was hunting again, doing what The Goddess commanded, and she flew into the bosom of the sky and relived every moment she had lived since she was reborn. What she was and what she is and what she must do are all one and now she is whole and, in being whole, she understood that she was nothing. Nothing but the servant of the goddess. They were one. *Her voice, my deed. One. All else is as nothing.*

As she flew, in a long, wide arc around her target, far out of its view, she remembered Chila, the dusty, impertinent little beggar-thief of the city that once she was, following the scent of

carrion and death and decay in the hope of a meal. She remembered fights with other kites over scraps of flesh plucked from the dirt. She remembered the taunts of other birds about how lowly a beast she was in her former life to be reborn, this, a scavenger for dead flesh, a thing of dirt, an untouchable. And she remembered the day when she returned to her nest and her children were dead, and a white crow gloated in her nest, wet with their blood.

"When I kill," it croaked, "you are not reborn."

She remembered its stench.

She had tracked that scent across the world, and when she lost it, she questioned a crow to find it again.

She remembered the crow's weapons.

Fear. Pain.

And she learned from it.

She remembered the goddess.

Her gentleness. Her wisdom.

And Her command.

"Purge the White Crow from your life."

So she flew, following the crows, learning, one crow at a time, how to hunt. The crows, when asked, spoke of the Heartstone, the great buried stones in the earth that fell from the sky before any bird flew, the pulse, the signal that the birds feel, that she felt in the wind, in her mind, in her veins and in her wings.

The stone heartbeat was on an island, hundreds of days away. So she flew. Through life and death, fear and pain, cold and heat, thirst and hunger and weariness, over land, forests, meadows, hills, mountains, rivers, deserts, cities, tundra, lakes and seas and now she did not beg or scavenge: she hunted for her food – crows' hearts – and

she learned to use her weapons. Her eyes, her wings, her beak, her talons, her stealth. And fear and pain.

I am reborn.

I am so strong now.

Chila has lived.

I am Dusk.

The Goddess named me.

Dusk: *Red in the sky. Then night comes.*

She readied herself to kill now, which she would do with ecstatic joy to please the goddess. The little meat creature would obey and do its part and be the bait. She had broken its tiny spirit with fear and pain. First, with my talons. Then, with my voice. I didn't need to use my killing weapons, my beak, my will. But she would use them now.

I see you, my quarry. Dusk comes. Then darkness.

The hare was nothing, she told herself. Bait. One more in the war, expendable, therefore nothing. One. One minus one equals nothing. *Perhaps,* she considered, *if I have scared him enough... he will be fearless.* But most likely, he would just die. But the goddess's swifts had sent word that such a creature must be sent as bait.

She had flown high and wide of her target now. Catching a current beneath her, with a curl of a wing-tip, she turned and dropped towards the dark thing which was circling lower and lower towards the dead meat, unaware that she hunted as the goddess commanded her.

Yes.

She would serve the goddess with her whole oneness until she was nothing.

She who is peace has sent me to war.

She struck the crow hard in its back, and it dropped to the ground like a stone.

She landed by it.

"Shabash!"

Hare did not dare move.

"You may stop pretending to be dead now."

Hare opened his eyes. There was a crow on the floor, only a few body-lengths away.

"Well. How do you like my hunting? I think I am on *very* good form today. Did you enjoy being bait? More importantly, have you learned how to play dead?"

"You wanted the crow. Not me," he said, standing up, his limbs trembling.

"Yes! And see! I have the crow. Now comes another test. Can you watch what I do next? And not look away? Look away, and you fail. Yes?"

Hare nodded.

"Because I am worried that you are a very fearful fellow and will be upset. But you took this path, yes? Well, this also is on the path. And I would not want this to happen to you. Observe."

He did.

She turned to the crow and spoke softly.

"Following me. Foolish."

She stooped over the crow and began to do what she had come to do.

Its broken black body was twisted, and it wouldn't live much longer. It was consumed by fear and she sensed this. Her strike, she thinks, was *too* good: a mere broken wing would have brought the thing down, but I broke its back, and now it will die sooner than I intended when I need time. Her weapons… yes, now she must employ these.

With darting powerful pecks, she started plucking feathers from the crow's breast with her beak. It screamed, and she let it. She plucked on, tearing out feathers one at a time to get to the flesh beneath, the flesh that hid and protected the heart. She could hear the crow's heart pounding, and she knew how to use fear and pain to keep it beating. The crow begged and cried out and screamed until it could scream no more, until it had nothing left to beg for but death. And only then did she begin her questioning.

Hare watched, utterly still, barely breathing, and she questioned the crow: She wanted to know about the White Crow.

And the black crow didn't want to tell her.

Or couldn't, because it didn't know.

But *she* wanted to know.

And the crow didn't have long to live.

And this was why she was doing what she was doing. She knew exactly how much pain a crow could take. None better than she. And she knew how much time this one had, and it was short. So she began again: to wound and torment and hurt and frighten the broken-backed dying thing until its body and mind were so racked and ruined with pain and fear that fear and pain became the only things making its heartbeat anymore. With her talons, her beak, her voice, her eyes, her threats, her skill, her scream, and her patience, the crow broke as she knew it would. And he screamed and wept, but she understood: the White Crow had found

the Heartstone and awakened the dreamer and now The Ghoul hunted and every day brought it closer to its prey.

"Kill me now," begged the crow.

And she tore out and ate the crow's heart.

Then she turned, and she said to Hare,

"The Dawn Oak. At sunrise. You must be prepared. For your purpose. For your path. Tomorrow begins your training."

And she was gone.

Leaving a dead human and a dead crow.

And a hare who had never felt more alive.

SAI

In the heart of the roaring city, the plaza echoed with noise and milled with people, and the sky at dusk was tinged with a bloody red, against which background darted dozens of swifts.

They came all the time now, by day and night, bringing messages from Athena.

The White Crow has been found; the Ghoul is yet to be.

The White Crow is being watched carefully.

The bait you asked for is being made ready, but you must put it in place.

Mir had come from his screen to talk to Sai.

"The Ghoul. I'm pretty sure right now it's crossing the Chihuahua desert in Mexico. That's what the swifts are saying, too."

Sai nodded.

"So that would put it...?"

"A few months away from Carlo. But it's heading in the right direction. And it's not stopping. At some point, it will find Carlo's trail."

Sai did not speak.

"C'mon," said Mir, "let's get off the roof before a cat comes."

Back inside, they went to find Max.

"So you're sending someone to kill it?" Max pushed him.

And Sai still did not speak because he did not know what he was doing: either he was sending to his death an innocent who had done nothing to get himself caught up with MOON, or his thinnest-chance gamble would pay off... that a hare could lead the Ghoul away from Carlo, just long enough for Carlo to deliver the message. That was all it had to do, just run ahead and not be caught, just lead the thing away from Carlo. It didn't have to die, not if it just kept running...

In the end, it was better not to think about it.

He was sending an animal to its death, and he hated himself.

"Mir. differentjungles. Extraction."

"Where from?"

"England."

HARE

He woke long before dawn. After she left, he went to his burrow and slept. On waking, he stretched, and his wounds stung. But it was less pain than before, and the rips didn't feel so deep. And for some reason, he wasn't afraid of her anymore.

A purpose and a path, she had said.

Go. He started running, thinking, *this is squirrelnutjob!*

It was two hours away. He loped fast, feeling his speed feeling good. The oak came into view as the sun was beginning to creep over the horizon, and as the day began to light up, he stood at the foot of the dawn oak and saw her.

She was on a branch, standing on one leg, her wings outstretched. Her eyes were closed, she was perfectly still, and she was beautiful. And the sun began to light her up from her talons upwards until she was fully illuminated, and Hare gaped. Her feathers were like autumn leaves with the sun shining on them.

She opened her eyes and looked at him.

She didn't speak but instead jumped and flew away.

He stood and watched her disappear.

"Wh...?"

Disappointment and confusion rushed up inside him, and he kicked the ground angrily. In the distance, he heard birdsong.

He slumped back on his hindquarters and looked up into the oak tree. Then a squirrel popped its head out from behind a branch and screamed: "STOP PINCHING MY NUTS!".

Hare jumped for safety, instantly alert and fearful and ready to fight or run. The screaming didn't stop. The squirrel was coming down the tree now, chittering and angry and frightened, and it just kept on: "Stop pinching my nuts! I don't know! I don't know! I don't know!"

It was on the ground now, and it was running at him, and it wanted to fight. It was fierce-looking, it was angry, it was ugly and it had missing patches of fur. One of its ears was missing. It was smaller than he was, but it wanted to fight. Hare didn't know whether to run away laughing or hit it, and he was still deciding when she landed back in the tree with bright blood on her yellow beak. The squirrel scampered back up into the tree as soon as she returned. He stopped his squeaking and chickering. Hare trembled with the after-shock and the violent feelings in him that it had awakened.

Finally, she spoke. Hare could see blood in her mouth.

"There. I am very grumpy before breakfast so I like to eat upon waking. More or less. I hope you have eaten well because you will be very busy today. I said I would prepare you, yes?"

"Yes."

"Then let us begin. Follow."

She jumped and flew away. He ran after her.

At first, he thought it was fitness training. But it wasn't: it was her way of showing him how useless he was. She invited him to use his camouflage to hide, and he did, using all his stillness, all his sense for cover and his natural camouflage, but she found him. She invited him to use his speed and agility to dodge her attacks, all his feints and bluffs and quick turns and wrong-footing but she found him.

He ran, turned, banked, wheeled, dodged, and jumped, but she tagged him every time, and every time she did, she hurt him because she wanted him to know she was above him and to remind him about pain and fear. So he ran on. He sprinted, jogged, loped, sprinted again, his eyes in the sky trying to see her, follow her. She swooped low, tagged him, she caught thermals, rose, soared, then tilted a single feather and showed him what speed really was as she flew over his head and invited him to race.

They did this for hours until they had travelled far inland. Her flying seemed effortless. Hare had to give everything he had. He ran until he dropped, and he understood: he was never going anywhere. He couldn't fly. He could hide, but she could disappear.

He could hear, but she could see the whole world from the sky. He could run, but she could rise into the air and let the world turn and land anywhere she wanted.

She landed beside him.

"I hope you are not too tired."

He was trembling with fatigue and couldn't speak.

"Yes. You are too tired. Eat. Rest. Sleep if you wish. I will wake you when the time comes. We are here."

"Where are we?"

"At the frontline of the war."

And she was gone.

He ate and then slept in the shade of the tree. When he woke, she was back, and she was somehow more fierce than ever. She was in the tree, watching the woods up ahead. She was perfectly still and silent. Hare barely dared to look at her eyes, but he sneaked a glance upwards. If she ever looks at me that way, he thought, I'll know I'm going to die.

They waited like that for hours until she said:

"Come. We go."

"Where?"

"Back to where we met."

He ran for hours. She returned in minutes, back to where the human died.

The motorbike and the body were gone.

He had never felt more tired, and he could barely find his burrow before he fell dead asleep.

They met in the darkness of a tunnel, Sai on his way to find Mir, and Mir on his way to find Sai. There was nobody around the hear what they discussed.

"Extraction by different jungles for your agent is all set-up," said Mir.

"And delivery...? "Just where we said: very remote, and your agent will be met by forces friendly to our cause, just as you asked. They'll lead him to the area roughly where the paths of the Ghoul and Carlo are likely to converge. He's on his own from there."

"Will there be any human interference?" asked Sai.

Mir paused.

"No. Shouldn't think so. Erm... but..."

"What is it?"

"Well, you know I said he would be met by erm, 'forces friendly to our cause'...? They say they've got a better way of using your agent."
"What's   that?"
"They think they can use him to lure the Ghoul to its death. Some really dangerous place they've got. But it means your guy probably dies too."

"What is this place?" asked Sai.

"It's an area that's been strewn with anti-personnel mines."

Sai's shame and pain and guilt throbbed in his head in the darkness: he was going to have to sacrifice his agent.

"It's one life, Sai, for potentially billions," Mir reminded him.

"We go ahead," said Sai, bleakly.

HARE

"What did you mean, 'the war'?" he asked.

She looked down at him, and swallowed the last of the crow's heart.
"This is a war. I am commanded. By the Goddess."

"Why do you want me?"

"To help me fight the war." "Here? Against the crows?"

"No. In a new world. Another enemy. The Ghoul."

"Do I have to go?"

"Of course not. But I will kill you if you don't. I did not train you to have you say 'no' when I need you. Silly. Besides, you might speak of my purpose, and that would never do. Of course, I would kill you. Then I would find another."

"And Squirrel Nutjob? Was he like me?"

"Who?"

"Squirrel Nutjob. Today, at the Dawn Oak. That's what we call it round here... y'know?... a bit crazy..."

"How unkind. His name is Shelley. Yes. Yes. He was very like you. He thought that there was ever so very much more to him than he could be in this life, and I showed him that he was right."

"How?"

"I hurt him very much and made him very afraid. Then I told him he was a very good spy. I break him, do you see? And I put him back together in a way he likes better. Then I send him into the woods with some balderdash explanation but without telling him the real why."

"Why? Why not?"

"So that he could not speak of my purpose if asked questions."

"What happened?"

"He was asked questions."

"Asked... how?"

"The way I ask crows questions."

Hare saw it now: why "Squirrel Nutjob" was squirrel nutjob.

"So yes, I sent the squirrel into the woods, and he was tortured. They hurt him and pecked his delicate, most private places, most painfully, I am sure, and lengthily, to make him answer questions. But he did not know any answers. And he did not say why because he could not say why because he did not know. And so the hurtful pecking continued. All over his body. For several days and nights. I saw his wounds when they pushed him out of the forest. They sent him back to me, broken. In his mind."

"Who did?"

"Crows."

"The White Crow?"

She glared at him.

He went cold.

"You have heard the name. But you know nothing."

"So what was the point of sending him in?"

"Do you not know?"

And he did.

"He was bait."

"No. A decoy. As you were yesterday."

"While you were really hunting the crow?"

"Correct."

"So what other plan did you have going when you sent Squirrel Nutjob in?"

"Shabash!"

Hare started. She'd said 'shabash'. That was what she said when she made a kill, he thought. He dared to look at her. She was actually smiling.

"I had a mole. Tunnelling very quietly for oh-so-many weeks and months. Her mission... that was my... strike. It was very slow. And deep. And successful."

"The mole?"

"Alive. Well. Still on the path. She brought me information."

"To do what?"

"To help me fight a war."

"Against the White Crow?"

"Yes."

Hare had never felt so alive. He dared to say to her:

"You're like the Goddess of War!"

She blinked.

She seemed genuinely taken-aback.

She said:

"Oh, no. I have met the Goddess, and she is Peace. In a former life, I was called Chila, and I lived in dirt. Now I am Dusk, and I serve Her. And She has chosen you to fight The Ghoul."

THE GHOUL

I 'ave travelled vairy far now an' ma journey is every day more delightful. Behind me is ze desert which is vairy ot an' ze mountains which are vairy cold, but both 'av delicious sings to sample. It is all new. And so many sings! I 'av never tasted any of zis nouvelle cuisine before! It is an inspiration! In ze desert, it is little sings to try, but so many of zem... all different, always so crunchy an' succulent. An zey are everywhere... I snuffle and zair! les spideurs, les scorpions, so many little sings come to my mouth, I am in an' 'eaven of different flevveurs an' ma tummy creates new masterpieces everyday. An' I am 'eading south but zen one day I snuffle and zair! anuzzer new sing with a thousand petit legs comes to me... it is vairy slow but it is so many beautiful couleurs! I think, *this is materiel I must work with*!

Un petit dégustation. And vairy soon I am vairy sick. Oh.

Under ze moon an' under ze 'ot sun I 'owl an' 'urt an' 'av bad dreams. Ma tummy 'urts an' 'urts an' creates only poor thin watercouleurs, zair iz no texture, nothing solide in ze work, ze colour iz wrong, zey are all bad (well, some are quite good) but ze aroma? Pff! Horrible! Zis it not a medium I like an' I do not want to work in it again. Non. Ze sing zat I et was a bad sing an' I decide that I will not work with such bright couleurs again. Non.

Snff snff. What is zat I scent?

I snuffle an' zair! a bird's nest. With no *maman*.

Oh. *Two* eggs.

But one would be un oeuf, madame!

I am also vairy funny.

I 'ead sowsse.

HARE

Hare sat at the side of the road and looked up at Dusk perched on a fence pole. It was a cold night, with thin sharp drizzle.

"I'm scared," he admitted now. He looked at the cage with horror. So human, so obviously a trap.

"Do you believe you are going to your death?" she asked.

"Yes."

"And would it be any different if you stayed?"

No, he thought, it wouldn't, but he wouldn't say it.

"Then you must step into the cage and drink the water in the bottle."

He didn't speak.

"Choose. This is a war. You are a soldier. You kill or die. You can be one or nothing. Such is so. Choose."

He turned and climbed into the cage, choosing death but fearing her in a new way now, wholly unexpected: he was afraid to disappoint her.

"What will you do?"

"I will wait and watch. If my quarry flies, I will follow it. And if I can, kill it. I also have allies to seek."

"And what about Squirrel Nutj… Shelley?"

"Ah. I did not tell you. He has lived."

"You mean he's dead?"

She said nothing. The squirrel had begged her, as she had once begged The Goddess, for death, and she had granted him what the Goddess would not give her. She broke his back while he looked away. And used him as bait to question another crow.

The Goddess had given her a purpose.

The squirrel had served his.

All one.

Such is so.

"Hurry. A car comes. Drink."

He did. Sweet water, something bitter in it. It acted quickly. A huge, heavy sleepiness came over him. Darkness took him.

CHAPTER 9

The Killing Ground

HARE

His mind rose from sleep like mist off a river: thick, heavy dreaming still fogging his thinking but clearing quickly. He opened his eyes to bright light and bars of darkness. He became aware of the walls of the cage, and everything in him sprang awake - fear, fight, flight - as he panicked in the confined space, thrashing in terror.

"*Bravo*," said a voice. "That was some siesta, *muchacho*."

Hare's fear sent another huge jolt through his body again, and he span around, staring wildly.

"You gonna get out of that cage, *estupido*?" came the voice again. "We got it open already."

Hare pushed himself through the open door and closed his eyes against the bright sun. His mouth was dry, his limbs unsteady, his mind still dull.

"You look like *mierda, tio*."

Then he opened his eyes and turned his head and saw where the voice came from. It was smaller than him and grey. Its fur was thick and looked soft and was the colour of the edges of rainclouds when the sun shines through them. It was standing on its back legs, looking at him intently. It was unlike anything he had ever seen. But it was the *friendliest* face, he thought, that he'd ever seen. He

281

liked it immediately. He wanted to hug it. Until it jumped suddenly and bit him on the nose, drawing blood.

"You had better not be thinking I'm cute!" it snapped,

Hare snapped, fully awake.

It got right in his face, and it was not afraid.

It made an angry chirrup:

"Chu!"

Hare was silent.

"It's my name, *idiota!*"

"Chu?"

It... no... *she* stared him right in the eye.

"You have very big ears, so let me tell you something. You come to this place to die. I don't know if you knew that. We are fighting a war, and we have a thing we need to kill. You understand me, *muerto?*"

Hare nodded.

"*Bueno*. I'm in charge here. You don't ask questions. You do everything I say. You are going to die, but you're going to die when and where and the way I tell you to die, okay, *muerto?*" Hare nods.

"So don't get killed in the meantime. And that means don't *ever* think I'm cute again. I'll skin you, *ese*. You hear me?"

"Yes."

"Why are you here?" "To die."

"Good. Now shut up and follow."

Then she called out, a quick piping noise.

Hundreds of grey things just like her rose up out of their camouflage among the rocks and shadows, and silently followed her. Hare followed too, his nose really *hurting*.

CARLO

Mauro had flown off earlier that day to talk to some of his contacts in the forest, and he had been gone for hours. Carlo and Emilio stood by the edge of the river, looking out over the slow, powerful waters and then, grinning, they exchanged a glance of anticipation. Emilio slithered forward and disappeared into the water, emerging in the middle of the broad stream. He let out a long hiss of pleasure. Carlo followed him, and soon, he was paddling alongside Emilio, smiling.

In the water, he was weightless, and the coolness of the river soothed his poor, tired, sore claws and the aching of his muscles. He could move faster in the water than he could on land or in a tree, and the speed at which he was now swimming made him feel giddy and free and deeply, deeply contented.

He turned his head to the anaconda and asked:

"Could we get where we are going by swimming, Emilio?"

Emilio shook his head.

"No. The river cuts west soon. Takes us a long way from where we need to be."

Carlo sighed. How much easier it would be to be carried in the arms of the current, he thought, to let it transport him... how effortless and pleasurable it would be to travel this way... but he knew that this journey was not about ease, but urgency, and he knew that his path was on the forest floor.

"I'm getting out," he told Emilio, and with an effort, turned his body in the water and headed back to shore, and just as he dragged himself out of the water and onto the riverbank, heavy and sodden but cooled and refreshed, he saw Mauro returning, and with sudden concern, he saw the hummingbird's expression and knew that something was wrong.

He called to Emilio, who followed him back onto dry land, and together they looked up at Mauro, hovering just above them.

"There's a hit out on you, Carlo," said Mauro.

"It wouldn't be the first time," said Carlo, thinking of Luca, Scorpionne and Mario Puma.

"Yeah, but this sounds...real bad."

Neither questioned Mauro about his sources: he spoke to the birds and they saw everything.

"What is it?" asked Emilio, already thinking that any hit on Carlo would have to get past him first. And nothing was getting past him, he thought with fierce pride, not unless it was very, very strong, because all he would need to do would be to throw one coil of his muscular body around it and *squeeeeeze* and the thing would soon be dead.

"It's called Guli, or Giulio, something like that," said Mauro. "And it's not from round here."

Then Mauro told them everything that the birds had learned about it, and he told them about the trail of blood and death, leading thousands of miles north, and the appalling body count it left behind it.

"It sounds like... what? A small bear? A hunting dog?" said Emilio.

"It ain't either. Nobody has seen one of these before. But it's bad."

"Get the word back – to everyone in the forest... track it, corner it and kill it," said Emilio.

"And what if they can't?" replied Mauro. "I'm telling ya, this thing is baaaaad...."

"Then try and kill it... slow it up," snapped Emilio.

"And tell the animals who can't fight to get to safety," said Carlo, "then catch us up."

Mauro flew off the deliver the message.

"Carlo..." said Emilio.

"Hmmm?"

"We have to go. Now. Climb on my back."

HARE

"Wake up!"

Hare snapped awake to see Chu standing before him.

"*Oye! Muerto*. We have to go. Now. Follow. And don't do anything *estupido*."

He did not enjoy what came next, an agonising descent down a mountain. The fluffy things were superb on slopes and rocks, with legs perfect for them. They were agile and quick, they hopped from rock to rock tirelessly, with perfect judgment and balance and with complete ease, and Hare couldn't keep up. His back began to ache first, soon his paws hurt too, then his ribs and his legs. He'd fallen off a rock twice, missing his footing as he hopped down to the next boulder. He was bruised and sore and aching, and the grey fluffy things thought it was hilarious.

"Oye, dead guy! Don't get dead yet!"

Hare had again fallen behind them and was coming down at the best pace he could manage at the back of the group.

They moved. They stopped. They fed and rested. They ate. They slept. They moved by day and by night. For weeks now, it had been hard, steep, jagged paths, but now they had come much nearer to the foothills, and the days and nights of pain gave way to easier-going for Hare as the terrain became smooth stone hills

286

amid brush and sweet-scented trees, under skies full of birds of prey, as they headed towards the great green forest hiding under mist in the distance.

Everything was different, even the stars, and the moon was huge and bright and clear and the sun was much hotter. It was so unlike his last life. Hare could not believe it was the same life, except that he was sure he hadn't been killed. He had never felt more alive. And he liked it that way. As each day passed without his being killed, it was starting to become normal being here in this new world.

The grey things didn't let him out of their sight. He was half a prisoner, half a very special guest, but he had no idea why. He could sense they had some purpose for him but had no idea what that was. He had trusted Dusk and knew not to ask questions. And he knew or thought he did, that it was best not to ask questions here, too, certainly not of Chu, not with her temper. Nobody questioned her: she was in charge. And she knew how to lead. The grey things followed orders and her tactics, and they didn't move in a pack. They spread out. Nobody stayed in the same position. They took turns to scout ahead. Some hopped up to the front, and others, earlier leaders, fell back. They circulated within the body.

When Chu spoke to him - usually to tell him to move faster, or shut up, or stop fallin' on your *culo, idiota*, - Hare understood, but when the grey things talked to each other, it was harder to pick up. They spoke in clicks and chirrups and squeaks and called each other strange names - *Tocati. Flaquita. Loco. Chica. Cuate. Ese.* But they used one word, again and again, a quick chirrup: *muchacho.* They talked all the time, and Hare listened, and if there was one thing that he had come to understand, it was that the grey things were all squirrel nutjob: they couldn't *wait* to die.

"Today I am going to be killed by the volcano, *muchacho*!"

"No, *ese*, today it is I who will be killed, not you!"

287

"Cuate, today is my day to die. Knives will cut me into a million pieces of *carnita!*"

"No! It is mine. I will die a glorious death today. In fire. And in the mountains, they will sing songs of my courage!"

And they thought it was hilarious to tell Hare that he too was going to die, and as they ran they took turns to fall back, or run on, or lead, or follow, but everyone got their turn at the back with Hare:

"Eh, dead guy.. You think this thing gonna skin you or do you quick?"

"This thing… I hear it eats you a piece at a time."

"It's bad!"

"I hear it hurts pretty bad when it bites your *huevos* off."

"Not a lot of meat on you, *amigo*. It's gonna to have break your bones and suck to get a good meal."

"You gonna scream and scream *ese...*"

"Ain't gonna die quick, *amigo...*"

"You gonna die slooooow...."

before hopping away again, chirruping with laughter.

So eventually, everybody got to know the dead guy, and they showed him what was safe to eat.

"Tio, this seed… this is *rumpiato*…. Rico!"

"These white flowers, ese, *carbonillo*, the seeds are goooood..."

"The pink flowers here… *renilla*, the leaves are taaaasty, tio..."

and he learns to eat *pingo pingo* stem, *monte negro* leaf from the plant with the blood-red flower, the root of *cebellin* and *doradilla*-leaf. They let him have pieces of delicious *olivillo, quisco* and *copao*, but won't let him near the plants themselves: he doesn't know how to get past the spikes, he'll get cut, the cut could go bad and….

"If you prick your poor paw…."

"… on a prickly pear..."

"… and you get infected..."

"... you'll die – we won't care. Heehee!"

Until one night Hare asked Chu,

"Why are you all in such a hurry to die?"

She looked at him as if he wasn't worthy of an answer.

"Why are you?" she asked back.

"I'm not."

"You are. You come with us. So you can get to the place where you are gonna die."

She looked over at her *gente,* who he now knew called themselves *chinchilla.*

"We are gonna die soon anyway." And she told him about life in the mountains, on bare rock, getting picked off by eagles and snakes and men. Dozens of the chinchillas stopped their hopping and feeding to listen to her. When she had finished, she said:

"The eagles, they only kill you once."

And other voices joined in.

"Snakes only kill you once."

"*Los humanos?* They kill you four times, *ese.*"

"Take you from the mountains."

"Put you in a cage."

"Skin you."

"Until there's none of us left."

"And we cannot live like that," said Chu. "So we accept this mission, in the war. We die for something better. We sacrifice our lives to get you through *la tierra de trampas*. We will die to get you through there, to where you are needed. We were told to bring the one who will kill the thing that hunts Carlo. We expected a killer. Maybe a lion. They sent us you. So, maybe we are all gonna die for nothing."

Every eye was on him. So he said it:

"I killed a human."

And he told them about the game he would play on the road and a collective gasp came from them that sounded like: *"Hombre!"*

And the jokes about him dying, stopped.

DOMINO

"An' that's when we heard. A hit on the boss. An' everybody in the jungle just laughed. A hit on Carlo? Here? Yeah, right. Cos no-one ain't never gonna get to tha sloth, not here, not in our neighbourhood. I mean, this is not even a stealth hit, sneaky like Scorpionne. This is an all-out, in-the-open hit. And we even got a name: 'Guli'. Which makes everybody laugh, cos it means 'asshole'. But we don't know what it is, the guli thing. So we wait.

And everybody's talkin' an' everybody's got the word: find out who this guy is.

And word starts comin' back.

It ain't from here, it's travelled for a year to make the hit.

There's a trail of bodies goes back north where it started out from.

It ain't small, it ain't big. It ain't poison. Can't fly, not so good in water, and climbs trees a bit. Thick coat. It's done mountains an' deserts to get here, so it's tough, whatever it is. But nobody knows what it is. So we wait for word on what's comin' next..."

The Ghoul

Ah.... ze forest! Ze cold of ze mountains was invigorating an ze ot sun of ze desert was vairy pleasant on ze back of my neck. Mais zis! Oh! It is warm an' 'umid. It is so rich an' green. Only in mah very finest creations 'ave I seen a green so deep, so lustrous an' vivide after I sample zoze parrots. And 'ere... oh! Zair are so many birds an' sings in ze trees an' on ze ground, zair are so many new sings to sample. I am so 'appy, wiz all zese new things to try. Zey will be an inspiration. I will sample. I will create. I will sample all ze beauty zair is 'ere, an' zen ze slow thing will be ma masterpiece.

Oui.

I 'ead sowsse.

Domino

"An' then we get the word from the birds: if you think you're tough enough to kill it, kill it, but if not... DO NOT take it on. Let it come through. Slow it up, but let it come through. Do not take it on. Stay out of its way. Stay in the trees, in the air, in the river, or get outta there. Word is there's a guy comin' up from who-the-hell-knows where an' he's gonna whack this thing, so everybody inna jungle can relax. Like, anyone was relaxin'. Cuz

292

by then, by then the stories had started comin' in from everywhere about what this thing was really like...."

⟨THE⟩GHOUL

      I am in 'eaven. Zis is a paradise. I am 'appy, 'ealthy, an' welcome 'ere. An I 'ave never been so productif or genereux wiz ma art as I am 'ere. Only zis morning I unveiled a stunning piece, enorme, ze inspiration would not stop coming. It was huge in scale, a tryptych. It smelled exotique an' new, as powerful as a new world being discovered. It was extraordinaire. But 'ow could it be otherwise? I am inspired. I have unlimited resources 'ere as an artiste, an' I 'ave found it vairy easy to be creatif 'ere. Ze creatures, zey are everywhere for me to sample. Ere a butterfly, zair a lizard, zair a baby monkey who fall from ze tree... I 'ave only to snuffle and zair! annuzzer sing to sample. An' zey are all delicieux, perfect. It is so genereux of zem to feed me so well, 'ere, zey are so welcoming, such lovely creatures. I am vairy moved by zair welcome an' zair hospitality.

But I 'ead sowsse.

⟨D⟩OMINO

"I mean, I've known some cold, mean, baaaaad killers in my time an' I seen a lotta rub-outs I wouldn't want my kids to see. Hell, I even *took* my kids to see rub-outs like that, just so they'd know not to let it happen to them... but this Guli thing? is freakin' insane.

Me an' some o' the guys we go look for it. We're safe from it in the trees. Maybe it can climb a bit but if we see it comin' up da tree we can just jump to the next one, it ain't gonna catch no monkey. Well, not unless that monkey is real dumb. From up in da trees we can see the way it's come, cos there's blood everywhere, an' body parts, and feathers an' scraps of fur, bones... an' always a cloud o' flies followin' the stink of the trail o' death this guy leaves behind him. The thing just comes through the forest an' catches animals by surprise. There's animals just layin' there, torn an' broken an' ripped an' shaken to death. One guy's hangin' from a branch, all bled out. An' the thing, it just carries on fightin an' killin', an' I never saw nothin' like this..."

The Ghoul

It is unbelievable. I 'ave never been so inspired or creatif. Ze precision of ma palate amazes me. Ze combinations of sings I am sampling are so delicate, so 'armonious in flevveur zat ma art is becoming more powerful with each new mouvement. Ze beauty is all around me. I snuffle an' zair! a bird which do not fly with fezzairs like all ze couleurs I 'ave ever seen, an' zair! a snake, zat delicious flevveur, wrapped inside ze mosaic. An' zair is so much creation inside me! So many new works, ze inspiration does not stop coming! Today four -four!- pieces, all daring an' creative an' fresh an' so very aromatique. (Secretly I am 'oping ze creatures 'ere will start coming to ma exhibitions before ze 'orrible flies come and take zem away. 'Orrible flies. I do not like them, but they are everywhere.). But of course! I am doing all zis for ze creatures 'ere. Ze artiste is nothing if 'e does not give, so zat ze creatures can experience great art. Oui. Ma art will bring joy an' beauty to zair 'umdrum existences. I shall rest now for a few moments an' savour an' appreciate ze aroma of ze work I have just unveiled.

Aaaaaaaah!

Parfait.

I will put a little Eau de Julien ere... ah! quel arome! - an' be on ma way. Oui.

Now.

I will 'ave something to eat.

Zen I 'ead sowsse.

OMINO

"I mean, it makes sense to be fierce, sure, but this? Killin' an' eatin' all day, an' all night, more than anythin' got a right to or need to? Young, old, feathers, fur, eggs, bugs, anythin' that comes near it, it kills an' eats. An' it doesn't just kill 'em, it savages them too, tears 'em up wid its claws, snarlin' an' groolin' an' droolin'. It howls, it growls, it grunts, it snarls, nobody can understand a freakin' word it's sayin', it stinks, it's crazy, it's killed animals we knew, animals we didn't know, animals we liked an' animals we didn't like. But after it had killed 'em an' they were gone, you felt like you knew the animals you didn't know an' liked the animals you didn't like, an' then, after all the killin'… this thing? this thing the whole neighbourhood is callin' 'The Asshole'? squats right there in the middle of where everybody eats, an', yeah... takes a shit. Yep. Curls out the biggest stinkiest mos' disgustin' crap ever, with everybody watchin', an' then, right in front of everybody, it takes a long, good smell of it an' then marks a tree with its disgustin' scent… an' it was like the whole neighbourhood an' all the five families jus' came together on this thing. Cuz everybody is thinkin' the same thing: Where's the respect? C'mon…

Slow it up?

Let it through?

Kiss my ass.

Let's kill it.

Every way we know how."

HARE

Chu led the pack on. She took her directions from the sun, and they moved on, further towards the deep green forest. And she told him about the pit, to the east, where the *humanos* were, the place beyond where the forest ended, the place beyond the desolation: a sheer-sided hole in the ground a mountain deep. At the bottom was a septic lake. The pit walls swarmed with life but everything around the mine is dead. The earth had not been tunnelled but stripped, a belly torn away in the hunt for one tiny choice organ. "Es el oro," sighed Chu. You could see *humanos* in it, she said, but they were tiny, flies in a giant burst stomach. A thousand of them, more, worn down to specks, climbing into and back up out of a pit, day and night. Lights glow around the cavern. If you walk towards the edge, they say, its nothingness draws you to the edge, to the drop.

"So we don't go there?"

"No. We go somewhere worse."

La tierra de trampas. The land of traps. If you step on one... all the *chinchilla* have told him about *las trampas*, the traps.... how *humanos* placed the traps in a war about the coca leaf that *chinchilla* don't eat because it make a chinchilla crazy... some of the traps fill the world with noise and red fire, like a volcano, others spit tiny tearing metal mosquitoes through your flesh. Others slice you to pieces. Most are buried in the ground, but some are on the surface. They look like *caca*, knives come out of them.

"'Caca'?"

"Mierda, *hombre*. Like a llama just took a big dump next to you."
"Oh. Right. And ...'llama'? Is that like a cow?"

"Cow take a shit where you eat?" "Yes." "Then yeah. It's like a cow"

"And we've got to cross this trap country?"

"Si."

"Do you know where the traps are?"

"No. That's why they're traps, *estupido*."

Chu explained:

"We have to walk across the land of death to protect you, *muerto*. We gotta set off all the traps an' die so you can go on through an' stop this thing."

Everything inside Hare at that moment said "No" to her. Everything except Dusk.

"So I can live to be bait, and die."

"Si. I told you... this is a war. Gotta be ready to die if you in a war. You gotta find this thing and lead it away from Carlo. Stop!" Chu squeaked.

"*Llegamos*. We are here."

She gave the signal to spread out. The other chinchillas scattered. She signalled 'forward', and with a great mass squeal of joy, the chinchillas started hopping and jumping and bouncing into the land of death, singing:

"Today is a good day to die!"

Hare didn't move but watched the chinchillas leaping in crazy zig-zags all over the ground, intending to land on a trap, spring it, lose their life, just so that it wouldn't kill him... but now it was happening, he couldn't let it, couldn't let these animals die for him, and he too stepped into the *tierra de trampas* and started walking forward, but gently, gently, one careful paw at a time, agonisingly slow progress, until when he had taken a hundred careful paces into the killing-ground... he stopped. He sensed something. Just a ripple along his spine and into his head, but it reminded him of something from home, that feeling that came when he ran under the black cobwebs that crossed the sky and connected the great grey metal trees together, the lines that hummed and thrummed with that strange energy he felt when he ran beneath them … that almost-like-you've-been touched fur-shiver that knows… it's human. He stepped around the ground in a wide circle around the *feeling,* and the energy faded, then he stepped near again. The feeling got stronger. His heart was pounding. He had never felt more alive. And then, ahead, through the trees, a trap went off.

One moment, she was alive - Flaca, her name was, Hare was sure... she brought him *olvillo* to eat - the next, there was a whistling noise like clean, sharp breezes across crevices in cliffs, and she was in pieces. Still, the chinchillas moved forward, following Chu. Two more traps sprang in quick succession. First, a volcano erupted, an agonising noise, a giant roar louder than thunder, and the ground beneath their feet rippled, and a rain of hard stones and scorched-smelling earth came down. The noise left Hare flinching, stunned and reeling, his hearing gone except for a thin, keen, painful ringing. Then another trap went off. This time, it sounded like the whine of flies, thousands of tiny flies that ripped through flesh. More dead. Many more wounded and crying in pain. All the joking about dying had stopped. Hare couldn't think. He looked around at the chinchillas. They were scared. They were angry. Their glances asked him: *This is all for you?* Chu was shouting,

"Stop! Stop! Don't nobody move!"

and they all came to a complete stop where they landed, each looking about at the ground around them, trying to guess where the next death traps were.

"Muerto! Where are you?"

"Chu! I'm here! I've found something."

It looked like dung, but it didn't smell like dung. It was wrong. It didn't belong here. He sniffed it again. It smelt of nothing.

"Hey, are you sniffin' *caca*? That's disgusting, ese."

One of them looked over at the caca.

"Yeah, that's llama."

Chu called over again.

"What's happening there?"

"This," Hare told her. "It's not real."

"Sure looks real."

"Smell it."

"Eee! Do I have to?"

"Yeah."

She took four very careful hops over to Hare, and the object, and sniffed it.

"Yeah. It's wrong. You think it's a *trampa*?"

"Yes."

Because there was that something else about it. Hare sensed it - that thrumming it gave off. The energy that he knew was human.

"Are you okay, homes?" asked Chu.

"Yeah. Turn back. I can get through this on my own."

"No."

"Why not?"

"I don't want your help. You can follow if you want, but more of you will die, maybe all of you. I've got to find a way though myself."

Chu looked at him without speaking, then turned and squeaked her orders:
"Back! Carefully. Remember to follow your paw-prints til we're out of the traps."

To him she said only:

"*Adios, muerto*. Good luck."

He waited until they were out of sight, and until he could no longer even hear them.

Completely alone, again, he set off to find the thing that would kill him, sensing traps all around him.

DOMINO

"An' cuz there was no sign of the supposed badass comin' in to whack the asshole Guli thing, the Five Families had a sit-down, an' they made a truce so they could start a war. We're used to wars here, gotta be one every few years, let the bad blood get out, 'cept this time everybody's bad blood was all about one guy. An' the truce says the killin's gonna stop until this Guli guy is dead because this guy?... bad as he is, he is one guy, remember that: jus' one. Here, one is nothin'. We got hundreds of natural-born killers right here in the neighbourhood all working for Carlo – we're talkin' snakes, eagles, jaguars, aligators, piranha… guys who whack other guys every day, eat, go home to the wife an' kids an' sleep just fine. An' this guy thinks he can beat anybody, *everybody*, in *all* of the five families? Then take a shit? He's gotta deathwish an' his wish is gonna come true. We're gonna throw everything we got at this guy but not all at once, cuz that ain't how we do it here. We got muscle, yeah, but we got moves, too. We been doin' this a long time, pal. This guy? He's in a world of pain. He jus' don't know it yet. Welcome to the neighbourhood, asshole. The Five Families wanna meet ya."

The Ghoul

I am far from 'ome but I feel so safe an' 'appy 'ere. Ze creatures 'ere adore me, for all that I give: ma parfum, ma art, ma delicate an' discerning palate, an' ma generale je ne sais quoi. An' ze place is beautiful, so alive wiz ze thrilling spectacle of life all around me. I am so 'appy, it as if I am ze only sing in the world an' all of zis is made for me. If only Maman et Papa could see me now.

Oh.

Zis thought makes me sad.

I 'ead sowsse.

ᗪOMINO

"But we're watching. It's heading south, all the time. This we know. In the trees an' in the air we got guys watchin'. Monkeys. Eagles. Condors. All the birds in the forest. Eyes by day, eyes by night. So we know where it is, like we don't already know from the trail o' bodies an' the smell o' the huge piles of crap it leaves all over the neighbourhood an that disgustin' scent it sprays everywhere. But at least it means he's easy ta follow on the ground an' we are lettin' him get deeper in an' deeper in, right into the neighburhood cuz the deeper he's in, the deader he's gonna be soon. Guys are jus' linin' up to take a shot at this asshole. The eagles ain't got a clear hit 'cos of the trees, but they are watchin' to see if it steps into a clearin', an' if it does, if there's a chance, they'll hit it, boom! break its back an' then carry it up real high an' drop it on a mountainside an' then the vultures can clean up the mess.

On the waterfront Fat Paulie an' Enzo's crew an' the crocs are watchin' the shore to see if it'll take a drink from the river, cos if it does? it's dead - it's gonna get snuck up on an' snatched, crocodile-style. Then it's goin' in tha water where it's gonna drown, or get bit in half or maybe

just cut a couple times so it bleeds in the water and let's see what happens: the piranhas will know soon enough an' they'd just *love* to tear this guy a new one. Hell, we could even get the leeches to just suck it dry. The river'd be death for this thing. But it never goes near the river…."

The Ghoul

Ah, ze rivvair. I would love to spend some time by ze water, gazing at ze light on ze water, and ze beautiful reflections of ze trees and ze clouds. Ze rivvair makes me think of 'ome. Ow inspiring it would be! Ow peaceful! To spend some time 'ere. I would like to take some time and create something truly beautiful by the water's edge, a work inspired by the sunlight an ze beautiful couleurs, a new creation, steaming and shiny fresh from ma tummy, ze womb of ma creation… I would do zis of course just to say sankyou to ze beauty of zis place an' ze kind creatures oo 'ave welcomed me 'ere.

But, alas.

Voila – un petit squirt of Eau de Julien… an' I must leave zis place, although now I think I should call my beautiful scent 'Goulot! Le parfum'.

I am not sure.

I 'ead sowsse.

Domino

"But that's still the plan: get it in the water. The big cats went in first an' who was gonna tell 'em no? - an' they hunted it. They like the idea of the river, an' the plan is that they're just gonna play with it, get it to river. Nice an' quiet they come on it from four different directions, an' try to push it to the water. But the thing is fast: fast to dodge a hit, fast to hit out, fast to turn. Covers all angles. Stands its ground and fights. Teeth, claws, real strong, real aggressive. Three cats get bit. One of 'em didn't make it. Meanwhile, the asshole's still killin' an' things are gettin' dead an' eaten all over with this thing no nearer to bein' cold and stiff. S'bad. We gotta come up with another plan."

The Ghoul

Some vairy friendly bobcats zey come today to meet ze artiste. But zey interrupt me in ze act of creation an' I was a little cross wiz zem an' I 'ave artistic disagreement wiz zem. Zey are all approaching ze artiste an' I am protesting, "Messieurs, 'ow can I create if you are watching? Ze artistic process is intimate, delicate, ze artiste an' 'iz oeuvre are one, you are distracting me...please gentlemen, you can return an' examine ze work when I 'ave completed it." But non! Zey were so very demanding I 'ad to drive them away. Although one of zem 'ad quite good taste, it turn out once I 'ave sampled im.

I 'ead sowsse.

Domino

"So Vipero Scacchi puts out the word, an' the snakes set up. Poison. One bite is all it'll take. An' even if that one bite don't kill it, it'll slow it up enough to put in more bites, however many it takes until this thing is *cold*. So they set up an' wait. Twenty, thirty guys all along a long stretch of the neighbourhood, all of 'em stone-cold pro bushwhackers, all camouflaged, hidden in good spots, waitin'... an' the thing came through 'n' they hit 'im. They hit him from behind rocks, from under rocks, from outta bushes, up outta holes an' from up in the branches. But the fangs couldn't get through that fur an' he's too quick, an' he gets everyone who takes a bite at him. Tears 'em up, eats 'em. Then it goes out

killin' an' eatin' again. An' it keeps curlin' 'em out for everybody t'see, jus' to let us know: I'm badder than every one of ya. Come 'n' get me."

THE GHOUL

It is extraordinaire. Ma art as attained new levels, new forms.

I am creating new ways for ze creatures to see ze world.

Even I, le Julien, am surprised. I am overwhelmed by my own genius. Forme, materiel an ze artiste 'ave become... one.

I 'ave recently been working wiz the concept of ze snake, because ze shape of ze snake is fascinating and because so many come to me these days an' I must be spontaneous in ma art! Zis is ze new concepte. I did not know what to expect after I sample so many snakes, 'ow zey would inspire me, an' when ze time come for my tummy to create, it is a vairy extraordinary piece I unveil. It is so firm, an' long, an' multicouleured, ze scales sparkle in ze sun, an' it looks vairy much like... a snake.

And ze aroma...?

Also snake.

Bizarre.

I 'ead sowsse.

DOMINO

"So the scorpions and spiders go in next, quiet an' deadly. None come back an' by now it's lookin' like what we need is a tree-frog with a death wish. Them tree frogs. All them colours. All them different poisons. I seen chumps eat treefrog before: dead fifty different ways. Others just sleepin' it off, so asleep it's like they're dead but they got big smiles on their face like they're dreaming somethin' sweet. We're hopin' the asshole'll eat the other kind. But nah, he don't eat none of them…."

The Ghoul

… an' zair! Oh. It is beautiful. It is ze petit frog in iz tree. But 'e is so small an' froggy. I 'ave sampled les frogs legs, oui, many times, I like zem vairy much. An' zis? Ze couleur! E looks so delicieux! An' zair! Annuzzer! An' zair! An' zair! What would it be like to sample zese perfect couleurs? Zis would be a masterpiece, non? An' zen I remember ze zing with many legs an' many couleurs I 'ave eaten in ze desert, et… Non.

I 'ead sowsse.

DOMINO

"An' after everything, after the cats an' snakes took a shot, after the scorpions an' the spiders had a pop, it's still there, still killin' an' eatin' an' takin' a dump. It's frightenin' everybody's kids an' insultin' the dead an' the livin' an' all the pain an' fear it's caused an' it's still crappin' all over everywhere we eat and then smellin' it, an' we can't slow it up, we can't stop it, we gotta let it through.

Slow it up?

Let it through?

Hell, we can't wait for it to go.

So I talk to my boys, all my monkeys, an' we decide to give it a nice send-off…."

THE GHOUL

What is zis? They throw things from the trees.

I snuffle.

Interessant. Ze scent.

I snuffle. Zair. Annuziar an' annuzair an' annuzair, falling to ze ground around me.

What is zis?

Regardes! It iz a near-perfect replica of an early work of mine from ma mountain period.

Non! Impossible!

Can it be?

Forgery?

Non!

Homage!

An attempt to create… as I create.

Finally, iz it someone oo recognise ma genius?

More copies of ma work fall by me.

DOMINO

"We threw shit at it. Hey, whaddya gonna do? it's a monkey thing, y'know, like, poop in ya palm 'n' pelt! ping! pong! pow! poo-ey! 'an' it didn't hit 'im or nothin' but it came close an' he jus' stops right there. So everybody else starts throwin' crap too…."

THE GHOUL

Oh. Oui. Enfin.

I 'ave travelled. I 'ave suffered. I 'ave known pain an' fear an' cold an' always 'unger.

I 'ave suffered for ma art.

Oui.

But now...

I 'ave arrived! Je suis lancé! At last! Zey recognise ma genius!

Papa, Maman... if you could only 'ear 'ow zey applaud your petit Julien.

An' ze uzzairs, ze 'erd, ze cowards oo refused to recognise ma talent before?... now, zey understand an' are no longer afraid to embrace ze truth of my art... one of zem 'as understood, an' now... ze uzzairs, zey too, dare to follow, an' zey begin to shower zair praise on me.

It is zair love, an' gratitude.

For ma art.

I 'ave set zem free.

DOMINO

"... until the guy is just bein' rained on by a thundercloud of crap, thrown by every monkey for miles around, screamin' at him about how much we hate him an' how dead we wish he was an' what an asshole he is...."

THE GHOUL

Zey scream zair appreciation of ma genius. It is musique. It iz a symphony of 'appy creatures, united in love. For art. For beauty. Et for moi. Moi. Julien. An' I am so 'appy!

Maman et Papa you would be so proud of your petit Julien.

But zey do not know! It is so sad, so poignant!

But zey will 'ear one day: I 'ave become a famous artiste!

Ze world az recognised ma genius.

Ze creatures in ze trees throw their homages at me! They are only pale shadows of ma work, of course, zey are not as complexe in bouquet an' texture an' colour as un Julien but they are... from ze 'eart.

312

Do not be 'ard on zese simple creatures, Julien.

Zese are good, simple sings, trying to understand ze beauty of art.

Many of zem 'ave good taste.

I should know. I 'ave sampled enough of zem.

Zis iz zair tribute to ma genius.

Zey understand.

Sankyou! Sankyou!

Non, you are too kind.

I accept your invitation.

I do not 'ead sowsse anymore.

I will stay 'ere.

Merci.

... but what is zis... ma tummy tells me that I 'ave annuzzair masterpiece in me an' zat I must create.

Oui... ooh... zut alors!

Ze power, ze force of ze creative urge... irresistible!

... it emerges... it builds...

... it takes shape and forme and...

... voila!

Forme et parfum in perfect 'armony.

Zis is for you, ma adoring publique!

Zen, I snuffle and zair!

Quoi?!

Oh.

Non!

Impossible!

Jacques-lapin?!

DOMINO

"... it stops, it squats, it takes a giant crap an' smells it like it's smellin' flowers, an' it's gone. Just runs away. Yeah. We beat it. Me 'n' my monkeys. Me an' my crew ran that asshole right outta the jungle. So, a little respect huh?"

HARE

He came through the jungle now and the going was little easier than the mountains. Perhaps the mountain running had left him wiry and stronger in his legs and with greater stamina. This was hard-going though. Fallen trees were everywhere, the floor was dense with plant life, the huge trunks towering above him were thick with creepers and yet... it was quiet. He couldn't hear any animals. He stopped, listened again, and caught faint noise off to his side. He moved towards it. It wasn't clear what it was but it was animal noises. He moved on, hopping from fallen tree to fallen tree, onto boulders, off boulders onto floor, then back up onto the next fallen tree trunk... and then he saw something and stopped. It turned to look at him, and he saw it.

Squat, square, twitching and growling, the creature looked at Hare with tiny eyes. Things in the trees were pelting things at it and screaming at it. One word kept coming through the cacophony of screaming: "Ghouli".

This was it. Hare flinched. He wanted to pee. The creature had not broken eye contact, and its eyes were tiny, bloodshot and yellowed. Yet it was no bigger than a badger. The snout was half-open, the teeth were bared. It slavered and gasped, panted, growled and snarled.

Run, thought Hare.

He turned and ran, and the thing followed.

The Ghoul

Viens, viens, Jacques-Lapin.

I 'ad not expected to bump into an old friend from 'ome an' I am 'ungry. I sink I shall invite you to dinnair chez moi. On ze menu... you.

Ah, but zis is a delightful ballet an' could not be more lovely entertainment before dinnair. Monsieur Jacques-lapin is vairy nimble but 'e 'ave to 'op over all ze fallen trees an' zis will make Jacques-lapin vairy tired. Many times Maman et Papa taught me 'ow to prepare Jacques-lapin, an' 'e will be like a little taste of 'ome. 'E iz 'eading for ze open ground where 'e thinks 'e can out-run me, but Julien 'as danced zis dance before, oui. So we are dancing togezzer now an' soon 'e will dance into my mouth.

'E 'op one way, I follow iz lead. E 'op anuzzair, I follow. 'E will tire before I will tire an' e will put a paw wrong somewhere an' zair! ze dance will finish, an' it will be time for dinnair an' zen I will 'ead sowsse again.

HARE

All his senses were telling him: It's on you. It's following. It's taken the bait and it's coming for you. Stay just ahead, never let it lose sight of you or the scent of you, and keep it focused on eating you so you can lead it away from Carlo.

As it loped along after him, Hare tested it, risking his life to gauge its speed and agility. He needed to test it to see how long he could lead it away. He slowed, to let it nearer, to see if it would attack. It put on a burst of speed Hare never knew it could produce and he had to jump to evade it. He veered right over a boulder. It followed. He zigzagged right-left, bouncing between a rock and a tree-trunk, it followed. He feinted right, it sensed the feint. He feinted left, it sensed the feint. He speeded up, it speeded up, he slowed down… it speeded up... trying to get near enough to make one final pounce count: because it had revealed a hidden skill: its lunge. Its lunge was incredibly quick and it made up twice its body-length...

Hare kept running, just slow enough to keep the thing on his tail but fast enough to stay away from its teeth. Ahead he knew, was the *tierra de trampas* he just crossed over and he stayed just ahead, knowing that the traps would soon be all around them, thinking that he could lure it to its death, even if that meant his own....

THE GHOUL

Ah! Vairy nearly 'ad 'im zen. But zen... where would be ze fun it zat? Ze game is delightful... ze dance... an' ze delay of the plaizir of ze taste of jacques-lapin shall make 'im all ze more delicieux! Ma mouth waters. 'E as slowed down, 'e is tiring... I snuffle an' oh...

Ma tummy.

It is telling me.

I must create.

Enough wiz zis silly Jacques-Lapin... zair are many more delicious sings to sample an' zen I must 'ead south.

But first... Art!

It begins... ze mouvement... I 'ave sampled so many sings I 'ave forgotten what medium I 'ave been working wiz, zis piece will be vairy surprising even to ze artiste, hmmm...

Oh, ça arrive...

HARE

... when the creature gave up and stopped chasing him. Hare could hear its feet stop behind him, and its growling become fainter, but he kept running on, and when he guessed it was safe to do so, he turned back and saw that the thing had stopped to take a crap.

Hare gaped, not believing what he was seeing. The creature was squatting, its face alight with pure bliss as it produced a long turd. It was gurgling and moaning in pleasure, trembling with ecstasy and snarling:

"Oui! OUI! OUI!!"

And when it had finished, it started sniffing over its mess with a delight that made Hare want to throw up at first but then...

THE GHOUL

Ah! Superbe!

Perfect in form an' execution... another oeuvre de clef de Julien... naturellement.

'Ow my genius is developing, ze style, ze form, ze meaning. Zis - ma latest creation - is more than just a montage of ze many creatures I 'ave sampled an' styles I 'ave worked in, it is the pinnacle of ma achievement as an artiste so far. Oui. Of course, I 'ave not yet sampled ze slow sing so it is not ze pinnacle of ma genius... but ze aroma! Ah! It is 'eaven for my sensitive nose... delicieux! Parfait.

Quoi?

Is someone mocking ma art?

... he started laughing as hard as he had ever laughed in his life. The creature, this thing he had feared and dreaded and heard spoken of as his certain death, was whimpering with joy as it sniffed its own crap. Hare laughed until his fear was nothing, until he accepted, I might be going to die, but I'm going to die laughing.

The creature turned from its pile of mess and looked at Hare with cold fury.

Then it started running at him, screaming.

Hare turned and ran, knowing exactly where to lead it.

The Ghoul

Come back 'ere! Come back 'ere! 'Ow dare you?! 'Ow dare you mock ze art of Julien de Goulot?! I, ze artiste an' parfumier! I oo 'ave travelled half ze world an' suffered for ma art an' created ze finest tableaux with my faecal genius - I oo 'ave done nothing except to live for ze beauty of art for all to enjoy... you laugh AT MOI?! I will kill you, Jacques-lapin! I will kill you! I will kill you slowly in every way I know will 'urt you... I will take your skin off you a little piece a time.... I will bite off little pieces of you so you do not die.... I will eat you while you watch... I...

Hare

The crackle along his fur told him that the *trampas* were all around them now, so Hare slowed down, stopped and looked around. He trod gingerly, keeping his senses fully focussed, especially the shiver in his fur... he could sense the buried things around him, and behind him, he could hear the creature coming after him at full pelt, still howling and snarling. Death was all around him, and behind him, and ahead of him, and Hare had never felt more alive. The joyous release and relief of his laughter at the creature's pathetic habit still exhilarated him, and his senses were thrillingly sharp to the wind stirring the leaves, the dappled sunlight coming through the trees, the warm, moist air rich with the vibrant perfume of life and death, growth and decay. Hare remembered the way to the *trampas*, the ones that weren't buried, the ones that look like *caca de llama*...the man-crackle coming off it, the way

it made his fur shiver the way it did under the great metal trees with the black cobweb lines back home...

There it was.

He pulled up and stopped right in front of the *trampa*, and waited.

The creature arrived very soon after. Across the floor, they looked at each other, and the jungle was quiet.

THE GHOUL

Zair. You. Are. Jacques-lapin. You 'oo laughed at ma creation, ma art, ma genius... an' made me vairy angry... I 'ave come for you...

HARE

321

He stood his ground in front of the *trampa*, hiding it from the creature's view. His heartbeat was even and his breathing was slow. His fur crackled along his back.

This... he told himself... is where you die. How you die. And what you die for. Not all those other places where you've nearly died. Here. Now.

It felt good to know those things for sure.

He would wait. He would stand his ground. The thing would come for him and he would let it, and let it, and not run, he would wait until it was almost upon him, then throw himself on the trap and they'd both be dead.

The thing started coming towards him, snarling and whining. Hare could understand nothing in its sounds but rage and hate and it kept coming nearer.

The Ghoul

You 'urt me. You did. Oui. You 'ave 'urt ma feelings vairy deeply, Monsieur Jacques-Lapin. I wanted us to be friends so that you could remind me of a taste of 'ome an' Maman et Papa... but you ran away... an' I am now lost an' now I cannot remember which way is sowsse...

HARE

And now he did want to run because he could hear the horrible noises it made and see the flesh in its teeth and the bloody drool around its jaws and he could smell it and it stank, stank like all the dead animals he'd ever come across, all the maggot-wracked road-kill he'd ever found rotting in the sun by the roads, dead things only good for crow-food.

THE GHOUL

I only evair wanted to be friends an' share ma genius with you, to make you into a work of art an' beauty for ze 'ole world to see an' inhale an' enjoy... but you ran away... an' would not be my friend.

Oh. Pauvre Jules. 'Ell is uzzair creatures... zey are so cruel.

But I am an artiste... an' I will forgive you, Monsieur Jacques-Lapin. Oui.

I will not eat you or 'urt you. I would like to give you an 'ug and we can be friends.... then, I think, I will turn around an' go 'ome... let us shake paws like gentlemen.

HARE

It was only a body-length away from him now. And it had gone still. Then it lunged with a claw and snarled.

THE GHOUL

Bonjour. Ma name is Julien de Goulot…

HARE

And Hare, his instincts stronger than his determination, flinched and jumped sideways.

THE GHOUL

But do not be alarmed, monsieur... mais quoi?

What is ZAT?!

HARE

And the creature saw the *trampa*. Hare's heart started wildly and he saw his chance of killing it slipping away.

THE GHOUL

But zis is vairy interesting... shiny an' lustrous like the newly-created art, yet blending in parfaitement with ze nature... I, too, work in zis medium, but, monsieur... zis is on a scale I 'ave not yet myself achieved. It is enorme... 'ow do you get so large a work of art... out of such a small... you?

HARE

The snarling continued, ever-menacing, and Hare thought
now! Jump on the trap now! But he couldn't, because the creature
had stepped between it and him.

THE GHOUL

May I smell your work, monsieur?... eet iz ze only way to
appreciate ze great art.

HARE

It began sniffing the *trampa* suspiciously, growling and
snarling.

THE GHOUL

Zair is something wrong, 'ere... zair is no smell... yet zis is fresh, is it not, monsieur? You 'ave only just created this but 'ow 'ave you achieved zis? Zair is no smell so zair will be no flies an' dung-beetles to destroy it. Zair is no decay: it is... *immortel.* Zis is not naturel, non.

HARE

Then it turned to sniff him, almost nose-to-nose, growling into Hare's face.

THE GHOUL

Monsieur, I say again: 'Ow 'ave you achieved zis? What 'ave you et? Wozzit a slow thing? Because if you 'ave eaten ze slow thing, when I 'ave come so far...

HARE

And Hare readied himself to jump onto the trap and its flames or tearing whistling knives.

THE GHOUL

I cannot accept zis. Non. Ma art is destroyed by 'orrible flies an' iz forgotten... while yours... ZIS?! Zis endures... I cannot bear zis... wiz all zat I 'ave suffered. I apologise but I cannot let zis be...

HARE

Then Hare watched, frozen in amazement, as the creature rose up to its full height and brought its forepaws down with all its strength on the *trampa*.

328

THE GHOUL

Ugh!

HARE

And Hare leapt back to escape the flames and destruction and the blaze of light and the earth-shattering noise but all that happened was a slender, shining spike sprang noiselessly through the creature's belly and impaled it.

THE GHOUL

Ah, Maman!

HARE

And then its last breath came out, and it went limp.

Hare spent a long time looking at the dead thing. Soon, flies came, and began exploring for places to lay eggs. The maggots would eat it away to bone and fur. If they had the chance: because overhead large birds of prey were circling, and they would take theirs first. He thought of Dusk, his heart bursting with how proud she would be, how pleased she would be that he'd *survived.* And he had never felt more alive.

DOMINO

"An' the word went out, all over the forest, birds puttin' it out everywhere: it's dead. We couldn't believe it, but the condors was keeping an eye in the sky an' they sent the word back that yep, it's dead: big spike through it, some trap, an' it was the guy we heard they was bringin' in to fix the problem. Whole forest went crazy. We were so happy this thing was finally dead.

An' the guy that got him? Nobody knows. Nobody saw 'im, nobody got a name. He jus' came to whack the guy they sent to whack Carlo, whacked it 'n' like that... he's gone. Now that's a guy you send to do a job.

Hell, we all helped to kill it, or tried... from the biggest cat to the littlest guys. The ants. The mosquitoes. The bees. Anything that stings or bites. They held him up. An' the flies?

They cleaned up after this asshole, so we didn't have to look at our dead friends' bodies no more.

An' they cleaned up the thing's shit too.

 I never had much respect for no flies before.

I do now."

HARE

The flies were thick and loud around the creature's body now and they were starting to land on him, too. Soon, the smell would bring something else: something hungry, something that would fight for this. The place wasn't safe and Hare had no idea what to do, except to move and the only way he could think to go was back the way he had come. The thick jungle was no place for a runner who liked open ground, so he criss-crossed his way through the traps and cleared the *tierra de trampas* as dusk was coming, and the temperature started to drop.

Ahead of him the low rocky hills rose and his eyes followed the rise til his gaze met the summits of the mountains he had come down from. The snow on the sky-high tops was stained with the light of the bright blood-red dusk sun and the darkness was coming on behind them. The only sound here was the wind. Hare closed his eyes and listened, hearing beyond the wind to the pure silence, and lost himself.

When he opened his eyes again, he was surrounded by chinchillas.

"Gonna get yourself killed you let your guard down like that, ese," said Chu.

She hopped up close to him.

"Word is you killed it good."

"Well..."

He couldn't take his eyes off her. She was so pretty, but he remembered what happened the last time he had looked at her that way, and his nose throbbed with the memory. Her eyes were smiling into his, and he could hear his heart beating wildly. She came even closer. In a voice that made him gulp, she whispered,

"*Bravo*,"

leaned in and kissed him on the nose. She turned to the others:

"*Vamonos! Muchachos!* Let's go home."

WhiteCrow

Under the moon, I seek you.

My Ghoul, my fool, my tool.

You are not there.

I inspired you with dreams, to love me and serve me, but Houyi has released an arrow in the war and it has found your heart.

Stupid wretched useless meat thing.

Rot. Serve the maggots.

You failed me.

Another serves me now.

Not one like you. One beautiful like me.

And we will see how Houyi likes my shield.

Mir was jubilant.

"You got it! The birds confirmed it. The Ghoul's dead. Carlo's safe."

Inwardly Sai was glowing but, "Hardly me," was all he would say.

He looked out over the plaza. How long ago had it been since *that night...*

"So - now it's Carlo, right. Think he still remembers the message?"

"Yes."

"Listen, Sai. We need to get word to Athena. We're entering the last phase of the operation. We need this White Crow out of the picture."

"I want you to get my agent home first."

"Oh. Right."

"If you don't mind."

HARE

The chinchillas didn't talk to him as they began their way back up the mountain, but they were looking at him very differently now. There was no more 'muerto', no more jokes about being killed, there was a respect now, and maybe even a little fear, because not all of the chinchillas would look him in the eye.

Before they started climbing, the first thing they did was find food, bringing him the delicious seeds and leaves and roots they had eaten on the way down. When the finally started climbing, they didn't hurry this time.

Coming down had been hard enough, Hare remembered, but they had been moving urgently, with a target and a purpose in mind. Now, going home, the chinchillas slowed down so that he could keep up. But the going was hard. His back ached horribly, his paws were sore, the air became thinner as they rose and breathing came so hard sometimes he had to stop and beg for a chance to rest and breathe, lying on the rocks, panting. This time they didn't laugh. They stopped and waited, standing over him, telling him how to breathe. They huddled close to him at night and kept him warm. When they climbed they took turns to guide him towards the easiest paths and jumps.

As the days passed, Hare got used to the thin air and the hard climb, and the aches and pains gave way as his body learned to meet the demands of the terrain. For days and days, Hare and the chinchillas climbed, and he hadn't even started thinking about what he was going to do when they got to the top, when they got to the top and Chu told him: "You go home, homes."

She led him to where they had met, by the road. The cage was still there, dirty and weather-beaten. Hare looked at it in despair, and couldn't speak. He felt tears coming, and to stop them he took a long deep breath of thin cold air and let it out slowly in a long sigh.

Chu hopped close.

"Mountain's no place for you. An' before you say you could have stayed in the jungle... uh-uh... the truce between the animals down there... is *over*. It's back to normal, eat or get eaten. You stay there, *ese*, you die. Nobody knows you are this killer of *monstruos*, and someone will want to eat you. Anyway, I got a message."

"Who from?"

"A little bird: 'Your war is not over.' That's from Dusk. Said you'd know who that was."

Dusk. Calling him back.

"Sounds like you have somebody else to kill," said Chu. "*Adios*."

Away in the distance, Hare could hear a sound he remembered from home, a sound he hated, faint but growing.

It was a car.

He knew what to do.

He stepped into the cage.

CHAPTER 10

Where The Paths Meet

HARE

His mind was blurred as his dream split apart and waking began to happen; still stupefied, his eyes were not fully-opened or focused, and his legs were useless but he could smell human and feel hands on his ribs as they lifted him out of the cage and gently placed him on the grass on his side and then the human walked away. He heard the noise of the car pulling away and staggered upright. Memories rushed back. The deafening horrible racket of the cage in the car, awful screaming hours of it, agony to him. The change of cage, from the old one to another, larger, cleaner, with food in it, and a water-bottle, and the long drink from it then... oblivion. Until here. Now. He shook himself fully awake.

"Dusk", he whispered.

From somewhere in a tree behind him came her soft mew:

"I am here."

"So what now?" Hare asked.

"You won your battle. Now, together, we must win the war."

"The White Crow?"

"Yes."

"How do we do that?"

338

"You know how we do this."

"I'm bait."

"No. A decoy."

Hare's blood jumped, then went cold.

That's what she did to Squirrel Nutjob, he thought, and remembered the screeching terrified thing it had become, torn-up and wretched.

A whimper came out of him:

"No...."

"*No?*"

"I'M SCARED!!" he yelped. "They'll tear me to pieces!"

Her voice softened to an absolute pitch of gentleness, and he felt his will being bent, again, to hers, and he was helpless.

"You have faced worse. And you killed the ghoul... shabash!... I am very proud of you...."

"I had help!"

"... and you will again... I did not train you to throw you away... I will not do that... "

"I won't do it!"

"... listen to my plan...."

*　　*　　*

Hare lay perfectly still, breathing evenly, and peered into the woods ahead of him, the trees thick and dark. In the branches of the trees were crows' nests, clots of shadow, but there was no sound other than the soft, steady, drizzling rain, like a thin hiss across the meadow. Half the sky was clouded over, and the moon appeared then was covered again. He dreaded its light falling on him, as he dreaded its light disappearing, because Dusk had told him where the moon would be when he went into the forest.

He knew there were eyes in the woods looking out, and that the White Crow was inside, and that it was almost certain death to go in but he would... and the time was now. The moon came out from heavy cloud and its light sparkled on the raindrops on the grass by his nose, and he started forward, low to the ground, one paw at a time, and the woods so near now...

DUSK

She is almost pure now, she thinks: her soul, her being, her wings, this air. She comes for the White Crow with all the speed and the fury of the weapon of the Goddess, at the head of an army, now in light, under the moon, now in darkness, under cloud.

The darkness means nothing: she sees. The rain means nothing: it cannot blunt her weapons. She has killed, tortured, betrayed and plotted to deliver her strike and she cares nothing for what she has done, only what she must do: obey the Goddess. Her hare will die or not, she thinks, as he has before. Such is so, it matters not, because her mole has described the woods to her, and in her mind's eye she can see it and feel it in the very tips of her talons: through the gap in the canopy made by the ring of trees which grow around the Heartstone and put no branches over it, so that it is always able to feel the sun and the moon.... that is where the crow will be, there, on the Heartstone.

HARE

It's just different jungles, Hare told himself, *that's all. This one - full of threat, and death, and pain, but you've survived worse than this, haven't you? And you saw a new world and learned how many lives you can live, and how many times you can die and come back because Dusk showed you.*

Suddenly he could remember the taste again of *pinga pinga* and *olvillo*, and he could remember the smell of the mountain air and he could hear chinchillas calling him *Muchacho! Cuate! Muerto!* And he could feel, in some part of him he had no name for, a pain that was telling him that all he wanted now was to do this, for Dusk.

It was dark and quiet, and he stopped, again. Beneath his feet the floor was damp, mossy, and littered with twigs and branches and leaves, and going silently was going to be near impossible. He took a deep breath and took a few more steps, deeper in among the trees, and the darkness wrapped him up. He put all of his focus into his hearing, and heard nothing and then he sniffed the air and the smell was... a shock to his whole body. It worse than any dead thing he had ever smelt, and he knew that must be where he had to go. There was no point in stealth, he decided, if you're going into a fight you know you're going to lose, that's where you'll find the courage to fight. I've died before, I can do it again.

He stood up and started running towards the smell. Ahead, the woods seemed to clear, and he thought he could see the sky through a break in the -

They fell out of the trees, hundreds of them and they mobbed him, landing on him, surrounding him from all directions, caging him, clawing into his back and along his spine. He was weighed-down, pressed flat, squashed into the floor, his paws caught, twisted agonisingly beneath him. He closed his eyes and told himself not to scream, but then the pain started and he was, into the moss, face down, suffocating, as crows stabbed their beaks into his ears and screeched, the noise splitting his mind from his body. Others came, and the pecking was all over his back, each stabbing jolt another wave of pain and he could feel his warm blood starting to flow as they plucked his fur, tearing little pieces of his flesh one at a time, skinning him.

Then it stopped. The crows stepped off him.

It was entirely quiet.

He was hollowed-out with pain. He couldn't move. Didn't dare open his eyes. His ears were ringing in pain, but the smell… the smell was right upon him now. Road-kill, rot, death, a world of it, a world where this was the only air to breathe. Then a voice came into Hare's darkness:

"When does Houyi come?"

Hare said nothing.

He felt two sharp, shocking pecks inside his ears, and the screaming started again.

Dusk

She hears them, behind her, flying in the formation of the fork of her tail, her legion, her army. Fewer soldiers than the White Crow has, for certain. But bigger, stronger soldiers than the White Crow has, and of the purest loyalty. It is the army of the Parliament of Rooks, summoned with a single command. They will obey her strategy. Half of them will enter before her, half behind her and they are to kill only black crows for the white crow is hers, as the goddess commanded. Even from this far away, she can smell the white crow, foul, unmistakable, a distant memory of a nightmare of a violated nest. In her breast, her rage is pure white light in the darkness.

Hare

The screaming in his ears stopped. Hare was pulled, pecked, poked until he turned over, his belly vulnerable. He kept his eyes clasped shut. The stench was horrible, and the voice came again.

"When does Houyi come? LOOK AT ME!"

Hare opened his eyes. All around him, night-black crows, shining in moonlight, their eyes sparkling with malevolence; all still, waiting on the voice.

Hare struggled to his feet, looking at the floor.

"Look at me."

He looked up.

It floated towards him with its wings spread but it did not move its wings. It seemed to be made of light and as it landed noiselessly before him, only then did it gain any solidity, and there it was: the white crow.

"When does Houyi come?" it asked again. "The archer killed my ghoul."

It floated up into the air.

"In return I have a gift for Houyi."

He swept back a wing, inviting Hare to look, and the crows, hundreds of them, all moved aside as the White Crow floated away to land next to a white dove.

DUSK

The moon appeared from behind cloud and illuminated the forest beneath and there was the gap in the trees above the Heartstone and she saw not the foul thing's head but its white wings spread wide and she mewed, once. The left flank of her army broke their formation and dropped into the forest and she struck.

344

HARE

The dove's wings were raised and it was trembling and terrified. Hare understood. The white dove was a hostage and a decoy. If Dusk saw the dove before the crow, she'd kill it. Even if she saw both at once, she would be distracted, even if only for a tiny moment, but that would be enough to deflect her strike, and then she would be mobbed by the sheer numbers of crows. Hare broke inside. Dusk would die here.

"When does Houyi come?"

The White Crow was standing in front of him again, on the ground, solid. The smell was worse than the pain all over his body.

Hare coughed and gasped.

"No more… beg… you..."

Buy her time, he screamed to himself.

Dusk! Hurry! he screamed to her.

"Her name's not Houyi. And I killed your ghoul," he told the White Crow.

The White Crow came closer, and stared hard into Hare's eyes. Hare stared back defiantly. Then the White Crow's head darted forward and he speared Hare's left eyeball with his beak.

Hare screamed, half his world gone. Crows started pecking him and leaping on him and as he went down he thought that he saw even more crows arriving from the sky, and his hope died.

And then he saw red in the moonlight - not blood in his blind eye, but wings in the other - and he heaved himself upwards, throwing crows off his back, and jumped on the White Crow.

DUSK

Down through the trees, and she saw the white of the thing she would kill, bright in her eyes and she adjusted her body and pointed her talons, her flight angle true and her target sure. And suddenly she caught white - again! - in the corner of her eye and her strike faltered. And then she screamed and hauled back her wings as she saw that she was about to kill a white dove. She dropped to the floor. All around her was the raging black storm of war as rooks and crows fought and killed each and looking out she saw the hare.

He was screaming,

"Dusk! This one!"

He had pinned it.

She leapt off the ground and covered the distance in seconds as the hare rolled onto his back, his paws hugging the crow against his breast.

She did not miss.

Her talons came out through the back of the White Crow's skull.

HARE

Hare grunted softly as he felt her talons pierce him. With his one eye he could see her tearing the White Crow to pieces. Whatever it was, it was made of flesh: Dusk had its heart in her beak. She was splashed with its blood and its feathers lay all around. She swallowed the heart and looked around. The rooks carried on killing and now crows were fleeing, trying to escape and the rooks were letting them fly. Hare could feel… not warmth leaving him, but cold filling him slowly… and he was numb where her talons cut into him, over his heart.

No pain. No fear.

He just *knew*.

Dusk. This time you've killed me.

It went dark, and he died.

DUSK

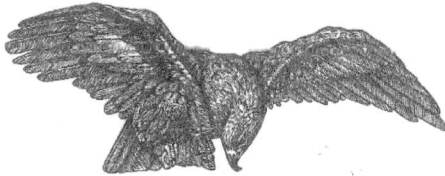

Rooks were taking to the air to pursue and slaughter the crows, as she had commanded them. Now there was only her hare and the dove, which was unharmed. Dusk jumped and fluttered over to Hare, and he was not moving. His breast, torn, blood on it,

347

was not rising or falling. She saw his burst eye. She mewed in pain for him.

"No... no... no...."

She stroked his face with her wings, spoke into his ear, nudged him softly to waken him, and when he did not, she shouted at him:

"No! I did not give you permission to die!"

She jumped onto him, sank her talons in, and she began to flap her wings, and rise into the air, hauling the limp hare's deadweight to the Heartstone. She dropped him with a dull thump and landed, raised her wings and sang inside her soul: a song of purest, truest gratitude to have loved and served the Goddess, to have killed her enemy and been healed. Dusk threw back her head and spread her wings wide as the pure beauty of the Goddess filled her with light.

HARE

Hare opened his eye. The torn body of the White Crow was scattered in pieces on the forest floor and the noise of the battle had stopped. Dusk was floating upwards, consumed in flames, a heatless silver fire, curling and swirling around her like mist over water, her flesh giving way as more flames flowed through her and carried her upwards as weightless as light. Hare could feel warmth and strength and love filling him back up again: he was alive again – never, ever, had he felt so alive - and as Dusk floated upwards into the night, he climbed to his feet to look at her. The fire was dying, fading, softening, breaking down into sparkling droplets of light. The flames passed in front of the moon.

He saw the last of her flesh dissolve.

And she was gone.

CARLO

They could hear it now: machines roaring and the scream of trees falling. Through the trees ahead they could see light, light which would once have been blocked out by trunks and vines, lianas, leaves and flowers. Wherever they were, they were there now, where Sai had told them to go: the edge of the rainforest, where the devastation was, to reason with men.

"Ready?" asked Emilio.

"Yes," said Carlo.

"Get on then."

Carlo clambered gracelessly onto Emilio's back, and with Mauro hovering over his head, they moved forward, and emerged from the jungle.

The man saw it through the bulldozer's dirty windscreen, something moving towards him, indistinct but low to the ground, like a big cat stalking. There was a gun in the cab but he didn't reach for it. He turned off the engine and wound down the window and put his head out. Then he recognised what it was with a start:

"*Es un oso perezoso....*"

It was a sloth.

    The man climbed out of the cab and as soon as he did he saw that there was hummingbird hovering over the sloth's head and the sloth wasn't walking on the ground, it was... riding - *dios mio!* - an anaconda. He reached for his phone, and started filming.

Carlo saw the man ahead, and noticed the little object in his hand that Sai had told him to look out for. As Emilio flexed beneath him, propelling him forward he ran through the white rat's code again in his mind. They were moving on soft dirt, on soil that would soon be planted with only one crop, land upon which no animal would be permitted to live.

While the human stood there, holding the object to his face, Carlo let himself topple slowly sideways and fell onto the soft, warm earth.

    The man kept filming. The sloth and the snake had stopped in front of him, and his heart was pounding but he kept the phone steady on the sloth and he readied himself to jump or run if the giant snake moved, but it had come to stop and wasn't moving. He followed the sloth as it moved towards him, came to a stop, and looked directly into the camera with a huge smile. Then it started scratching in the dirt.

Carlo pressed softly in the soil, and it gave beneath his claw.

A snake going between two round rocks: **S**

A snake crossing another snake's path: **T**

A snake trying to eat its own tail: **O**

A snake going around a tree-trunk: **P**

Then he smiled again in to the camera, and walked slowly back to the snake, climbed on its back, and they went back the way they had come.

By the time they had reached the line of the forest again, and disappeared inside it, the man was already thinking how much money the film would be worth, and, although he couldn't know it, Mir had a copy too.

Epilogue

"… I mean, it's great film, it looks great. You were right, Sai, you can't get humans to listen to reason but they're suckers for cute… Carlo looks great. That 'stop' is really clear..."

Mir's claws tapped again at the tiny keyboard. He watched Sai out of the corner of his eye as he showed him the progress of the film of Carlo. Sai stared at the screen as shots of where the film was cropping up, across the world, began to appear.

"It's spreading, Sai, it's gone viral, nobody can shut it down. Here - look: social media, YouTube, news channels, talk-shows… the whole world's looking at it…."

IS THIS SLOTH TALKING TO US??!

OH MY GOD ITS A TALKING FRIKKIN SLOTH!!!!!!

IS THIS REAL?????!!!!

OMG!!

WTF??????!!!!!

ITS SO CUTE!!!!!!!!!!!!!

CGI!!!!!!!!

"You did it, Sai," said Max.

"Let's wait and see…" said Sai.

352

Mir turned to him.

"You know, Sai, I've been thinking… you know that thousand square miles of plastic-bag slick floating in the Pacific Ocean… what if we could persuade a lot of whales and dolphins to swim around it and spell out 'wtf?' or something and somehow film it?"

"What does 'wtf' mean?" asked Sai.

Max told him.

"Certainly not," said Sai. "But we should do *something*. I wonder… Mir?"

"Yes?"

"I've got an idea…."

ATHENA

The scent of jasmine and marigold garlands hung thickly in the warm air and she sniffed with intense delight and some sadness. It was time to leave. Later that day, a car would be arriving at the temple and she would once again be picked up by gentle human hands and be placed in a cage and differentjungles.com would transport her back to the city, to its noise and commotion, and to Max, Sai and Mir.

Part of her yearned to stay here in the temple, free and unencumbered by the burden of being the goddess. But part of her now accepted that what she could do as the goddess could – sometimes – bring about something *good*. The Ghoul was dead.

The White Crow was dead. Carlo was alive and he had succeeded in the mission Sai had given him. She wished she could meet him, this sloth, this remarkable animal. But she knew she would never see his jungle, although, most likely, there would be other, different jungles for her to see, she supposed.

She found herself looking forward very much to seeing Max again, and with a smile she thought about how Max would react when she proposed to him, as she planned to, and become his queen. And there she would stay. And live happily ever after. Until whatever was going to go wrong did. And then she would become the goddess again.

DOMINO

"...but jus' listen to it, pal...the river, the trees, the birds... no men, no fires, no machines, no stinky psycho-killers crappin' all over the neighbourhood, everybody in the five families all livin' quiet, jus' like it used t' be, jus' like the old days. Carlo did that. An' Emilo, an' Mauro. None o' the other animals couldda done it or even wouldda tried. They jus' didn't care enough if things was goin' okay, but when it goes boom an' the trees fall down they come bleatin': "Help us, Don Carlo." Hey, who else y'gonna ask? I'm tellin' you, buddy, you wanna save the forest cuz it's gettin' cut down an' your own capos have sold out on it, don' wanna do nothin' jus' talk, you got no-one else to turn to? You need to ask the sloth - he'll get things done quickest."

HARE

Hare stands in the field looking up into the sky with his one good eye. It is sunset, and golden-red and orange clouds are floating gently past. For him, now, it is not waking in the morning that matters anymore, but making it to evening and the rest of sleep. Every night now, he watches the sun go down.

High, high up in the sky he sees a buzzard circling, and Dusk comes immediately to mind. Somehow she healed his wounds, but he is scarred and ugly, and his missing eye frightens other hares and they avoid him, which he prefers, because the story he could tell them would make him sound squirrelnutjob.

He feels the tiredness of his body, and a part of him knows that one night he will go to sleep and he will not wake up again. He can feel it in the slowed pace of his running and in the shortness of breath that comes now after only a short run and in the aches and pains in his limbs. But it won't be tomorrow, he thinks, and even if it will not be long now, he is not afraid. He is no longer afraid of anything, even death. He isn't even sure if he even believes in death anymore. Mountains, forests, *trampas*, Chu…. all rush across his mind's eye, and he can taste in his memory delicious *doradilla*-leaf, *renilla, quisco, copao, rumpiato, maracuya* and *pingo pingo*.

He turns his back to the sunset and lies down to sleep.

He wonders if he will dream about her again tonight, and he smiles.

Sleep begins to come, and he surrenders to it.

He hopes he'll dream of the mountains.

He hopes he'll live to see another morning.

And he hopes he'll live to see another Dusk.

The End.

Acknowledgment

I would like to thank Betsy Wentzel for her encouragement and advice, Jenny Florio for the inside cover art, and Polly Stopforth for the cover art.

About the Author

Damian Ward was born in Yorkshire in 1966. He attended London University before moving abroad to teach in France, Crete, Spain and India. He now lives and teaches in Gloucestershire.

Printed in Great Britain
by Amazon

52688011R00205